EBUR

CALL IT C

Nona Uppal is a New Delhi-based author, marketer and content creator. Her debut novel, *Fool Me Twice*, was published by Penguin Random House India in 2024 and is now a national bestseller. *Call It Coincidence* is her second novel.

CALL IT COINCIDENCE

NONA UPPAL

EBURY
PRESS

An imprint of Penguin Random House

EBURY PRESS

Ebury Press is an imprint of the Penguin Random House group of companies
whose addresses can be found at global.penguinrandomhouse.com

Published by Penguin Random House India Pvt. Ltd
4th Floor, Capital Tower 1, MG Road,
Gurugram 122 002, Haryana, India

Penguin
Random House
India

First published in Ebury Press by Penguin Random House India 2025

10 9 8 7 6 5 4 3 2 1

ISBN 9780143471547

Typeset in RequiemText by Manipal Technologies Limited, Manipal
Printed at Thomson Press India Ltd, New Delhi

www.penguin.co.in

MIX
Paper | Supporting
responsible forestry
FSC® C010615

To all the boys I've loved before:
For legal reasons, this isn't about any of you

'Phir miloge kabhi is baat ka wada karlo,
humse ek aur mulaqat ka wada karlo'
(Promise me that we will meet again,
promise me one more meeting)

—S.H. Bihari, sung by Asha Bhosle and
Mohammed Rafi

THREE YEARS AGO

'What's the verdict?'

'Late, *obviously*.'

Here's what my profound yet wholly regrettable experience re: first dates has brought to me—a rock-solid sixth sense that can scope out, within seconds, if a date is going to suck or end up in me taking them back home. (You can stop reading here, Mom.) This is the third one this week; so, I'm either too desperate and the likelihood of the universe sending an eligible bachelor in place of my date is indirectly proportional to the extent of my desperation ... or, every single man within a five-kilometre radius of where I live comes to dates with a non-negotiable fatal flaw in tow.

Not *this* one though.

He's just . . . late. Which, before the pitchforks take for my scrawny throat, does not mean he's late by five—or even ten—minutes, but a whole forty-five! A little south of an *hour*! And he hasn't once apologized for it, unless you count a 'Hey, running twenty minutes late' by-the-way text sent—mind you, after I had already been waiting for the last twenty minutes—as an apology.

So, it's not about being late, really. It's the *callousness*. It's the not caring about it. It's the whiplash of an excellently written bio countered by a man who can't be bothered to do the single most important thing on first dates: show up on time.

'I wouldn't normally be this pissed, you know?' I squeal into my receiver, finally padding towards the bar counter my date is standing up against, waiting for me, after I've spent close to an hour loitering outside the restaurant, biding time—god forbid strangers snicker behind my back, exchanging gossip and dissecting, as filler conversation, the story behind that girl sitting at the bar who has most certainly been stood up. (Fine, I know this because *I've* done this to people.)

All at once, our eyes meet, the glimmer of familiarity softening his sharp gaze around the room. I look at him, feign a smile, bobbing my head to tell him to give me a moment, and add: 'But like, be decent? Apologize?'

Sarina, my childhood best friend, the platonic love of my life and the only person who not only tolerates but, secretly, enjoys my persistent bickering before first dates, sighs from across the line, 'I get it, Naina, but it's not really their fault, *na*? When are boys ever taught to apologize growing up? Remember Nitin from school? The one who put gum in your hair and laughed while I had to cut it out with safety scissors during lunch period?'

'Yes, and I had a crush on him, Sarina. Maybe I'm attracting these men,' I say, shifting my phone from one ear to the other. 'Anyway, he's here. I'll call you when I'm done.'

I watch my date gawk at his phone from all the way across the room while I stand still, considering my choices of intoxication. A margarita would get me *just* tipsy enough to want to stay a little longer, maybe even flirt a little, and I've already had enough sugar in my coffee today for a cosmopolitan, so a tequila soda it is—classic, tough to mess up no matter the bartender's relative inexperience, and easy to knock back through an hour of tired small talk.

When did this become my life—willing myself to survive dates I never thought I'd have to go on? No, I was done. At twenty-five, I almost had it all. A great—although slightly soul-sucking—job straight out of college, a wonderful—Fine! Decent!—boyfriend and a normal family life, as normal as it can be. I was happy. I had enough. I was *content*.

Until my ex, he-who-shall-not-be-named, decided that this 'stability' thing was too much for him, that his twenties with me by his side were a little less roaring than he'd expected, and that he wanted to have more fun before the clutches of adulthood took him hostage forever. He could've just said what he really meant—*I want to have sex with other girls, Naina,* which is an activity he promptly took to a week after our break-up—but I spared him the horror, read between the lines, and said goodbye like it wasn't breaking my heart, *and* my plans, *and* my bank.

Like today, my date for the night is scheduled at South Delhi's poshest new restro-club Django. I'd suggested the place: I knew a friend who knew a friend who could get us a pretty decent discount. And this way, I got to put down my card for the dinner in advance so the guy doesn't pick up the bill; I don't want to feel pressured to agree to a second date just because he paid for this one.

But life, as they say—rather tritely but hey, if the shoe fits—is full of surprises. As I curve along the U, my date and I finally close enough to properly register each other, knowing now for certain it's *us* we're looking for, I suddenly feel the built-up dread wash away. The anger and anxiety give way to something softer, calmer, something . . . wait, these can't be butterflies? I inch up closer to the man I am formally bound to spend the rest of the evening with. With a gait that can only accompany a stature and built like that, he saunters over towards me and, with his arm outstretched, opens the conversation with, 'You must be Naina. I'm so sorry I'm late.'

Turns out, six foot two is awfully tall on a man—and while height has never been a criterion of mine, *oh my god*. Maybe my luck isn't rotten after all.

'That's okay,' I sputter out, having totally lost my ability to make sentences when confronted with a man handsome enough to roll out of bed and still look put together for the fanciest party.

'No, really, my car broke down, which I know is the most clichéd excuse in the world, but it's true,' he says, half-giggling, a tacit sheen of self-awareness on his face.

'It's honestly all good,' I say, unable to imagine just how mad I was seconds ago, how easily he's managed to douse a potential fire.

His photos on Tinder or his face from afar, neither match up to how gorgeous he is up close—like a painting that takes shape, expands and contorts into new forms, the longer you spend gaping at it. He is just doe-eyed enough that it cuts through the rest of his uber-macho demeanour as he's dressed in an impeccably tailored navy-blue suit that fits like it was stitched keeping *just* him in mind.

Suddenly, I'm excited for the night that lies ahead: this is the first Tinder date where, although late, my match hasn't revealed himself to be slightly south of a pathological liar within a few minutes. While the first one lied about his age (a literal minor to my twenty-five—I bolted out of the restaurant), the second one took the cake by catfishing me with photos of a semi-famous guy I used to know back in school. Ever since, it's been a disappointing rut, one after the other, and this guy was decidedly my last straw.

And what a rope I've been thrown.

'Find this place easily?' I ask, settling on the bar stool he pulls out for me as he leads us towards where he was sitting. Right next to him, I see a glass of what looks like scotch on the rocks.

'Tequila soda, please,' I request the bartender, needing something to calm the nerves that have just decided to show up, before turning towards Nikhil. Right, I forgot to mention, that's his name.

His gaze is sharp, intentionally focused on me, like there's nowhere else he'd rather be. The attention feels like drugs injected straight into my veins. 'Mm-hmm, I actually work right down the road.'

'You *work* down this party street? What, do you bartend? Play live music?'

'Something like that.'

'Something like that?'

He crosses his arms across his chest as he says: 'I actually own a restaurant on the party street.'

I prefer to go into my dates blind. Which means I schedule a date the moment a guy meets my basic criteria; this way, all the actual small talk and getting to know each other happens in real time. So, suddenly, all the scattered pieces of him on his profile finally fit: the dorky photo with the chef's hat, the hospitality degree from IHM Pusa, the multiple stills of expensive-looking food littered all over his profile.

'Fancy,' I say, tempering my amusement. 'Someplace I might have heard of?'

Nikhil swirls the ice in his drink before taking a swig from the corner of his mouth. It's such a scene from a first date in a movie, he's so Shah Rukh Khan, casually charming with his sly smile and exhilaratingly attractive brown eyes. I'm not the swooning kind, but I'm not sure it's entirely voluntary, what's happening here.

'Maybe,' he shrugs.

'Maybe?'

'Yeah, if you've heard of Curos.'

I almost drop the tequila onto my lap—partly because the coaster is a chunky piece of metal with no architectural integrity, but mostly because I am sitting across from the owner of a restaurant that the who's who of New Delhi frequent. You know, the kind of place that has a photo wall of all the celebrities who have ever shown up—and you stand there, transfixed, with your friends, matching up the faces you do or don't recognize? Yep, *that*.

'You *own* . . . Curos?'

'I'm afraid so.'

'As in, Curos from across the street?'

'Unless there's another one I'm not aware of, in which case, I'll have to call my lawyer,' he chuckles, like it's totally casual to *have* a lawyer on speed dial.

'You mean the same place that said they'd be happy to give me a reservation for my birthday *this* year . . . three years from now?'

Nikhil guffaws, an all-thirty-two-teeth-on-display kind of hearty smile that instantly endears him to me. 'We're unfortunately very booked, but I'll see what I can do about your birthday.' Somehow, he manages to sound humble saying this.

'I mean, it did just pass, so you have a full year to make it up to me,' I say, the tiny sips of the tequila fuelling my confidence speaking to a guy who has quickly revealed himself to be very, *very* out of my league. I curse my choice of pleather jacket with plastic ripping off at the underarm seam; the baggy jeans I wore because I prioritized a loose waistline over my usual high-waisted denim. As luck would have it, of all the dates, I had to show up in my least-bothered outfit to *this* one.

'So, Naina,' Nikhil says, his eyes looking straight into mine—the kind of reckless confidence that is infuriatingly attractive on men—'tell me why you rescheduled this date thrice.'

I gape at him, open-mouthed. The jump from pleasant small talk to direct verbal assault is baffling, but I like how this conversation already feels comfortable. Familiar. 'Because.'

'Because?'

'Because I had a few other dates already planned. And I can only eat so many meals outside in a week.'

'So, we're *shopping* now, are we?'

'Aren't you?' I ask, my eyebrow raised in intrigue.

'Yeah, but I'm a different kind of a shopper.'

'And what kind is that?'

He pauses, softly looking at his drink before he answers: 'I only try on things I really, *really* like.' My inhibitions come loose at his easy flirting. I can feel goosebumps rise on my arms. 'You want to shift to a table?' he asks, before I can say anything in response. I nod in response.

This almost never happens to me on a date. In fact, most dates end with me questioning if I am into men at all, considering how little most of them make me feel. But not this time. Nikhil is far too gorgeous and a little too well spoken and smooth for my internal organs to not quiver at the thought of him *maybe* touching me. I never thought a man could be *sexy*, but here I am, proven wrong.

'So, Naina, tell me something about yourself,' he confidently commands.

I'm hanging my bag around my chair as I try to look anywhere but his eyes. Distractedly, I answer: 'That's a loaded question.'

'I ask only because your profile was so unbelievably cagey about anything of actual significance about you. The only thing I took away was that you have a cat.'

'I attract a lot of creeps, so I keep the personal information to a bare minimum,' I say, half-blushing at how well he's had me read, how he remembers the one detail I let on.

'And here I thought I was being catfished.'

'I thought *I* was being catfished, hello,' I say, gawking at him.

'Then I guess this is a nice surprise for the both of us.'

'The jury's still out,' I say, looking down at the menu and smiling. 'So, something about me.' He stares at me straight on, his gaze so piercing it's drilling nails into my body as it lands on me. 'Well, the basics are that I'm twenty-five, newly single, slightly jaded from the whole experience, I work in marketing but I'm slightly jaded with that too, and I'm looking for, I guess, I don't know . . . something to feel excited about, again, I think?'

The thirty-second monologue comes out more honest than I expect—under the sudden glare of this man, I feel all sorts of vulnerable, as if a polygraph's electrodes have been attached to my skin—and I can see him processing everything I've said in real time, the wheels whirring in his head.

'And I'm also an oversharer, so that's another thing for you,' I add with a nervous giggle. 'Okay, your turn. Tell me something about yourself.' I almost add: *please feel free to unleash your deepest, darkest secrets so I feel better about myself.*

He extends one leg towards me, the other tucked close to him, as he leans back in his chair to answer. 'You know the essentials,' he shrugs. 'Own a restaurant, live in there for more hours than I spend at home, sometimes wonder if I should get a cot and make a makeshift room in there, and that, honestly, pretty much sums it up.'

'There has to be more, come on,' I tug at him. *Open up to me.*

'I'm *also* fresh off a pretty brutal break-up, so that's one thing we have in common. Cheers to that,' he says clinking his glass to mine—right as his phone starts buzzing. He crinkles one eye and lifts a finger, the universal 'one sec' sign, before answering the call.

'I'll just do a quick run to the washroom,' I whisper, interrupting. He nods as I grab an emergency pouch out of my bag, already lost in conversation.

As I criss-cross through the restaurant's dizzying seating arrangement towards the washroom, I pat my heart under my chest. Like, *physically*, because I fear it's beating too hard. *Stop it, we're not there yet*, I try to reason with it, but it's on its own speed, jumping so far ahead of the finish line that I can't even see it long enough to pull it back.

I wait outside the only washroom in the restaurant, clutching my make-up pouch in my hand, running over every way in which this could still turn out bad—even when it's started good. The scenarios announce themselves easily—and I'm currently running through the fifth one when my spiral is suddenly interrupted by the door unbolting. Out emerges a man not much taller than me as the latch turns and our eyes meet—his face ovular and pasty-white like the moon, his hair buzzed close to his ears, which are ridiculously jutting out of his skull, a troubled scrunch in his eyebrow. Those are the only three things I notice about him before he walks away.

Until suddenly, I hear the wind rustle behind me.

The air fills up with an unfamiliar sound. 'You're not going to believe me,' he says, hurried and anxious and so pointedly averting my eyes, 'but that smell, that was already *in* there before me. I promise.' And because that is so far off from what I was expecting him to say—which was nothing at all—I just smile awkwardly, say thanks, and lock myself in. Inside, it's not half as bad, thank god.

As if on a timed mission, I quickly dab off the excess sweat under my armpits and the extra shine on my nose with a powder puff, following it up with a subtle lipstick refresh. Spritzing my perfume and walking straight into it like they show in the movies, I count my breath to ten before unbolting the door to make my way back to this unexpectedly high-stakes date.

Instantly, my eyes land on Nikhil right as I step outside and . . .

No.

That can't be.

He *obviously* isn't bailing, is he? That thing you do when the second your date is out of your line of sight, you waltz away so you don't have to have an awkward hour-long conversation with someone you don't even find attractive? That thing I did to the last guy who wouldn't stop droning on and on about his anime-whatever collection? No, that can't be—I wasn't imagining that witty banter, that instant chemistry, was I?

Just as quickly as Nikhil has gotten up and out of our table, I catch the silhouette of the same man I bumped into outside the washroom taking *my* spot, sitting casually in my chair across from Nikhil mere seconds after he has left.

'Excuse me, this table is taken,' I grunt at the guy, having maniacally padded towards the table in hopes of catching Nikhil somehow.

He blinks, genuinely confused. 'Is it?'

'You see that bag?' I say pointing to Sarina's purple cross-body bag I borrow for dates hanging on the chair. 'What does that tell you?'

'Oh, right. Sorry, the guy sitting here just told me he was leaving so the table was all mine,' he says, standing up, instantly releasing my seat, clueless that I'm minutes away from crying.

I unhook my bag from the chair and sigh, 'You know what, have it.'

What's going on? My brain squeals like a thirteen-year-old who's being told periods are a permanent monthly occurrence in her life. Nikhil's one-eighty-degree shift in interest in me feels like a sudden car crash on an empty street. Wasn't this going . . . well? Or am I so lonely that I was up in my head, imagining the first good date I've had in months?

'Everything . . . okay?' the guy asks, reading the horror, the disappointment of the night showing on my face. How can he not? My date just *live*-ghosted me. There is no rock-bottom left to hit—this is it, gravel and all.

'Yes, splendid,' I reply with gritted teeth. So much for not wanting gossipy bystanders to make up scenarios about my sad date night. 'Have a nice dinner,' I say as I turn around to beeline for the restaurant exit—hoping I open the door to a time-loop sci-fi vortex that'll let me disappear into it forever. Whatever it takes to not go on a first date ever again.

~

It's raining when I make it out of Django, which is just as well, because when my bad luck rains, it pours like the Mumbai monsoon. I stand waiting for what feels like thirty minutes straight as Uber and Ola pretend to be working hard to get me rides, tempting me with notifications like 'many drivers are nearby' while clearly not a single one of them seems to want to take my ride. Because why shouldn't more men reject me tonight? Why would just the one, tall, handsome, straight-out-of-a-Karan-Johar-movie guy be enough?

Right on cue, my phone buzzes in my hand.

Nikhil Tinder: hey, have to head out, emergency at the restaurant, so sorry! Please have dinner, have put my card down for it

What emergencies are there at restaurants? Someone burned a pizza? A chef cut a pinky finger slicing onions? Oh my god, a guest left without a tip after that massive service charge we hide in the bill?!

I slide to delete the notification before also deleting Nikhil's contact. That might seem extreme, but at this point, it's an aggressive form of self-preservation—taking someone's treatment of you at face value instead of looking for a deeper meaning where there is none. That doesn't mean it doesn't sting, though—the deflation of this hope that was bubbling in my stomach all of the last half an hour, the expectation that life was finally on the precipice of change.

And pop!

In the puddle collecting on the dug-up ground outside the restaurant that charges you for so much as breathing in its premises, I find my morose reflection glaring back at me. She looks like she's been through the trenches, the woman in the grimy brown water, having survived the humiliation ritual that is a first date. I smile at her and promise the era of dating random men from Tinder and Bumble has come to an end. She half-heartedly smiles right back, not believing a word I'm saying.

Another ten minutes pass and after agreeing to pay a little north of the price of a kidney for an Uber ride,

I finally see the headlights of what seems to be my ride edging inwards towards the parking lot. I hold my arm out, courting the driver in my direction, when his sharp turn splashes puddle water all over the brand-new heels I'd whipped out for Nikhil. *Of course.*

'OTP madam?' the driver asks before I've had the chance to plop my butt down.

'*Ek* second,' I say, struggling to find enough overhead lighting for my phone's facial recognition to activate. '5149,' I recite, and as the ride dings in confirmation, I throw my head back.

'Thank you, madam,' the driver chimes from the front, '*bass* one more pick-up.'

'One more pick-up *matlab*?'

'*Doosra* passenger, madam.'

He accelerates only to brake forty meters ahead of where we're parked, right outside the restaurant complex, guided by a man holding out his right arm. As the headlights of the car shine a light on who's going to be my co-passenger, my vision clears. *Please, no.*

'What are you doing here?'

'This is my ride,' he says matter-of-factly—the stinker-upper of washrooms, the observer of my first date's demise, the stealer of visibly-occupied tables—before telling the Uber driver his OTP. '4342'

'This is *my* cab!' I screech, loud enough to alarm the driver, who is, let's be honest, simply doing his job. But pleasantries are so far out the window; my patience is at an all-time low.

'It's also my cab?' the guy responds nonchalantly.

'How is that even possible?'

As the cab zooms out of the parking lot, the guy turns to look at me. 'You know, there's this brand-new feature on Uber where you can pool rides.' At once, I scour my phone for the Uber app. The guy trudges on, 'And what happens when you select that feature is that sometimes,'— his tone is so condescendingly didactic I could gouge his eyes out—'someone else gets the same cab as you. Which means it's not your cab, it's *ours*. Pooled. Shared.'

Annoying as he is, he isn't wrong. I did, in my rain-induced frustration and general proclivity for a good deal, book myself an Uber Pool. Or maybe that was the only thing available—I'm not sure.

'Great, this just keeps getting better and better,' I say, throwing my head back against the seat again, resigning to my fate that this night couldn't possibly get worse.

'Accidentally booked a Pool?'

I stare at him in disbelief. 'No, I actually specifically called Uber headquarters and asked them to pair me up with the guy who stinks up washrooms.'

He moves closer towards me, his chest almost at a fist's distance from my shoulder. 'Okay, be real for one second, if it was me, would I not just escape as fast as I could instead of giving you that disclaimer?'

'Or it was a classic misdirection tactic that you used to distract me and shirk off blame,' I say, shrugging.

'You know this wasn't some high-stakes heist, right?'

'Pretty high stakes to be a stinky public-washroom user,' I say, lightly chuckling as he gasps at me in a natural end to this small talk. As the engine roars and shuts every few minutes at the signal right outside Mehrauli, we sit in sudden silence and a strange . . . comfort. In the background, the cab driver shuffles through radio stations, settling on a crackling sound bleeding into a sixties Bollywood song I can't quite place.

He breaks the stillness of the moment as the music fades out and the radio jockey comes back on. 'It wasn't me, though, I'd just really like the record to state that.'

My mind spins in a different direction. 'Didn't you *just* take my seat, by the way? How come you're leaving already?'

From the corner of my eye, I feel him turn to look at me. 'Half an hour ago,' he says. 'But yes, fast nonetheless.'

'Bad date?'

He shakes his head. 'Job interview.'

'At 9 p.m. in a club?'

'You'd be surprised at the number of things lawyers prefer doing drunk.'

'So, you're a lawyer.'

'I'm trying to become one, yes.'

'How's that going?'

'Poorly,' he laughs, looking away, and I don't know why—it's not particularly funny, I don't even know the guy—but I laugh too.

'What was *that*, if I may ask?'

'It was a . . . date.'

'Didn't go too well?'

'Hey, what makes you think *that*?'

This time he laughs. 'I think I bombed my interview too.'

'Half an hour is decently long for an interview.'

'He was fifteen minutes late and spent five minutes asking the waiter about the specials, so,' he shrugs. 'Bombed, for sure.'

'There are more jobs.'

'And there certainly are more men,' he says right back.

'Really? I wouldn't be so sure about that,' I chuckle, looking out the window.

'You sound like you're forty when you say that, when you're, what?'

'Twenty-five.'

'Twenty-five,' he says, nodding. 'Not the age to be giving up on love.'

'And you say that at the wise old age of?'

'At the *extremely* wise old age of twenty-eight,' he grins.

'Right, so you know.'

'I do know,' he says, confidently. 'It'll happen for you.'

I look at him to ask: 'What will happen for me?'

'Whatever you're looking for,' he says, simply.

At the hint of another song coming on, both of us quiet down. For the next few minutes, he gazes out the window while I try not to cry to 'Pyar Diwana Hota Hai' as it plays in the background. Only about halfway into the chorus do I notice the guy lightly singing, murmuring alongside Kishore Kumar.

'Nice song,' I mutter—this time it's me interrupting the tranquillity of our shared silence.

'It's the best.'

A verse plays along as the both of us sit there, motionless, humming together, on cue. For the rest of the song, we sing the lyrics, first quiet enough to go unnoticed over Kumar's bellowing, and then, all at once, feverishly loud.

'Do you remember when you first heard it?' I ask as the song fades out and something else plays on the radio before the driver changes the channel.

'This song? No, not really. My dad sang it for my mom all the time, though, so I heard it on repeat for years, basically,' he says, pausing for a moment, as though to ruminate over what he just said. 'Do you?'

'I used to listen to it on my nani's Walkman after school.'

'I never had one of those.'

'What? How is that possible?'

'I don't know, I guess I was always a radio guy. I liked not knowing what would play next.'

'But what if you really wanted to listen to a particular song?'

'I'd just wait for it to play on the radio, then,' he says, casually, absurdly, especially in the era of playlists upon playlists and extremely curated music preferences. I stare at him, saying nothing.

'What?'

'That's slightly serial-killer-sounding, I'm not going to lie.'

'Or I'm just a really patient guy,' he says, smirking.

We cross the Hauz Khas Fort, where the night is still alive, while the two of us are on the tail end of ours. He lives behind the fort, in *gallis* too narrow for the cab to realistically be in, but despite my initial grumpiness, I'm grateful for the company, for the diversion.

'You know, I always thought it was Dear Park? Like, "dear Naina" *waala* dear,' I say right as we cross it.

'You're not being serious.'

'No, I'm so serious. I thought it got its name because people went there to make out, so like, *that* dear, I figured, made a lot of sense.'

'And you never thought to question that when you saw actual deer frolicking about?'

'Somehow it never quite clicked that they would name an entire park Deer Park just because a few deer lived there, you know?'

'That logic is simultaneously so iron-clad tight and absolutely ridiculous,' he says, shaking his head. 'Is it safe to assume your name is Naina?'

I nod, extending my hand towards him. 'Vatsal,' he murmurs, meeting mine with his. For the first time, both of us look straight at each other. Up until this moment, I wouldn't have recognized him if I bumped into him tomorrow.

'Naina, this is me,' he says my name out loud, a quiet exhale that breaks the electric moment where our eyes meet in sudden familiarity, as the cab comes to a halt in front of a rickety colony gate. 'Thanks for letting me share *your* ride.'

Unsure why, but I blush. 'It was nice meeting you, Vatsal, however terrible the circumstances.'

Time seems to stop—the moment feels endless, but it has also just begun, and neither of us seem to want it to end. It does end, though—with the sound of the door unlocking, whooshing and bursting open in front of us. His foot thuds against the pebbly road as he steps out of the car and shuts the door, simultaneously signalling me to roll the window down. I take my sweet time with it—and once down, he props his forearms atop the open window and leans into the car, a little too close to my face. He takes a beat to say nothing, to stare at my face like he's reading scripts off of it, until his eyes wander elsewhere. And then suddenly back to mine.

Before he walks away, he says: 'For what it's worth, Naina, that guy is an idiot.'

NOW

The first thing I do is hide behind the shelf of Kellogg's cereal. That's the one place I know, for a fact, he won't ever be caught dead loitering, what with his 'processed food is the new cancer' spiel.

'No, cancer is the new cancer,' I would reply.

'That's what Big Cancer will have you believe.'

I don't give myself any time to wonder why he's here. No, the priority right now is to disappear.

Okay, Naina, focus. How do we get out of here without him spotting us?

I look ahead and try to assess the path leading up to the main entry door in this 24Seven. Geometrically—Ha! And they said I'd never use maths in real life!—it's laid out in a perfect square. I'm hiding behind one of the last rows that runs vertically, only slightly wider than me so that my entire body fits, thank god, very precisely behind the faux wall of sugary treats masquerading as breakfast. I'm positioned in a way that I can beeline for the exit without being spotted . . . or, if my bladder complies, I could just wait for him to leave.

As he peruses five different yoghurts and their ingredient lists, I take my time to assess my options. Every few seconds, I peep from between the cracks of the egregiously colourful boxes to get a peep at him examining the label contents of, now, what looks like a protein bar. God, it's *definitely* him. He's checking for the healthier options before he flocks for the chips. The hypocrite.

I thought I'd forgotten. And then it only took one glimpse. Funny—time changes how you dress, how you part your hair, even your godforsaken posture—but it rarely ever changes what aisle you flock to the second you step inside a 24Seven. For me, it's straight to Lays'—yellow, in particular. Vatsal, the protein bars—the extra sugary kind. Every second I take him in, watching his movements in secret, he goes from a flicker of my imagination to real flesh. Standing there, motionless, I realize the brain can try and erase memories but the bones remember; you can turn off the lights in your head, but your heart will still beat to the sound of someone who has broken it apart into a million pieces the second they're close, that your nose will sniff them out like a dog the very moment they're in your peripheral vision. That love, when unfinished, will try and race its way to the home stretch, no matter how hard it hurts when you stumble and fall on your way there.

I promise I'm not being dramatic.

If it were anyone else—even my crush from the ninth grade who put glue in my hair when I scored higher in a test—which, hello? Serial killer behaviour?—I'd have gone and said hi. I would've struck up a conversation, initiated a hug, found some middle ground, maybe even said something overly clichéd but slightly genuine, like, 'Let's keep in touch?' and mean 'Let's like each other's Instagram posts occasionally?' But not with Vatsal. Not after everything.

He doesn't know it yet but I'm watching him like a security guard watches an unexpected car at midnight; my eyes—feral, my vision—fixed. He's wearing cargo pants that I recognize—how have they held up so well?—and a T-shirt that *seems* new; the shoes could be brand new or a month old, give or take. This exchange, this observation from the outside, too, could be old or new, give or take. It tastes familiar, though. It looks like something I knew like the back of my hand three years ago.

Look at him: how dare he look that good, his hair still behaving as though they've just been blown out while being perfectly buzzed from where his ears start.

'First, bold of you to assume I even know what a blowout is,' he would say.

'You don't?'

He would shrug. 'It sounds awfully sexual.'

Jerking my mind out of this loop that I automatically fall into the second thoughts of Vatsal crop up, I take on texting as a distraction. Scrolling, emailing, anything to stop myself from cartwheeling from one proposition to another; hey, maybe I'll even update Sarina on the shocking turn of events of my afternoon. She'll enjoy this—the ever indulger of my life's 'What the fuck?' moments.

Which would all be great *if* I could find my phone.

I glance up from scrambling for it in my bag, finding it missing as it usually is—only to realize that he, too, is no longer where my eyes left him. One second, and poof.

Gone. My heart sinks into the pit in my chest—did he really leave without spotting me? Was all this effort to hide away from him just a way to conceal how desperately I wanted *him* to find me?

Gaping at the empty space where he once was, I finally let out the exhale I've held in my stomach for what feels like hours, at this point. I fling my bag back on my shoulder as I reach for my back pocket—suddenly remembering where my phone usually is.

The lack of a bulge jolts me as a familiar voice looms over my head.

'You know it's not particularly safe, keeping your phone in your back pocket.' The half an inch he has over me suddenly feels like ten. And right on cue: the rising goosebumps on my arm. The erratic beat of my heart. The drying up of my throat.

I turn around, already knowing what to expect.

'Hi, Vatsal.'

'Hi Naina,' he replies, holding his hand out to me, offering me back my phone, untying the knots on a part of my life I'd kept boxed up and shut inside a dark corner in my mind. 'It's been a long time.'

I rescue it from his hands, ensuring our fingers don't touch, and put my phone back in my pocket—he notices my careful precision. His smirk is telling. I wish I could wipe it off.

~

Everything happens for a reason. That's what they say, don't they? A bird shits on you before an important presentation because that shirt you were wearing was actually *so* see-through and you only realized it when you went back home and changed. Or you miss your flight because there was going to be a drunk man who pees on passengers and you were going to be seated right next to him. And, so, fate intervenes and sprinkles something bad in your life to prevent something much worse from happening—and when you look back, you have to be grateful for the bad stuff, too.

That's how I have always explained away the disasters of my life. But there is no way to explain something like this happening without it seeming like the gods are doing it for some *mirch-masala*, for TRP, or for some cheap entertainment.

'So, how have you been?' Vatsal asks as I stare at him, mouth flung open, the opposite of the Cool Girl energy I should be channelling right now. 'Clearly your preference in chips hasn't improved,' he says, pointing to the basket in my hand topped with yellow Lays'.

I scratch my head, willing my brain to form a sentence. *Something*, I plead. *Anything will do.*

'It is the best flavour,' I reply, flatly. 'I'm doing good, busy with work. What about you?' I say, the palm of my right hand stretching out towards him, accidentally poking him in the stomach. I move back an inch to introduce a safe distance between us. 'Still in London? I mean, not at the moment, obviously,' I ask, masking my nervous stutter with a forced giggle. Internally, all vocabulary across my two spoken languages has been wiped clean out of my system; the only thing that remains is a single phrase. *What the fuck.*

Here's the thing people don't tell you about unexpected run-ins: your mind instantly activates auto-pilot. You think you're fully there, more alive than ever before, so fully present with your faculties intact. But that is bullshit—I have no idea what I'm doing, what I'm saying. My brain has left processing this to a later time, while my mouth makes up sentences that can half-pass as coherent. Because . . .

Because he is not supposed to be here, or in my city, *or* in India. He's especially not supposed to be at *my* 24Seven, within ten feet of me, close enough to see the new pimple that has sprouted up on my head just this morning. And yet, here he is: live, in flesh, as striking as I remember him, with a few white hair. Probably too stressed. Possibly not sleeping well. His face, too, is fuller—his once-scrawny jaw has some meat on it, like life has primed him with soft fat to keep him warm. Dresses the same, stands with his left knee bent, his hand on his hip just the same. Beautiful, all the same. Still head-turning enough to make me pause if I ran into him at the mall. Still compelling enough to be an instant right swipe. Still breathtaking enough to make it all seem worth it—even though the cut still bleeds every time I so much as run a finger over it.

Stop it, Naina, snap out of it, I scold myself.

'It's been a while, but no, London's in the past. Back to India for good now,' he replies.

'Oh, wow, how come?' I ask, like it's a totally casual fact to me that he's back *for good*. He shrugs like it's no big deal—like he hasn't spent the last two years walking by King's Cross, Instagram-storying his morning coffee in the foreground on occasion. (Thank *god* for fake accounts.)

'Same old story, I watched *Swades* on Independence Day and instantly put in my papers. You know, *mitti ki khushboo* and all.' Classic Vatsal. 'No, I'm kidding, of course. It was actually *Lakshya*.'

Another click in the puzzle—his favourite movie—and he's clearer in my mind. I'd forgotten this piece, but there it is: this fact presented to me again, the picture forming right back up in my head. And with it comes the barrage of related and unrelated strokes of remembrance—how he once asked me to guess what movie he was watching and I guessed *Lakshya*, how shocked he'd been when I was correct ('Oh my god, do you have cameras in my room?'), how he'd once sung 'Agar Main Kahoon' for me but changed *mohabbat* to *naffrat* and then pinched my cheeks when I'd scrunched up my nose in defence. How we'd almost kissed then. How many times we'd almost kissed until we actually did.

'But it was about time,' he says. 'I think I've reached my saturation of how many fancy coffees I can have that would justify living in a four-by-four and working with white men who won't learn how to pronounce your name even if they see you every single day.'

I nod like I get it. 'So what now?'

'Wow, you sound just like my dad,' he chuckles as he sifts through my basket, rummaging through the stuff I'd stacked in. Overfamiliar, as always. His friendship hinged on inserting his way in; he never asked. His hands move in wonderment—grabbing the frozen yoghurt I'd picked for a portable choice of breakfast, reading its nutrition contents half-heartedly, cringing at the ten packets of chips I'd added in. 'Nothing, really, I have a few offers from firms in India and honestly some really good ones from London, too. I'll take whichever feels the least soul-sucking. But I want to stay here, mostly. Until then, I don't know, freelancing for some tech bros to draft up contracts you can find templates for on Google,' he says, shrugging. 'Doing god's work, basically.'

'*Is* there such a thing as a law firm that doesn't suck your soul?'

He laughs—the same way he used to before, slightly delayed, like his brain is working through the joke and then suddenly, all at once, with his entire head, his upper body, and not just his mouth, in a way that I can see all of his perfectly white teeth—and says, 'Unfortunately for me, you are right. But not everyone can do marketing for super cool start-ups, you know?'

He remembers.

'Yeah, I'm the lucky one,' I say, smiling meekly, when all I want to do is ask: What else do you remember?

'Fuck, Naina, I can't believe I'm bumping into you at a 24Seven of all places,' he says, after a short pause.

Another piece of the puzzle, retrieved from years ago: 'When you become a hotshot marketer with your own agency and when I am Chief Justice and we've not talked in years and years and years,' he said, high as a kite on my cheapest bottle of gin, resting his back against my bed with his legs sprawled out on the floor, 'I'll bump into you at a grocery store.'

I scoffed at him. 'You think the Chief Justice does his own grocery shopping?'

He was too drunk to compute my response. 'I'll bump into you at a 24Seven and I'll say HI NAINA OH MY

GOD I CAN'T BELIEVE IT'S YOU and we'll become friends again.'

'Of course. Hotshot marketing agency owner and Chief Justice of India. We'd *obviously* have so much to talk about.' That made him laugh. Oh how I loved making him laugh. 'And why won't we always be friends, exactly?' I asked, mildly offended at his suggestion that there'd be a time where he would have nothing to do with my life. Absurd—that's what it sounded like. Even though he'd just arrived into my life, he didn't feel new. *We* didn't feel new.

'Because.'

'Because?'

'Because you'll become too cool and forget about me,' he said, turning his lips down into a puppyish frown. 'You'll become rich and famous and forget me.'

'What if *you* become a hotshot criminal lawyer and forget *me*?'

He took a moment to think—long enough that I thought he was about to throw up. Then he said, 'I could never forget you,' before suddenly passing out. His saliva dripped on my shoulder as he instantly started snoring against it.

I could never forget you. He had said those words once.

Then proceeded to show me all the ways he could.

THREE YEARS AGO

With one hand, I unlock the door to my house. With the other, I unhook the muddy heels I put on specifically for this date because some Hollywood rom-com said they do great things for the butt. Then, with my phone between my hands, I delete all my dating apps one by one.

Hinge? Gone. Tinder? Uninstalled. This random app that matches you with people based on your taste in memes? In the bin—I matched with a guy still in college. I don't know if that says something about my humour, or his.

I shut my phone off and leave it on the dining-room table as I walk to the kitchen, wondering who will show up to claim my body when I die alone at eighty, my carcass being fed on by my ten cats. On command, Bittoo comes padding towards me, his little tippy-taps on the marble floor announcing his arrival before he's in my peripheral vision. At once, I get down on my knees to greet him hello; I scratch his ear at that one spot that renders him completely hypnotized.

'Hi, handsome, did you miss me?' I ask as he violently rubs his head against my leg, purring into my jeans.

Seven years ago, I brought Bittoo home with the bravado of a twelfth grader, courtesy rebellion and teenage hormones. I'd figured that after months of feeding him out of my pocket money and making sure night and day that no scooter-wallahs ran him over, I owed him—myself—this. I'd simply fallen in love and couldn't take another colony cat scratching him up anymore. My parents, while not entirely thrilled, relented—Bittoo was shockingly low maintenance and I vowed to return to the streets with him if they said no. What they thought was an irrational decision to me was just something they would never understand: I needed Bittoo's company about as much as he needed my care.

Here's the thing: I grew up loved. But I grew up alone. And sometimes, in all that consuming loneliness, that love got lost. My parents and their time, care, affection was always at odds with their work—two sought-after neurosurgeons, regarded by everyone's friend, cousin or uncle to be the best in the country, and logically then, perennially busy. Lucky for them, though, Nani volunteered to raise me for most of my life—I called her maa until I was ten years old—which was good, until I was old enough to realize not everyone was raised by their widowed grandmothers.

I grew up with many such odd frames of reference. Because my parents were never home and the only time they'd ever show up to places was if things were punched in on their diaries or into their calendars, I naturally grew up believing that I, too, had to schedule appointments with them for when I needed more than twenty minutes of their time. I'd mentioned this to my mother once—I had to block her time for a parent-teacher meeting at school—and she panicked and rage-threatened to quit her job. I heard her crying in the bedroom to my dad about how she thought she was a pathetic mother. I'd been morbidly excited at the prospect, until the next day, when I woke up for school, Nani told me my mother was already off to surgeries.

And so, here's the thing, dramatic as it may be: Bittoo saved me. On those days when Nani slept a few hours too long in the afternoon because age was catching up to her and the house drowned in silence, Bittoo was my distraction. Feeding him, petting him, playing with his folded ear gave me something—anything—to do after all the homework had run out and it was too sunny to go out and play.

I'm scratching his ear as Bittoo continues to purr against my leg. Because no one's home yet, I talk to him like he understands, like he's one of us, the way I have always done. I ask: 'Are Sarina and Nipun home yet?' He meows once, then once more after an intentional pause. 'They're not, that was a trick question. You're a very good boy. You're so smart!'

Bittoo watches as I fill his bowl with food. Half of his head disappears inside it as soon as I instruct him to eat. And because no one's coming around to feed me, I walk over to the fridge, praying for leftovers.

Leftovers: *that's* what I feel like. The hodgepodge plate of *stuffs* hiding at the back of your fridge, a little bit of everything collected in a pile, remnants of a party where two pizza slices from different boxes were left behind, a half-eaten slice of cake, a few lone, soggy chicken nuggets.

I open the door to the fridge and the white light instantly washes the dark kitchen with a cool blue light. I crouch down to stock-check the shelves, when I'm surprisingly face to face with a bright yellow sticky note atop a Tupperware container. 'No man is good enough to avoid carbs, eat up <3' reads the note, written in purple glitter gel pen. Inside, chicken biryani with beads of condensation trickling down the plastic walls—the Sarina special, the Hyderabadi kind, one that takes hours to make and a special garam masala that she has to call a 'supplier' to find for her. A recipe I love so dearly, one she makes on days I don't beg for it.

I flick the sticky note off and heat the container in the microwave. As it dings to a finish, I serve myself a portion and watch the layers of biryani collapse onto the bright white of my plate. The smell of kesar fills the house as I take a bite. It's probably her best yet, this dish that says, loudly, through its overwhelmingly fragrant announcement: *You're not leftovers for me.*

~

I find it hard to not correct people when they use the phrase 'we go way back' for a friend and mean the first year of college after they're only a year out. It's a petty thing to have a gripe with, but life is too short to not have petty gripes, so here's the thing—you don't get to flaunt that tag if you haven't earned it in years the way Sarina and I have.

Sarina and I go way back.

Like back before all my teeth were fully formed and when I would still, occasionally, wet the bed. Back when life's perimeter was the spoked boundaries of my colony and days stretched on for what felt like years. Back when I was five and she was eight and our mothers, acquaintances from school, bought houses right next to each other, and my parents decided that a literal child was qualified to look after another child.

Little did they know that Sarina would be looking after me for the rest of my life, and I, her; in my babysitter, I found my best friend.

'Sarina, there is blood in my panties,' I said one day, crying on my way out of the washroom. 'Am I . . . dying?' Thick beads of tears trickled down my unformed face, trailing over my puffy cheeks and the three volcanic pimples that had erupted on my chin.

Sarina, thirteen then, hadn't yet had her period. Instantly, she started crying, too—I knew then that this was the end. Together, we wrote an obituary—after Sarina was finished hunting through all the old newspapers in my house to see how it's done, having skipped the English period where we were taught the suddenly-very-useful skill of writing to-let and obituary advertisements. It took five drafts and a lot of red-penning of my vision by her, but eventually we arrived upon two full sentences—*To whomsoever it may concern, our beloved Naina is now no more. She lived a short, but rich, life of ten years and died doing what she loved most, spending time with her best friend, Sarina*—and then got sidetracked by the most important question of all: would my crush, the same one who would puke in my backpack days later, show up to my funeral?

Through it all, the penning and the editing, the sobbing and the giggling, Sarina had nodded so sincerely that it hadn't felt scary: dying.

'You'll mail it to them?' I asked, holding the sheet of paper with our tear-smudged obituary for a ten-year-old, clutched right to my chest.

Anyway, my parents landing home at 8 p.m. ended the charade. Mom taught me how to stick a pad to my underwear, calling me a 'woman' with tears glistening in her eyes—the first of the very few times I have ever seen my mother cry—and my dad shared a good laugh with Sarina as she read out what we wrote to him. It was stupid, but that near-death experience—it's still near death if you *think* you're dying—superglued us into one unit, forever.

Sarina, alone, nursed me through all my teenage heartbreaks and I held her hand as she convinced her mother to let her quit medicine and become a DJ. (Yes, a DJ.) We have grown up together and we've had moments of growing apart, too—but all the winding roads have always led us home to each other, and now, to our house, literally, in Rajendra Nagar, a stone's throw from the heart of New Delhi.

It happened just like our friendship did—overnight, right as I was finishing college and starting a job as an account manager at the same marketing agency I work at today, while she was one month into quitting medicine and starting her apprenticeship under Delhi's most famous DJ.

'Imagine if we lived together, we could do this every night,' she said, chugging a pint of Kingfisher we'd snuck inside my PG, two days before I was due to move out and find a flat of my own. The travel from my place in Rohini to my job in Green Park wasn't worth the hours it demanded—not when my parents came home long after I was asleep and left for work, again, before I was awake.

'Why don't we just do it?'

'Do what?'

'Move in together,' I suggested, casually, and she looked at me like I'd lost my mind. And then I realized that wasn't what the look was. It was: 'How the hell did *I* not think of that?' No longer did Sarina have to live in her hostel—and between having to move back home and explain her life choices to her parents every day versus living with me, the latter was the clear winner.

And once we thought about it, there was no looking back: instantly, we found a flat with rent as cheap as its ceilings were steep in some corners, but it felt like home and it fit the budget. For two twenty-somethings, that's all that mattered. A stint of bad flatmate interviews later, we decided to foot the extra rent and drink only cheap beer to save cash over living with a stranger who would always be an extra third.

'Promise me that if we're unmarried by forty, we'll adopt lots of kids and dogs and live happily ever after,' Sarina said a few weeks into moving in, half-drunk on the sangria I'd made out of a red wine I'd pilfered from my dad's decade-old collection. We were watching our fifteen-thousandth rerun of *Sholay*, this time in *our* living room.

'Cats and you've got a deal.'

'Cats *and* dogs.'

'Dogs that are afraid of cats,' I countered. We pinky swore on it and glued our eyes back to the screen.

Imagine—we *pinky swore* on it. And then she found her happily ever after exactly two months and five Hinge swipes later.

'His name is Nipun,' she confessed one day after I finally confronted her about being MIA for three weeks straight, missing every last one of our movie nights while offering explanations like 'Work has been crazy.' Sarina is a DJ. Her work was *always* crazy.

'Nipun?'

'Nipun.'

'Is he . . . forty?'

'Shut up, Naina,' she said, collapsing dramatically on the couch, dropping her head between her knees. 'He's a year older. Works in finance, unironically wears half-sleeved shirts and . . .'

'And?'

'And I think I'm in love.'

It all went freakishly fast after that. Sarina and Nipun dove deep into crazy love and just like that, our wallets got a little heavier; Nipun moved in.

And although far from forty, Nipun *was* twice as grown up as the two of us combined. Without asking, he took over all the dad duties—meaning there were never no eggs in our pantry, all of our favourite fruits were stocked in worrying quantities and the bills, somehow, were magically paid on time. He stole my best friend, sure, but he also simultaneously made both of our lives so much easier—it was tough to not feel grateful.

It's been a year of this arrangement and, of course, my parents or Sarina's don't know Nipun lives with us—we're not crazy. According to them, our third flatmate is a very lovely but docile Bengali girl who promptly manages to make herself disappear to Kolkata whenever our parents come over.

Ever since, life has been an endless rotation of Sarina labouring over the stove for hours while Nipun and I divide the boring chores—I set and clear the dining table, Nipun washes the plates squeaky clean and spotless, and the leftovers are stuffed in the fridge by whichever one of us calls dibs on them for lunch the next day. We're a proper *system* together and every part of it has been just as mundane and exhilarating as I had grown up believing adulthood to be.

Tonight, though—I eat the biryani alone, perched against the kitchen slab, the rice still half-thawed from its time in the fridge. The flavours are perfect, but it doesn't blunt the edge on the embarrassment that was the night—how ridiculous I feel about becoming a caricature, at best a 90s rom-com trope of the damsel being left at the altar. And so, I stuff enough spoonfuls in till the only thing I can feel is satiated and order ice cream just in case, for some extra padding. Alone, I clear the kitchen and wash the dishes as the world quietens; Kishore Kumar bellows on 'Yeh Shaam Mastani' and crickets fill the gaps between the chorus and the verse.

And then it hits me, a maddening cliché: there's something missing. Something amorphous, but something I can swear I will know the shape of the second it lands in the palm of my hand. But it's not here yet and this emptiness when I clutch my palm shut is all I can feel. It's not here, but it lingers in the two-second pause between the songs changing, the single plate of food, the lack of someone to request to wash the dirty utensils because you're so tired. It's not around, but it's everywhere, all at once: the lonely footsteps in my bedroom, the nightstand on the right side of the bed lying empty, the room for one with space for two.

This part of adulthood, no one prepared me for.

~

A remix of my alarm and a recent earworm—a trendy Instagram song I despise—buzzes in my ear as I rouse to a semi-conscious state, roll over, and turn it off.

Five more minutes. I need to see how this ends.

It's the same sequence every night. In an *Inception*-esque scenario, I wake up from a long slumber to find that I'm lying on a bed of leaves in the middle of a dark forest with no recollection whatsoever of how I ended up there. Instantly, my limbic system goes into overdrive and I start running aimlessly, panting like a feral dog as I cut myself all over, trying to make it past the dense shrubs. Even unconscious, I can feel my heart racing, the rough stems scratching my bare arms as I claw my way through to catch the light at the end of the greens. And yet every morning, without fail, I wake up right before the first ray of sunshine hits my eyes. I find my way out of the dark each time for just a flicker until snap, and gone—close, but never close enough.

My therapist recommends meditation.

'It's a classic scenario playing out,' she said in one of our first sessions, when the only thing I could think to bring up with her was this dream that wouldn't leave me alone. 'You grew up lonely, you internalized that feeling as a personality marker, and now your body is telling you that you need people.'

'But I *have* people. I have Sarina.'

'You need more than one person, Naina,' she said, taking off her spectacles and holding them in one hand, the left temple pointed towards me. 'Sometimes, we need a whole village.'

I groan as my eyes pop open—the bright morning sun piercing through the sheer curtains and straight into my corneas as I roll off my side of the bed and then, literally, fall onto the floor. Sometimes I feel like my life is a bad script green-lit by a network extremely low on talent but good on budget.

'Morning *meri* sleeping beauty,' Sarina's voice fills my room as I lie there, not unlike my dream, contemplating casual stuff. Like the point of life or whatever. In her hands, Sarina holds a steaming cup of coffee.

'Get out of my face,' I say, rising up, shoving a pillow in her direction.

'*Arre*? What did I do?' she squeals, putting the pillow back down on my bed and following me as I strut to the kitchen.

Most mornings, Sarina makes me coffee and brings it to me in bed; she is part of the reason why my standards for men are skyrocketing. Dutifully, Sarina follows me, wallowing, 'Why are you mad at meeeeeeee?'

'I'm not mad at you. I'm mad at myself. And the world. And all the men in this world,' I scream, opening and shutting all the cupboards in our kitchen, searching for equipment to make my coffee.

'What exactly are you doing?' she asks, one hand on her waist, towering right behind me in the kitchen.

'Making coffee.'

'You know I just made you a cup, right? It's in my hands?'

I turn around. 'Yes, and I need you to stop getting me coffee in bed because *you've* spoiled me enough already and I'm never going to find an actual *guy* who is ever going to get me coffee in bed and,' I say, breathless.

'And?'

'And I need to figure out how to do this on my own. I mean, it can't be that hard, right?' I say, twisting open the box with the roasted coffee grounds.

'That's *chai patti*,' Sarina replies.

'Sarina, I'm going to die alone *and* un-caffeinated,' I resign, putting the box back, next to its counterpart holding sugar.

'I take it the date didn't go so well.' I stare at her with eyes that could cut glass, and she physically backs away from me. 'Okay, oh my god, I won't say anything.'

'Good.'

'But what *happened*?'

'The worst.'

'Will you just tell me?'

'You don't *want* to know.'

'Oh, I really, really do.'

I take a pause before I can get myself to say it—until I realize that nothing, no amount of context, is going to make this any less embarrassing. 'He walked out on me when I went to the washroom.'

'Oh my god, Naina . . .'

'And then he said there was an "emergency" at his restaurant,' I add, sighing. 'We all know what that means. I know what that means because *I* do it to people.'

'Maybe he *did* have an emergency?' Sarina asks.

'Come on, Sarina.'

'But . . .'

'But nothing. I just . . . I *hate* him, and I hate being single and going on dead-end dates and I *hate* how hot Nikhil was and—'

Somehow, Nipun walks in around the same time as my early-morning breakdown and Sarina cups her hand against her face and whispers, 'Bad Tinder date,' in the way couples do when discussing the woes of their single friends—as though the memories of *them* being on the other side have been wiped off by their bodies flooding with oxytocin. God, I hate couples.

Almost as much as I hate Monday mornings.

There comes a point in your time at a particular job when you realize: this is it, it's time to go. It's tough to predict exactly when it'll happen; but you'll know it's happened when you feel like a sandpaper all sandpapered out. You can no longer do your work without feeling like there's intense friction all around and most mornings, you'd choose something pretty ghastly happening to you over the idea of actually showing up to your desk. That's when you know it's time to cut your losses and put in the papers.

Like I'm going to do today. Or next week, for sure.

I joined Zupiter fresh out of college, the starry-eyed graduate who thought she could craft the next '*daag acche hain*' copy for a brand and change the world. And, well, the world has changed, but I've played no part in it. Most of my work has been for mind-numbingly boring clients like sustainable energy firms or golf apparel brands that only fifty-year-old uncles buy. For the last year, especially, my creativity has sat in a cage long enough that it no longer bothers to flutter its wings; now, I slap a Tiger Woods reference on an ad and call it a day.

In the shower, I rehearse the conversation I *need* to have today with my manager, Sujata.

'I'm so, so sorry Sujata, but I must go.'

'I gotta go my own way, Sujata.'

'Hey Sujata, Naina out.' Third. It's definitely the third one.

So much for having options, though, when it's Sujata who beats me to the punch.

'Are you fucking kidding me?' This is the first time I—or anyone in this office, to my knowledge—has so passionately sworn at work. A certified rationer, I'd saved up all my fucks and shits and motherfuckers for moments like this one. But now that it has arrived, I realize none of them cut it. I need a road-raging-Scorpio-driving-uncle-swearing-at-the-traffic-cops super-combo to match up to what is happening right now.

'I'm really, *truly* sorry, Naina,' Sujata murmurs from across the table.

This was meant to be a standard performance review—one that happens every quarter. It had been on my calendar for months now, so much so that I'd overlooked it. Barely given it any importance. I was a star performer; what did *I* need a review for?

So, when I walk into a boardroom with Sujata and her higher-up, ten minutes after my calendar pings, the last thing I'm expecting is to be served a termination notice. No, the last thing I'm expecting is for Sujata to tell me she's quitting the job and handing over her title and package to me because I deserve it way more than she does. That's about the last thing I'm expecting. Not *this*—not being broken up with when you were going to pull the plug on the relationship.

'We're really, *extremely* sorry to do this, Naina,' Sujata announces, finally shutting off her laptop, as the HR team and her boss look over, emotionless. I see one of the guys nudge Sujata in the shoulder as she says this. Instantly, she corrects herself: 'What I meant is, we're really sad to see you go.'

I've seen this in *Suits* or some other legal drama Nipun keeps watching—not admitting culpability by saying sorry. Dumbfounded as I am, I truly debate whether I'm fully awake—it's possible that somehow, I've run from the forest right into my worst nightmare.

I feign unconcern, even though it's obvious I'm seconds away from crying. 'May I ask why?' As I speak, I can already taste the salt in the corners of my mouth.

Even if I didn't like the job, I need the money. I *literally* survive on it, after proudly rejecting any support from my parents that wasn't absolutely necessary the day I started earning. My plans to leave this job were going to be cushioned by a two-month notice period and a job hunt. A pay hike. A next step. A twelve-step plan! What now?! Sure, I had some LinkedIn leads that seemed promising— but nothing was going to convert this soon.

'It has nothing to do with your performance, I can assure you,' Sujata says flatly, like it has everything to do with my performance. 'You were a . . . star.'

It's not you, it's me, Naina, my ex's voice creeps up out of turn in my head.

'If it doesn't have to do with my performance, why am I being fired?'

The HR lady sitting to Sujata's right interrupts. 'I'm sorry Naina, this isn't firing. Just a voluntary resignation. The final decision is totally up to you.'

'So . . . you're telling me I'm fired, but I *get* to decide if I want to leave or not?'

HR lady nods. 'Right. But there's not really an option.'

'So, I *am* being fired.'

'No, you're voluntarily resigning.'

'Because you're making me.'

'Correct.'

'So, I'm being . . . fired.'

Before HR lady can respond, the man standing behind Sujata intervenes. If I'm placing him correctly from the two *total* meetings he's bothered to show up to for the department he's *president* of, both of which he spent mansplaining to both Sujata and me, his name is Malik. He's one of those people who have a last name for their first name.

'This back and forth isn't necessary,' he says, curtly, to Sujata.

'Oh, I can see that,' I snicker back. 'I'm not entirely sure why this conversation is being had if my firing has nothing to do with my performance. Or if I have absolutely no say in whether I get to stay or leave.'

Sujata nods as though she's in complete understanding. 'You're right. There is not much to discuss other than to say we've thoroughly enjoyed your work and wish you the best in all your endeavours. I'd be happy to be your reference for any of your future applications.' And with that, the curtain falls. I have officially been fired from my first job.

I don't think you understand. This is not just bad. This is like being dumped-by-the-guy-you-were-dating-out-of-pity bad. This is like finding out that your Tinder date walked into the restaurant, saw your face, and left bad. This is what-am-I-going-to-tell-my-parents bad. This is . . . oh my god, how am I going to feed Bittoo?

Storming out of the building, no box in hand like they show in the movies because all my work was digital and I barely ever decorated my desk, I let the tears stream. *It's okay, Naina,* I console myself, talking out loud. *You can cry about it.* I've left behind that one photo I have of Bittoo push-pinned on the board in front of my seat, the only evidence I was ever there. The realization makes me cry even harder as I sit myself down on the pavement across the building of my now former workplace.

'*Didi, ro mat,*' a little kid says, touching my hair, after I notice him running to me from across the road. '*Kuch nahi hota.*'

This absolutely unexpected act of kindness from a stranger causes my tears to sputter out uncontrollably, like lava out of my eyes; he stands there, smiling cluelessly as he fetches an Alpenliebe from his pocket. Through sniffs and sobs, I shake my head and say no.

'You keep it.'

'*Lelo,* didi,' he says, smiling, before bouncing away and back to his corner of the street.

I pop the toffee in my mouth and realize I need to get out of here before someone from Zupiter sees me like this. Instantly, I dial Sarina. Skipping any salutations, I ask, 'Where are you?'

'At work. What's up?'

'So early today?'

'*Arre,* there is some mixologist event and the brand that's hosting it could barely pull a crowd. No influencers they spoke to turned up. So Sahil asked everyone to come in early and pretend they're a part of the event.'

'Mixologist as in . . .'

'As in, I'm currently on my third cocktail of the day and it's only 11 a.m.'

'Great, can you tell Sahil you're bringing a plus one?'

While Sarina's freelance DJing gigs are aplenty, and intensely lucrative might I add, she does have a daily job at a restro-pub called Bruno's where she DJs most nights. Its vibe is kind of like Curos, if you squint your eyes really hard. Like really, *really* hard. As I walk inside, the overwhelming smell of cranberry and orange juice that is less fruit and more cane sugar nauseates me—all of Bruno's smells like a fruit salad.

'Is this some special work assignment?' Sarina asks as I drop my bag on the counter and take a swig from her glass. Within seconds, I down her drink. Handing her the glass back, I wipe my mouth with the back of my hand. 'Where's this bartender mixologist dude?'

'Okay, hold up. What's going on?'

'Cocktail first.'

With a fresh drink finally in my hand, fittingly blue to match my mood, I sit down on the bar stool right next to Sarina and recount the events of the morning. It takes me three separate cocktails to get through it all. Somehow, I avoid breaking down twice, until it finally happens when the story reaches the point of leaving behind Bittoo's photo and the little kid outside my office.

'Honestly, Naina, take this as a sign from the universe.'

'If you said that when I was sober, I would've punched you,' I say, taking a fat sip of my drink. 'But since my mental faculties are compromised, I do think that's an incredibly wise thing for you to say and have you maybe considered quitting your job and philosophizing full time?'

'*I* think maybe you've had enough,' she says, grabbing my glass away from me.

'Why me, Sarina? What have *I* done? Why do *I* get the shitty job and the shitty love life and the shitty goddamn metabolism while everyone else is just out there doing it all and making it look so fucking easy?' I crash my head on the bar counter like a child napping away during history period in school, rising up moments later.

'Bartender, can I get another, please?' I request, raising my empty glass towards a figure in black that has just appeared before me. 'Extra strong, thanks.'

When my drink is placed in front of me, with a loud thud atop a coaster that is on its last life, I suddenly come to my senses; it's no longer Sarina sitting next to me. And that's not a drink. It's a glass of water.

No, it can't be.

'*You*. What are *you* doing here?'

'Hello to you too,' Vatsal says. 'Nice to see you again, Naina? Was it?'

It's either the alcohol or I'm dreaming—this can't be happening, right? But it is. It is him, isn't it?

I reach out to touch his face to confirm I'm not dreaming. When I actually feel his skin under my fingers, I retreat, realizing what I've done. 'Sorry, I had to . . .'

'You had to?'

'Make sure you were real,' I say, only realizing how ridiculous it sounds once I've already said it. 'What are you doing here? Are you stalking me? Do you want to kidnap me? Who sent you here? It was Sujata, wasn't it?'

Vatsal gapes at me, dumbfounded, before asking: 'Is this an investigation?' When I don't soften my eyes, still incredibly suspicious, he adds, 'Oh my god, no, I'm not stalking you. I'm meeting a bunch of old friends and they're running late. I was having drinks at that table all the way over there when I saw you napping away, and realized, hey, that's the Uber girl!'

'Should I be calling you the washroom guy, then?'

'I'd prefer it if you didn't.'

'I wasn't napping,' I say, clarifying.

'Sure you weren't.'

'I was just resting my eyes for, like, a second.'

'I believe you.'

'You're sure you're not stalking me?'

'Positive,' he says, raising his hands. 'My friends are on their way, if you'd like to meet them. *Just* to be sure.'

'You're meeting your friends *here*?'

'You know this isn't some undercover speakeasy bar you've discovered, right?' he says, smirking. 'Delhi just happens to be a really, really tiny city.'

'And yet I never bump into Shah Rukh Khan.'

'Probably because he lived here thirty years ago,' he deadpans. 'What's . . . wrong with you by the way?' he says, pointing to the nest that my hair has become and the mascara that has, I'm sure, given me raccoon eyes.

'Oh, right,' I say, realizing the state I'm probably in. 'Got fired.'

'Ouch, oh no.'

'From a job I was going to quit . . .'

'No . . .'

'*Today.*'

'Oh my god, we need to get you another drink. Bartender?' Vatsal calls, pointing to the mixologist—who glares back at us with venomous eyes.

'He doesn't like being called bartender.'

He turns back around to look at me. 'So, clearly this is a job you didn't want. What am I missing? Why are you . . . this affected by it?'

'I mean, yes, but even then, being *asked* to leave is humiliating.'

'Did they tell you why they were firing you?'

'Apparently nothing to do with my performance, which, *duh*, my manager literally couldn't pull off a single meeting without me,' I add, mildly slurring my words. I've lost track of time—just as much as I've lost track of how many drinks I've downed. 'I'm genuinely concerned how she's going to handle a presentation we have lined up on Friday,' I say. '*Had.*'

'Well, good thing it's not your problem anymore,' Vatsal says, shrugging, and I know it's intended as placatory, but something about the finality of it all brims my eyes up again. 'Wait, wait, wait, that's supposed to be a good thing, Naina.'

'I worked so hard on that presentation. How could they fire me?' I say, wiping off tears with the back of my hand. I am an adult, meeting another adult for the second time in my life, and I'm crying like a toddler. 'I'm so good at what I do. I literally don't take a single day off, like, ever,' I say, wailing like I'm pleading my case for class monitor.

'It's just a job,' Vatsal says, patting my shoulder, trying to comfort me. It's awkward, mostly—we don't know each other at all, yet he has found himself in this weird position of having to make me feel better when I don't know better than to unload on him. 'You'll find another one, obviously.'

I sit up straight on the bar stool, quietly attempting to somehow return to sobriety. 'Yeah, you're right,' I say, nodding.

'I often am,' he smiles, now on to his second drink with me.

'Speaking of jobs . . . what is it that you do?'

'Will you keep asking me questions until you're convinced I'm not stalking you?'

'I don't know. Maybe?'

He raises his eyebrow at me in intrigue.

'I mean, you have now shown up where I am two nights in a row and I would be stupid to not consider the possibility that you have a hit out to kill me or kidnap me at the very least, and so . . . I'm just collecting all the evidence.'

'You do know that if I actually killed you, you'd *have* no evidence to present?'

'I have to say you're not making a great case for yourself,' I say, inching up close to his face.

Vatsal looks at me—like, really looks at me, in the way that you do when you, for the first time, consider a person as more than just a person in your orbit—and I catch a hint of a blush. He quickly hides it by returning to my question. 'If you'd really like to know, I'm in Delhi interning for a bit before I head to London for school.'

'What are you studying?'

'Law,' he says, matter of factly, like he has no qualms with me interrogating him all night long. 'I mentioned it the first time we met, you know?'

'Forgive me for not remembering that day, I try to block out traumatic memories,' I say, shrugging. 'Isn't interning at your age really embarrassing?'

I gag him with this comment and he laughs in my face, unabashedly.

'I guess you're right, there is something slightly embarrassing about it.' I nod approvingly. Vatsal continues, 'Not more embarrassing than getting fired from a job you wanted to quit though.'

I *would* lunge at him but he pokes me in the stomach quickly enough—like we're already familiar, like this is who we are, like we joke around each other all the time. Like . . . like we've already been friends forever. 'Come on, Naina, you know this is a sign, right?'

'Why does everyone keep saying that? Maybe it's not a sign, you know? Maybe it's just a shit thing and there are no consequences to it other than the fact that I now don't know where my next paycheck is coming from,' I exhale, mildly annoyed. 'Can we let a shit thing be shit or do we have to pop-psychology the hell out of it every time?'

Vatsal isn't deterred by my drunk chiding. That's when I realize he's not any less drunk himself.

'I don't know, I just truly believe there are no coincidences in life. Like, I think when you're too afraid to take the steering wheel, like in your case, not quitting this horrible job, life intervenes and takes that turn you're so fucking scared of taking.'

'I disagree. I think sometimes life sucks and things are bad and that's it. There doesn't *have* to be a reason.'

'Okay, but tell me this. Would you have quit if it weren't for today?'

'Yes. A hundred percent. I was going to quit *today*!'

'Were you, though? It doesn't sound like it, not with that presentation coming up.'

'Okay so maybe not *today,* today. But I would've quit.'

'When?'

'Eventually.'

'Eventually?'

'Fine. Maybe I wouldn't have quit. Maybe I would've stayed there forever. Maybe I would've been one of those people who never leave and are still at the same company thirty years later,' I say, breathless in my pace at this point. 'Maybe I am that person, you know?'

This time, Vatsal turns around—and only now does it dawn upon me, how close our stools have been this entire time. Suddenly, I feel his knees engulfing my waist, lightly trapping me in, the proximity of his touch suddenly sobering me up as his eyes on me cause nervous beads of sweat to trickle down my neck. The world has already been softening on the edges, the booze in my system drowning out the events of the morning and pulling my focus straight onto this boy in front of me. The added sensation of his body meeting mine is too much. He pushes in further towards me, his knee now nestled between my legs, opening me up to him as he drags his bar stool a little too close for comfort.

'Maybe. Maybe that's who Naina is. But is that who *you* really want to be?'

'They teach all this smart talk in law school?'

Finally, Vatsal grabs the stool and pulls me in—with all of my weight—towards him, until the legs of our stools clank against each other. 'No, this is all self-taught.'

NOW

'Ready to go?' Nancy asks, leading the way into the conference room.

'Born ready,' I say, feigning what I hope is at least a modicum of confidence, because the alternative—bursting out into toddler tears—is apparently not encouraged at the workplace.

God, I miss teenage romance.

Sure, it was more melodramatic than romantic and the first kisses were awful, but at least there was plenty of time to wonder and wallow. In the classroom, during lunch breaks, the bus rides back home: the minutes and hours stretched to *make* time for love, for its misery. In or out of love, it felt good to be able to feel so much—and have so much time to let those feelings simmer and spike and stir up waves inside my tiny heart. Because as much as I would like to starfish on my bed and think only and only of Vatsal, the absolute madness yet complete normalcy of seeing him again after all these years, the demands of adulthood no longer allow for that.

Today, the *day* after running into him, just happens to be the most important day of my career yet. It's our first meeting with the independent client that I brought to Marked—the full-stack marketing agency I clawed my way into as an associate fresh off of my soulless job at Zupiter—one that'll finally earn me a permanent spot in Nancy's heart. After all, it's the big guns—QuickCart, the quick commerce company whose pan-India app roll-out we're trying to bag.

This account is it. It is my *moment*.

'Vikas, Sushil, so nice of you guys to come all the way,' Nancy exclaims as she walks into the room ahead of me and shakes hands with the founders who I still can't believe are standing here—a friend I know works in the founder's office and one thing led to another, but we got an in that an agency our size almost never gets.

Be that as it may, though—on her way in, Nancy, in classic Nancy fashion, confirms their names with me.

'The tall one is Vikas and the one who looks like Manoj Bajpai is Sushil,' I whisper in her ear.

'Is that supposed to be helpful?'

'Just trust me.'

As we step in, Sushil, the co-founder who dons the role of the chattier one of the two, meets Nancy's hand first, followed by Vikas—who I presume is all the tech brains—and then I follow. Only when Nancy, Vikas and Sushil take their seats do I catch sight of a looming figure—until now eclipsed by Sushil's gait—lifting off from the chair that's conveniently kept him out of sight. Nancy leans over the table to greet him, having spotted him only now, just as I have, as I stand there, dumbfounded.

She turns to me quickly afterwards. 'Naina, could you ring Rajat from legal and ask him to join us?' she whispers softly in my ear. 'We'll just wait a few minutes to start? Someone from our team is running a little late,' she announces to the room.

This is pretty standard practice for when we're pitching our ideas to clients. Sometimes, we prefer legal to be involved from the start—our pitches have been stolen by prospective clients who backed out at the last minute claiming 'cost complications' only to later pull off big-budget celebrity shoots based on concepts we presented.

But what's happening right *now* isn't standard. In fact, it's so out of the ordinary, I wish I could physically slap myself awake just to ascertain that this isn't real life.

Somehow, I force myself out of my stupor when Vikas pulls the trigger: 'And that's our legal advisor, Vatsal. I don't believe you two have met before.'

Before I can respond, Vatsal looks at me, the fattest smirk washed over his face, and deadpans, 'Nope. First time.'

~

'You know we're going to have to confess, right?' I say as everyone exits the meeting room after an excruciating hour of presenting my pitch to Vikas, Sushil and *Vatsal* like I wasn't sweating out of all my extremities. The pitch, though, ends up semi-successful, despite the wrench in the works. As the room empties, I stay behind, clearing the table of loose papers and folders, switching my laptop on and off in desperate fury to do something with my hands, biding time until everyone's out; Vatsal, too, fetches something indiscernible from inside his briefcase for five whole minutes. The room finally empties and then all at once, Vatsal turns to look at me. Instantly, I take a step back and move five whole feet away from him, only now recalling that of all the ten steps of my morning routine, deodorant was the one abandoned because of my Uber driver's incessant calling.

'Why, exactly?' He asks, folding his arms across his chest, his eyebrow raised.

'This is obviously not . . . normal.'

Unflinchingly, he replies: 'I feel like the time to confess has passed. Besides, confess *what*, exactly? We're not dating.' As he talks, he takes several steps to undo the ones I took away from him.

I swallow my pride—the casualness with which he says this singular truth is so enviable; it's downright infuriating. Except, my face, my tone find it tough to exhibit anger. *Flustered* is all I can muster.

'I never said we were, but—'

'—so unless you think that me being around you does something to your productivity or objectivity, I find no reason to . . . *confess*,' he says, leaning in, whispering the word like a sleaze, all while inching himself close enough that I can feel his breath on my bare shoulder.

'No, I'm good. As long as you're good with being in the same room with me for the next few days without feeling the need to bolt.'

Vatsal looks at me like I've pricked a nerve—like *he's* the one who gets to take offence. He grabs his briefcase and puts it over his shoulder. 'So this is going to be smooth, then,' he announces.

'Totally.'

'Not unprofessional at all,' he asserts, moving closer to me, his palm cupping the front of the table, centimetres away from my chest, his entire body locking mine in place. I couldn't escape if I tried.

'No, we're both adults here.'

'Nothing to get our bosses worked up about.'

'It's all under control,' I say, confirming, as I notice the rise and fall in his chest, matching mine.

No two people have stood this close to each other in this conference room before. No two people have stood this close to each other without either lunging for each other's throats or kissing—period. But before I can figure out what we're about to do with this proximity, Vatsal's chest deflates. Against all my wishes and my worst, truest intentions, he retreats.

'If everything goes well on Vikas and Sushil's end, I'll have some paperwork emailed to you by tonight. Check with Rajat and send it back by tomorrow, please,' he says, conclusively, and then releases me from his gaze. The conference room door jingles open and then promptly whooshes shut—until it suddenly swings open again.

'And Naina?' Vatsal calls out to me, causing me to tense up all over just as I am finally breathing my first sigh of relief all morning.

I turn around to face him as he pokes his head in, already halfway through the door.

'Good pitch.'

~

When I'm confident Vatsal is out of the building, I panic-run to Nancy's office. Nothing in our stand-off about keeping things professional *felt* professional. It felt like a big, bold HR violation.

'Hey, got a minute?'

'I have,' she glances at her watch as she says, 'fifteen seconds.'

'Great, I'll be quick,' I say, taking the seat in front of her. 'Their legal guy, Vatsal?'

She looks at me poker-faced, waiting for me to get to the point.

'I have . . . hooked up with him. I mean, *had* . . . a sort of situation with him. Once. Two years ago,' I hesitate as I add the additional details. 'We've been out of touch all this while and I *just* ran into him yesterday and . . . Nancy, he's *their* legal guy. And this is *my* account that I have worked my ass off on and I had no idea he was going to be here and now . . . I don't know, I'm slightly freaking out.'

'Your question?' she asks, half-distracted by the beeping on her phone.

'Is this going to be a concern? Do we need to do something about it? Will you have to take me off the project?'

Nancy looks up from her phone at me. 'You hooked up with him?' I nod. 'Once, two years ago?' I bob my head up and down. 'And that's my business, how?'

'I just don't want to mess this up,' I say with such sincere vulnerability, the exact kind that Nancy hates, that I half-expect her to take me off the project just for showing how much I want it.

Nancy looks straight at me in her classic now-you-listen-to-me way as she says: 'Naina, as a woman, the biggest thing you need to learn is to stop underselling yourself. Or finding ways to self-sabotage. I don't care about your personal life; I care that you're the best employee I've ever had and that I need you on this project.'

'I know, but—' I say, interrupting.

'There's no but,' Nancy emphasizes. 'I'm sure that guy . . . Vatsal, was it, isn't going to Vikas or Sushil and confessing all of this, is he?' she asks me, her eyes narrowing. 'So why, exactly, are you telling me this?'

'Did I do something wrong?'

Nancy sighs, like people often do at the precipice of a teachable moment. 'Naina, your business is your business. You don't need to make it the company's business. I trust you to do your work objectively and that's all I care about,' she replies. 'Unless you think him being on the project impairs your ability to deliver your best. In which case, by all means, sign off.'

'Absolutely not. This project is my baby, Nancy, you know that.'

'Good, then, will that be all?' she says, back to looking at her phone.

'I . . . yes. That's all.'

'Great. Shut the door on your way out.'

I walk away satisfied that this Vatsal thing is not going to be a problem at work. I'm not going to let it.

Everywhere else, well, I guess I'll just have to see about that.

~

'SHUT THE FUCK UP,' Sarina yells from across the kitchen as she smushes the mashed potato mix onto the white bread for the Bombay sandwich she's making me. 'You're pranking me, *haina*?'

'It feels like the universe is pranking *me*, Sarina. The fact that I bump into Vatsal one day after three years and then bump into him again at my job, where we're somehow working on my dream account? Together, now, for some reason. *If* I get the account, that is.'

We're both quiet as Sarina loads the sandwich onto the grill. Instantly, the sizzle of the oil meeting the metal bars reminds me I've been famished for hours, too nervous to eat. I look back up from the grill to find Sarina gazing at me, an unrecognizable look in her eye.

'What?' I ask.

'I'm just thinking . . .'

'Okay, think out loud.'

'I just think, this is a lot of things happening together, all at once, to call it coincidence, right?'

'What do I call it then?'

'I don't know . . . fate?' she says, releasing the nicely crisped sandwich with the golden-brown crinkle coat from the grill. She sets it down on a plate, slices it into triangular halves, and adds a tiny mountain of ketchup before sliding it towards me.

'It's not fate if it's the guy who broke your heart, Sarina,' I say, instantly taking a fat bite. 'Fuck, fuck, fuck, it's boiling,' I say, spitting out the unchewed bits. I run my hand under cold water as I speak to her, and myself, out loud: 'He's . . . the one that got away. The one that ruined me. That's not fate, it's a tragicomedy.'

'Whatever you want to call it. I'm just saying, stuff like this is never random.'

'Yeah? That's what it felt like the last time,' I say, tearing the sandwich open to let the potato filling cool off. 'Look what happened then.'

'It could've ended differently and you know that.'

'I don't know, I don't think so,' I say, before trudging my plate to my bedroom. Back in my bed with half a sandwich, I run the scenarios over in my mind of all the ways this can go down. My brain throws up a single word: *bad.* The last time Vatsal and I got even remotely close to getting together, things combusted bad enough for us to literally never see—or talk to—each other again. Until now, that is. And sure, my heart ripped into teeny-tiny pieces when that unfolded, but this time, my career is involved. This time, *everything* is at stake.

As I wipe the crumbs of the sandwich off my hands, my phone lights up with a notification—the ding is Gmail, a sound that I have trained myself to be able to recognize in my sleep. Inside, a world of unfamiliarity.

Dear Naina
Requesting signatures.
Vatsal

Attached to the mail are the files he mentioned right before he left the conference room. His email persona is so unlike his actual self, it feels like we're playing pretend. I hit download on all the files, punch my signatures in, and send everything back in record timing. Anything to get his unread notification off my inbox.

Vatsal,
PFA countersigned documents.
Best,
Naina

I shoot off the mail and slide his name away from my notification bar. There. We're clean.

Dear Naina
Requesting your signatures please.
Vatsal

What's he on about, I whisper out loud. Annoyed, I open all the files one by one, when—yeah. Shit.

Two weeks ago, Sarina's eight-year-old cousin had come over for lunch and had seen me signing ten documents in a row on my iPad—with a wildly manipulative smile, he asked if he could sign some too. I humoured him with some older files, thinking I'll just go back and delete the latest signature, which my system automatically sets to a default. Smiley faces and all.

Vatsal,
Apologies for the error. PFA revised files.
Best,
Naina

I obsessively attach and download and delete and attach the files about thirty times before I half-shut my eyes and press send on the email to Vatsal. Once sent, I drag the cursor to quit Gmail altogether, when, suddenly, the top row of my inbox boldens in front of my eyes.

Dear Naina
Thanks, this works. Who is Amitoj?
P.S.
Free for a call?

Nervous beads of sweat *would* run down my forehead if that were really a thing, if people did spontaneously burst into perspiration at the onset of tricky situations.

Vatsal,
Amitoj is my assistant.
P.S.
Sure.

My phone rings the second I shoot the mail off. I'm certain he didn't even wait for me to say yes before he dialled my number.

'Hello,' I answer, trying to be my nonchalant best.

'I didn't know you had an assistant,' he announces more than says. The smile I can hear in his voice through the phone makes my worried frown disappear—but I promise myself to not let it sound through the phone, to not let him hear the joy in my voice the way I can hear it radiating in his.

'Yeah, he's really good.'

'Is he also four?'

'That's . . . beside the point.'

'No, I think that's the point, entirely.'

'What's this regarding?'

'*Regarding?*'

I'm trying so hard to not give too much of me away, not even as much as a smile, even though Vatsal continues to poke me in every way that feels familiar. 'Yes.'

'I thought you got rid of my number,' he says, randomly, and I want to bury my head into my pillow—I can't help but knock the feeling that he can see me. When I don't respond, he asks, 'Did you?'

'I generally clean out my contacts every six months.'

'No one does that.'

'*I* do that.'

'*Crazy* people do that.'

'Anyway, I didn't delete your number. Just forgot I had it,' I say, shrugging, convinced that he can see my put-on nonchalance through the phone. I have to pace myself, remind myself that he's not around, that he can't see me, but it's not working. I've never felt so . . . observed.

As though he's just now understood the rules of the game we're playing, Vatsal clears his throat and matches my seriousness tone for tone. 'This is *regarding* the documents.'

'Any problem?' I ask. Please, god, please tell me I didn't mess something else up this time. 'They look fine on my end.'

'Yes, everything looks good. I just need you to also get Nancy's signature on the NDA.'

'Will that be necessary?' I ask, already nervous in anticipation of what lies ahead.

'Sushil is very anal about the proprietary information, especially related to the app. And since Nancy will be heavily involved, I'm assuming, I need her to also sign it for the boss-men to get a good night's sleep. And me, by extension.'

'They know that we're a marketing agency, right? We're not going to one day randomly decide we want to make an app?'

'If the entire world operated on blind trust, Naina, there would *be* no need for lawyers.'

'And what a world that would've been,' I say, sighing, and I hear him snicker on the other end. 'Fine, I'll get you the signatures tomorrow. Anything else?'

I'm trying so hard to keep it short—untethered—with Vatsal this time around, but I can't help but feel like it comes across as trying *too* hard, if anything. Like he can tell that I not only care, but that I care a lot.

'Nope, that's all. Have a nice night, Naina.'

His phone clicks off before I can say it back.

~

'I'm not signing a fucking NDA,' Nancy yells furiously from across the room.

By all accounts, the day is already off to an excellent start. A long-term client has pulled out of the contract renewal process because their commercials no longer matched ours and our finance team was dead set on not getting low-balled for the second year in a row. And while that means more time on my plate to really prioritize QuickCart's account—a company larger than all the brands we handle *combined*—Nancy isn't happy.

'Have they lost their minds? Don't they understand that me coming on board literally means it's in *my* best interest that their launch plan does not get leaked?'

'Besides, what's so fucking proprietary about a quick commerce app?' Nancy adds as I stand still, too stunned to speak. 'Everyone's making one. My neighbour's twelve-year-old son is making one.'

I let Nancy have her moment—it's office lore, her disagreeability with NDAs. A former employee had put Nancy's signatures on one without consulting her, Nancy went and spoke about that project at length at a business conclave to educate young marketers on how to capture the right customer, and lo and behold, the client threatened to sue—something our legal team managed to put to bed by finding some loophole in the contract, thank god.

The employee was, *obviously*, fired.

'What do you want to do?' I ask, trying hard to not sound like I'm desperate. Being able to close this with Vikas and Sushil—and *Vatsal*—means that I'll be on the fast track to a promotion, even though I'm sure that will happen regardless. Nancy loves me. But this way *I* can be certain that I deserve it and not feel like an imposter when it actually happens.

Nancy doesn't answer—she just stares into oblivion, mulling over her choices. She hates NDAs, I know. She hates signing over the right to talk about her accomplishments with companies because it minimizes the public's perception of the volume of work she did. But she also knows, just as much as I do, that this account is too good to drop over this. The money it'll bring in will be fantastic for the agency—life-changing, even.

'Fuck,' she mutters under her breath.

That means yes.

'So, I'll sign it on your behalf and send it?'

'Yes.'

'The NDA. That they sent. I'm going to sign and email that.'

'Do you want to record this conversation?'

'Yes, please, if that's okay?' I say, half-joking, mostly very serious.

'Get out of here.'

Back at my table, I push send on the dreaded email, specifically choosing to not copy Nancy. The last thing she needs is a reminder.

Vatsal,
PFA countersigned NDA with Nancy's signatures.
Naina

My phone lights right back up.

Dear Naina
Thanks!
See you at work tomorrow :)

I stare at the screen for a solid fifteen minutes before I decide against emailing him back. What I *should* be feeling is dread. Instead, I can't wait to get into work tomorrow.

Three Years Ago

'How drunk are you?' I ask, pulling him inside the washroom. It takes a whisper in his ear—*Meet me at the back in two minutes*—and exactly two minutes later, Vatsal knocks on the one common washroom at Bruno's. I don't know what has come over me. Maybe it's the fact that he pulled me in; maybe it is the glimmer in his eyes that made me feel like he wants it too. Or maybe it's the sudden recklessness that the firing has invoked—this do-or-die mentality that has somehow switched on in my brain.

Or maybe all of that's bullshit and I am just wasted.

'Pretty drunk,' he shrugs. 'You?'

'Same.'

'Which means this is a bad idea.'

'Totally.' I nod.

We stand there, snug inside a tiny matchbox, close as much by necessity as by want. Yet, even within this cramped set up, Vatsal finds space to move in, to position

his hand on my waist and clutch me to his chest the way
he'd done with my barstool minutes ago.

I fear he can hear the jagged beat of my heart running
crazy. I fear I won't be able to hear his.

'We just agreed this was a bad idea,' I say, intentionally
coy, staring at him in defiance, dangling my waist under his
touch, feigning a need for release, needing him to hold me
even tighter. Even closer.

Like he can read my mind, his grip hardens, digging
into the skin on my waist. 'And I agreed.'

'So, you should leave.'

'Maybe you should leave,' he responds, both our
chests expanding and collapsing rhythmically. Even before
anything happens, we are already sharing all the oxygen in
this three by three. Vatsal continues to stare at me and as
much as it feels like it will immolate me if it lasts a second
longer, I hold his gaze right back.

'I don't usually do this.'

That makes him laugh, which makes him finally take
his eyes off me. For the first time in a few minutes, I take
in a full breath.

'And you think I do this, what, every day?'

'I mean, I wouldn't know.'

'You know if I had said that to you I would be in a lot
of trouble?'

I look at him and wonder what it would take for us to
stop talking, if I have it in me to take the lead. 'We could
get in trouble for this, too.'

He agrees. 'Which is why we shouldn't.'

'You're right.'

'So, you should walk out,' he instructs me, pointing to
the door.

'You leave first,' I say, challenging, but he just stands there, so I do it—I move past him, brushing against his shoulder, trying to grab hold of the door knob when, just as quickly as my hand wraps around it, his palm grabs the inside of my elbow. A quick pull is all it takes; Vatsal turns me around and pushes me against the door, which shakes with my weight being shoved against it. I stand there, dumbstruck, turning into liquid by just how much he wants me.

'Where exactly do you think you're going?' he whispers, his hands holding both of my arms glued tight to the door behind me, his grip firm and unshaking on both of my elbows, with enough give that I could just as easily fidget out of his touch if I wanted to. But that is the last thing I want.

'You told me to leave.'

'So you're telling me that if I just tell you to do things, Naina, you'll do them?'

I look up at him, into his eyes. 'If you ask nicely.'

'Do you *want to* leave?'

'Wasn't I the one who called you in here?' I ask, narrowing my eyes, his hands still holding me hostage.

'You could've called me in here for whatever.'

'Right, I called you in here for a conversation.'

'Cool, let's talk,' he says, moving his chest into mine even further, while he lets go of his grip on me. This time, it's his head nuzzled between my neck and my shoulder, breathing right over my skin while, once again, locking my arms in place, making me unable to touch as much of him as he is of me. 'What,'—his lips graze the outside of my jaw. 'Do,' he whispers, a warm breath against my ear, 'you want to,' his mouth hovers at my neck, 'talk about,' he finally asks, his voice muffled, as his lips gently latch onto my skin.

'Fuck,' I whisper as his mouth circles to the bottom of my neck and then right atop my collar bone, where he stops and looks right up at me. 'Let's talk about that shirt of yours,' I reply.

'What about it?' he asks, his lips still drawn apart on my collarbone.

'About how it's still on.'

We look at each other, half in challenge, half in unbridled desire—I haven't known this before him, before this moment, this feeling of such desperate, such heady need that consumes you till the neck-up, till you can't breathe, till you can't keep it from spilling over.

'What if somebody knocks?' I ask, nervously.

'They're just going to have to wait.'

A second later, Vatsal's lips, my lips, you couldn't tell the difference.

~

Making out with Vatsal—a total out of body, out of character experience—was one thing. Finding that in our impatient need to be with each other, we both forgot to lock the washroom door was a whole another.

And then there was the fact that it was Sarina, of all people, who walked in on us while Vatsal's hand was visibly on my butt. I don't know if it would've been better or worse to be caught by a stranger.

'Wait, what the actual fuck?' she shrieks.

'What are *you* doing here?' Vatsal asks, covering up the side of my shirt he's pulled down to feel more, touch more.

'I work here, you idiot,' she responds.

Still slightly jarred by being busted in the act, I ask, in my confusion: 'You two . . . know each other?'

'You know *her*?' Vatsal quizzes Sarina, puzzled.

'Clearly *you* two know each other,' Sarina replies. 'I'm going to give you guys a second to clean up,' she says, laughing, as she shuts the door. 'Lock it this time!' I hear her yell from the outside.

Vatsal and I don't talk as he puts his shirt on while I close the buttons he undid on mine.

'Your face,' I say, pointing to the red lipstick I was wearing, now smudged all over his mouth.

When we finally look half-decent, I open the bathroom door to Sarina still standing outside, her arms crossed against her chest.

'So, I clearly don't have to do the introductions here,' she quips. 'Naina, Vatsal. Vatsal, Naina,' she says, pointing to the both of us respectively.

'Yeah, we're a little past that point,' Vatsal smiles.

'Good first interaction?' Sarina asks.

Shyly, I add: 'This isn't . . . the first.'

'You haven't told her about the other washroom incident?' Vatsal looks at me, shocked.

'There's more than *one* washroom incident?' Sarina asks, her mouth flung open.

'Wait, I think there's some clearing up you guys need to do,' I say, interrupting. 'Like, how do *you* two know each other?'

'Right, right. Naina, that's Nipun's childhood best friend, Vatsal,' she says, pointing at him. At once, the name throws up factoids Nipun has peppered into conversations: school friend, stand-up guy, went to London, studies law, a bit of a player? 'Who he is supposed to be having dinner with right now.' *And of course, of course, the one guy I've ever spontaneously hooked up with has to be inextricably tied to my life. Great.* 'And Vatsal, this is Naina. My best friend.'

'Now,' she says as she plants her hands on her waist, bossing over us. 'Do you two want to tell me what's going on *here?*'

~

By the next morning, Nipun is in on it too—and I am mortified. Sarina, meanwhile, is having the time of her life with this turn of events.

'That's where Vatsal disappeared to?' Nipun asks Sarina, shocked, as she finishes narrating the story over breakfast, while I just watch, waiting to get a word in edgewise.

'While you were waiting for him at dinner, he was . . . let's just say, he was . . . '

Before Sarina can say anything more, I interrupt, asking Nipun: 'Who *is* this Vatsal guy anyway? I've hardly ever heard of him!'

'Childhood friend, kind of like you and Sarina. Except we don't live together and confuse people about our sexuality on the regular,' Nipun laughs. 'He's in town for a bit before he goes off to London for his master's.'

'Yeah, that much he told me.'

He does have such a lawyer look, now that I think about it. Cunning, over-smart, over-familiar.

'Anyway, he might come over to chill one of these days,' Nipun adds, grabbing the toast from my plate that I no longer have an appetite for, 'just giving you a heads up.'

Sarina takes the bait, adding: 'Right, just like Naina was giving him a heads up last ni—'

'I will murder you if you finish that sentence.'

'Okay, I won't finish that sentence.'

'Good,' I reply, getting up off the table.

'Just like you guys couldn't finish last night,' she cackles, finally throwing her head back with childish giggles as I collect the leftovers from breakfast in a Tupperware container. Nipun shrugs his shoulders, apologizing for his girlfriend. I'm less generous; I wave my middle finger at her.

'Can't you just take the day off, please?' I squeal at Sarina as she pads to her bedroom, trying, desperately, to redirect the conversation.

Being fired is bad enough. Being fired right at the brink of *chutti* season is almost maddening. While everyone is trying to close deadlines, finish festive deliverables, clear the next week's calendar to make space for Diwali parties, I have received a sum total of zero responses to the hundred job applications I must've sent out by now.

'Naina, you know this is, like, the busiest season for me?' she says as she's teasing her hair back, before filling the room with the scent of her hairspray. 'Eyes,' she instructs, and I cover mine and clip my nose as she douses her crown in hairspray that won't let her hair budge through an entire day of head-banging. 'Besides, don't you have to meet that friend of Nipun's today?'

'I do,' I say, crashing flat on her bed. 'But that's in the afternoon. What do I do until then?'

'Why don't you go work at the cafe where you're seeing him? Read up on what he does, send out a few more apps and all?' Sarina suggests, locking her bun in place. 'Get out of the house, Naina. You'll drive yourself crazy, *warna*.'

Despite Bittoo's strategic purrs right as I make it out of the house compelling me to stay back, I take Sarina's advice.

The auto ride to the coffee shop passes through the same primary school that I would glance at longingly on my way to work. Just like today, I'd hear the children wailing all the way to the main road and think: *same*. Except now, I wish I *were* them. I wish the way out of most problems in life was still to cry instead of having to figure them out on your own.

At the coffee shop, I take the table furthest away from the annoying couple—PDA is only okay when I'm involved—and turn my laptop on. It's a random landing page on Chrome, a website I'd last visited but never closed the tab for. But it sticks out like a sore thumb: A Google ad of a festive campaign for *my* account that *I* painstakingly designed with our crackhead visual artist that Sujata must now be taking credit for. Furious, I click on the ad with no intention of purchasing—just to waste the client's budget. When the shopping page opens, I add everything to my cart and then close the tab without checking out. It's my invisible 'fuck you' to Zupiter.

It takes fifteen minutes, but every last file—every pending document that I had up for completion for this week at Zupiter, every random image I'd stored but forgotten to delete—I select and dump into the recycle bin. I'm almost done eliminating the last few remnants from my screen, including my employment contract, when I feel the looming shadow, an inexplicable closeness, of someone familiar hovering behind me. I turn around, expecting a nosey waiter needing me to order something more than just an americano, now that I've been here for half an hour.

'Is that you?' the voice asks. It's not a waiter. I feel my cheeks firing up red at the sudden sight of him—his wet hair falling haphazardly on his forehead while he's dressed in a white shirt with brown linen pants, holding a briefcase in his left hand.

'Turns out it is,' I say, smiling through gritted teeth, the sobered-up embarrassment of our drunk encounter washing over me.

I'd really love to stop running into Vatsal.

~

'Listen, I want to apologize for that night,' I say before Vatsal can say anything else. It's so unlike me to be so out of control, I don't even know how to *really* apologize for it. Or for everything that came next. I try to stop the film from playing, but it rewinds back to the entire sequence: the grip of his fingers on my waist. The sweat of the palm of his hand between my legs. The arresting of my heart at his refusal to lose steam until I was breathless. How I'd screamed.

God, I'd screamed, hadn't I?

'What night?' he says, cocking his head to the right.

'You *know* what night.'

Vatsal grabs the chair in front of me and points to ask if it's free. 'Yeah, yeah, go ahead. I'm meeting someone, but that's not for a while.'

'Date?'

'*God*, no. Job stuff,' I say. 'And really, I'm sorry about being a sloppy drunk, I swear I'm not usually like that.'

'Don't be, I had fun.'

'Of course you had fun, *you* don't have to live with Sarina and Nipun after this.'

'I feel like we should've covered some . . . bases before you asked me into that washroom,' Vatsal says, jumping straight to the point.

'I doubt this would've come up,' I say, blushing. 'Anyway, Nipun doesn't particularly care, so we're okay.'

'Of course he doesn't care, he isn't the one who walked in on us.'

'Sarina . . . has seen worse.'

'Oh, so you do this often? With strange boys in washrooms?'

'Are you *seriously* judging me right now?'

'I was just asking a question.'

'And I'm refusing to answer it,' I say, hoping he doesn't read it on my face, the fact that I don't do this often. Or ever. 'What are you doing here?' I ask, swerving the topic into safer, less suggestive territory. 'What about the fancy internship?'

'The *fancy* internship,' he replies, 'does not have enough fancy seating to accommodate me on most days. So I work out of here. Or, like, any coffee shop that won't kick me out.'

'You're joking, right?'

'No, really. On my first day, I sat in this seat I thought was empty until this giant dude walked over and said, "I think you might be in my seat." Lawyers have such a temper, Naina, I thought he was going to kill me. Almost shit my pants.'

'Not the first day on the job impression you want to give.'

'Not the impression you want to give on any day,' Vatsal laughs. 'But this isn't too shabby. I like the coffee here. Plus, I've always wanted to do this working-out-of-a-cafe thing. Feels so fancy.'

'You're a piece.'

'A piece?'

'Yeah, one of a kind.'

'Thank you?'

'Wasn't a compliment.'

'Too late, already went to my head.'

Suddenly, an interruption: 'Naina?' A tall man towering over Vatsal calls out my name.

'Hey, Sambhav, hi,' I reply, rising up out of my seat, spilling some of my americano with the sudden jerk of the table. We shake hands as Vatsal watches, before he gets up too.

'Hey, man, Vatsal,' Sambhav exclaims, as Vatsal initiates a hug. 'It's been so long, dude! How've you been? *Where* have you been?'

Of course.

All of this is just . . . brilliant.

'Good, good,' Vatsal says, smiling. 'Just in town for a few months before heading off to London for law school.'

'You guys know each other?' I ask, trying to make sense of this interaction.

Sambhav puts his arm around Vatsal, 'Oh, we go way, way back. All the way back to college.' He turns around to look at him again, before patting his chest. 'But fancy, man. London again, *haan*? That'll be so cool. You're going to love it.'

They exchange small talk as I watch, stupefied. Vatsal notices and then looks over at me and asks, 'You were supposed to meet Sambhav about the job?' He says more than asks, a smirk on his face, because he knows what this means. That I can't escape him—no matter where I go. That he likes it this way.

'I had no idea you guys knew each other,' I say, shrugging casually. Which is the opposite of what I feel.

'That's funny,' Vatsal says, scratching his head. 'I'm going to head out and let you guys . . .' Vatsal says, hanging his words in the air. 'I'll see you, Naina,' he waves at me, a subtle goodbye, and grabs a table of his own at the other end of the cafe.

'So, Naina. Tell me a little bit about yourself,' Sambhav asks, as we sit down and get the pleasantries out of the way—how he knows Nipun, Vatsal, what he does at Marked, the marketing agency where he's been for three years now. I hadn't anticipated this being an interview, so it stuns me, slightly—I'd only prepared myself for an informal chat. I ooh and ah a little, buying some time, before I do a two-minute run down of every project I handled with Sujata. The conversation flows—from one account I brought to the firm to another I botched—I'm being more candid than I usually am in interviews, but Sambhav seems interested. Impressed.

'Launching potato chips. In this economy,' Sambhav scoffs. 'How did you manage to make noise for them in such a crowded market?'

'I made them launch a chocolate-coated potato chip.'

'That sounds . . . awful.'

'I know. It *was*. But it got everyone talking. An influencer made a video about it, pranking his friend with a bag of chocolate but then there's a chocolate-covered potato chip in there and the reactions were *phenomenal*. After that it became a viral prank to the point where every big-name influencer was doing it. And then sales,' I point to an upward-rising graph. Recounting this particular instance feels good even beyond just impressing Sambhav; for the first time in a few days, I don't feel like a piece of shit.

'I have to say, Naina, I came here to do Nipun a favour,' Sambhav says, stoic, as I try so hard to not let my face shift, preventing even a hint of a smile from appearing on it. 'But I'm honestly quite impressed.' Before I can get my hopes up, Sambhav continues: 'I hope you understand, though, that I'll have to run this by my team. Even then, Nancy takes the final call. No matter how much I think you're a fit,' he says, smiling.

'Of course, I absolutely understand.' I nod, remembering to strike Sujata off as a reference in my resume when I send it out to Sambhav. 'Any timeline that I can keep in mind?'

'Let's try and get you in for an interview with Nancy soon and then we'll see? Maybe we could try for a post-Diwali joining, if everything goes well?'

'Sounds like a plan!'

'Awesome. I'll call you,' Sambhav beams as he pushes his chair inward and waves goodbye.

God. Men. Working for them, dating them: you can't escape the wait for a call.

~

Walking out of the cafe some time later, I glance at the Instagram notifications on my phone; one stands out. @

vatsal_ has sent you a follow request. I bob my head to the left and right back inside the cafe—only slightly disappointed when he's nowhere to be seen—and finally walk out again after my Uber auto driver calls for the second time. In the auto, I slide the notification away.

I'll think about it when I get home.

NOW

'Shut the fuck up, you're joking,' Ira, a colleague, yells when the waiter arrives with a wine cooler so tall it takes me a vertical pan to take it all in. You *know* Nancy is happy when there's free-flowing champagne.

Before leaving, Sambhav told me he'd never been able to convince Nancy to get an expensive bottle of champagne in his entire time with the agency, no matter how massive the celebration; and so, Nancy, on his farewell, finally relented—for last time's sake. But that was different.

'To Naina,' Nancy says, raising her glass to the entire team as everyone joins in. 'To Naina,' the team chants together and my chest swells at the same time as my brain tells me to disappear to the bottom of the table.

This morning, the QuickCart account finally closed—paperwork and all. The final email that I shot off to Vatsal felt like guzzling a chilled bottle of water at the end of a long workout; a reinforcement that I'd done something right in my time at Marked. Even though I was handed a Mount Everest-sized hurdle in the way.

The real work begins now, but the champagne is well earned.

'Thanks, guys; thanks, Nancy,' I say shyly, taking a bigger sip than necessary, anything to dull the nerves. The adrenaline won't leave my system, no matter how many times I see the partnership confirmation email from Vatsal in my inbox. 'I'm just glad it all went smoothly.'

'This one is really going to put us on the map,' Shivani, an intern who recently joined us with the promise of a full-time employee, squeals.

'We're already on the map, kiddo. This one's going to take us to outer space,' Ira zooms her hand past Shivani in a dramatic flight as the rest of the table laughs.

Nancy interrupts. 'Let's not get too big for our boots before we've even worn them, people. This is an excellent feat, and this account is going to do great things for us, but let's not get carried away.'

To many people in the industry, Nancy is an overconfident, cocky know-it-all. Sambhav, too, had once expressed his disdain for her overbearing, controlling tendencies when he thought I wasn't paying attention. 'If only she'd be a little more agreeable, we could make Marked so much bigger,' he said at one of our office parties, slightly tipsy. But I knew then, even just a few months into knowing Nancy, that she was anything but cocky. She's a woman who is aware, painstakingly so, of the curse of being a woman in a competitive industry; she knows her confidence is such an aberration, it's instantly unappealing to an onlooker. But the real Nancy is humble. Controlled.

Almost impossibly measured. Exactly the kind of person I want to be.

'I agree,' I say, adding. 'They could pull out, still, or this could all go horribly wrong or . . .'

Nancy cuts me, too, grazing my forearm sternly and numbing the thought at bay. 'That's *also* what we're not going to do. We're not going to catastrophize this, Naina. This is a good thing. And we're going to celebrate.' She raises her hand to get the waiter's attention. 'Another bottle, please?'

~

It's close to midnight by the time I'm back home. Ira, gracious as she is, and also the only teetotaller in the entire agency, drops me right in front of my apartment building. 'Text me when you're inside,' she says as I jump out of her car. '*Pakka* we're at the right location, no? You're not drunk and disoriented?'

'I had, like, half a glass of champagne,' I say, pulling my bag over my left shoulder. The confidence wanes as I find my head pulsating on the stairs. Three woozy flights later, though, I find myself in front of my apartment door—the tiredness of the day finally settling in as I wrestle through the fifteen thousand unnecessary things in my bag to find my house keys.

I unlock my home to a scene from a potential crime docu-series: Bittoo sprawled out like a doped-up feline in *Vatsal's* arms, with Nipun and Sarina asleep on the couch. I step foot into my own house with Vatsal's annoyingly perfect face gaping at me like he's been staring at the door all night. I watch my step to have something to do instead of looking into his eyes that are so pointedly fixed on me.

'Should I be calling the police?' I ask, internally panicking at the sight of him. 'Why is everyone drugged up and passed out?'

Seeing Vatsal here, at my home, next to the people I love . . . it's déjà vu, a film scene on repeat: once Vatsal landed into my life, he showed up everywhere, all the time. Within days, he went from being a stranger to becoming a placeholder in each one of my life's mundane moments until he disappeared into thin air, like I dreamed him up, somehow.

'So, it's closed, huh?' Vatsal says, flashing his perfect set of teeth at me, scratching Bittoo's sleepy head as he purrs against him. 'How happy are you?'

All day today, Vatsal and I have gone back and forth on the final paperwork and the signing of the deal documents between QuickCart and Marked; I have practically received an email from him once every half an hour. Never before in the history of time has someone been this happy gawking at their screen for twelve hours in the day, waiting for fresh emails to come through.

In answering Vatsal, though, I curb my excitement, hoping to not come across as overeager. 'Just really tired,' I say, smiling, as I set down my bag on the empty spot right next to him. I, too, sit down on the armchair placed adjacent to where Vatsal's sitting on the couch. He turns around to be able to look at me when he talks.

'This one's still just as cute.'

'That's because he's asleep and not begging for food,' I say, trying to motion Vatsal to hand me him, but Bittoo's so peacefully strewn in his arms that I decide against it. 'Okay, actually, you know what? You keep him.'

'So,' I say, shifting my weight around the seat to find a comfortable position to sit in, while Vatsal's feet point at me. I settle on sitting cross-legged, my toes resting against his knees.

'You're wondering why I'm still here. Or if I drugged all three of them.'

'It is *slightly* concerning that they're all passed out and you're . . . the only one awake?'

Vatsal laughs, 'I'm sure you think of me better than to poison my best friend and his girlfriend?'

'Yeah, but not my cat.'

'That's low, Naina.'

'Okay, but what happened . . . here?'

'They weren't sure if you had keys,' Vatsal says simply.

I narrow my eyes at him. 'Not *quite* adding up, still.'

'So, we were all wine drunk and trying to stay up, waiting for you to come. And they weren't sure if you had keys, so we all just decided to wait until you were back, to be safe. They crashed, unfortunately.'

'I always have keys, they know that.'

'*I* didn't know that.'

I look away because I don't know what to say to that. Instead, I veer the conversation far, far away.

'We had a celebration dinner tonight,' I say. 'For the account closing.'

'You can say thank you anytime.'

'Why will I thank *you*? I've been working on this for months.'

'Yet somehow, I show up and it closes in a week.'

'You got involved during the closing stage!' I say, smacking his chest lightly. He grabs my hand before I can make it all the way through; the warmth of his palm could just as well set me ablaze at this moment.

Still, I somehow continue, 'Get your head out of your ass.'

Vatsal is still holding my palm straight to his chest as he says, 'I'm slightly disappointed, though.' I don't know how to demand my hand back.

'About what?'

'You know, with the contract signing and all, my work ends here.'

'That's usually how it goes with you lawyer folk,' I shrug. 'In and out.'

'Yeah, but that sucks because now I can't keep emailing you.'

I take my hand away.

'You can always consult for this next brand that I'm trying to get on board.'

Vatsal cocks his head to the right, holding his head in his hand, his elbow placed over the top edge of the couch. 'Or . . . here's an idea, I could just text you?'

'That's another way,' I say, looking at my lap, non-committal at best.

'So, what's going on with Naina?' he asks, turning the conversation over on its head. 'I hear she's doing pretty well.'

Another nod to the past—how he used to talk about my professional self in third person, how he would dissect my work personality, goals, dreams, ambitions as though we were talking about someone completely outside of me.

'It lets work not become your entire identity,' he'd explain. 'Also, I just really like your name.'

'Naina *is* doing well, especially now that the account is closed, thank you for asking,' I say decidedly.

'You seem happy here.'

'At Marked?'

'Yeah, I mean, in comparison to what you said you felt like at . . . Zupiter?'

I nod. 'Way happier than I was there. Hopefully not getting fired anytime soon, either.'

'Let's just hope this time she beats the management to the punch,' he laughs. 'Because I don't think there's enough liquor in the world for another firing.'

'I don't think there's enough liquor in the world to listen to a lawyer explain *mens rea* to you, either, but hey, nothing like a good business opportunity.'

'Right, and what does it mean again?' he asks, his eyebrow raised in contest.

'Let me think,' I say, scratching my head to make a point out of it. 'Something about what a person was thinking before committing a crime?'

'Impressive,' he says, his mouth upturned.

'Am I ready to become a lawyer now?'

'*I'd* let you defend me,' he says as he smiles at me delicately; like he, too, is holding on to this thing we're building again lightly—like it can break any second. 'No, but really, how *are* you, Naina? I feel like we jumped straight into work, didn't catch up at all.'

'I'm actually really good. How are you?' I ask. 'How is it like being back in India after all that time in London?'

'I'm good too. India is . . . good. I mean, I could taste the smoke the day I landed, but home is home, you know?'

'Yeah, who needs oxygen?'

With that, we arrive at that awkward point in small talk when the niceties have run out, the work and the weather have been exhausted, and one of two options presents itself: dive into the deep stuff or cut your losses. Talk about it all or call it quits while it's still civil.

How do I do it, though? How do I fall into a new rhythm with a person whose pulse once used to match mine?

'So, Nipun and Sarina,' he says, changing the topic.

'Crazy, no?'

'I still can't believe it,' he adds as he throws his head back against the wall.

'I know.' I nod. 'Sometimes I still have to stop, pause and shake Sarina to ask if she's even sure about this.'

'It doesn't sound like you're too thrilled.'

'Hello, I'm ecstatic! But we're all so young, still.'

'Isn't she, like, three years older?' he asks, his eyebrow raised. 'And they *have* been together for ages now, Naina.'

'*Accha*? I didn't know only.'

'You think they're going to go through with it?'

'I mean, the hotel is booked, and all the invites are out and there are literally, like, two weeks to go *and* I've spent two months' worth of my salary on new clothes so . . . yes, I hope?'

'Fuck, dude,' Vatsal laughs. 'I still can't believe he pulled that proposal off.'

I interrupt, adding, 'He had great help.'

'I'm sure he did,' he says, poking my waist. 'How was it?'

It plays like a film reel in my mind—the planning, the plotting, the hiding, The Day, but mostly, the look on Sarina's face when Nipun went down on one knee. The incredible ease with which Sarina knew, like she knew how to breathe, like she knew how to exist, that she wanted to say yes. And amidst it all, I remember the dread. I remember feeling, in every inch of my body, Vatsal's absence. I remember feeling this would never happen for me—but mostly, that it would never happen for us.

Obviously, I don't say any of this. Instead, I say: 'It was like a movie.'

'I would've loved to be there, you know.'

'I know.'

'Why wouldn't you tell me?'

I have to assume that Nipun, when inviting Vatsal to the wedding, told him about the proposal party; probably mentioned that I was responsible for the invites. Which is . . . great.

'I just didn't think you'd make it,' I say, like it wasn't a calculated decision. Like I hadn't typed in and typed out his name over and over in my Notes app, eventually striking it off because I didn't think I could stand to be in the same room as him. Like I didn't know he was in India at the time from the thirty different times I had looked at his stories from Sarina's Instagram account.

'I *was* in India, you know,' he declares.

I act surprised; I do such a bad job at it.

'And how was I supposed to know?'

'How you find out anything about anyone these days, Naina. You check their Instagram stories.'

Right, Instagram.

'I must've missed them,' I say shyly.

'Yeah, you must've missed them,' he smiles—because he knows. Of course he does.

Three Years Ago

On some days, I'm convinced my cat thinks I understand him. Why else would Bittoo meow furiously as I return home from meeting with Sambhav, as though saying, 'How dare you be away for so long?' after days of staying home, all day every day, in my new unemployment era? I pour extra food in his bowl, an afternoon snack, to win him over—luckily, my cat is smart but also so food-motivated it's hilarious—and as he chomps it away, I slip into pajamas so I can become one with my bed.

Over the next hour, my left hand pops fistfuls of yellow Lay's in my mouth while my right hits Easy Apply on any job on LinkedIn that I even remotely find interesting—when, suddenly, a notification zaps me out of accidentally applying for a job in a different department at Zupiter.

The glowing screen reads *@vatsal_ has sent you a follow request.*

I gawk in my phone like a kid; did he just send it *again*?

His profile photo has him dressed in a white linen shirt and black Ray Bans, standing in front of a cliff with the sea stretching in the horizon, his head tilted ever-so-slightly to the right with half a smile on his face. Even in the tiny circular photo on his profile that I have to screenshot to zoom in, he looks so ridiculously handsome that I feel myself getting annoyed. I've seen Vatsal up close plenty of times in the last few days but seeing him in a photograph really seals it for me: just how good looking he is with his, honestly, quite startling, model-esque features and uber-macho demeanour. And yet, for just how handsome he is, he is not douchebag enough.

I gawk at his follow request, hitting 'accept' and 'follow back' in a quick move before he cancels it again, abandoning my job search to shuffle through his entire life history, coded via Instagram posts and story highlights. He follows me right back too, which confirms to me that he sent the request, unsent it, sent it again, and then sat there on the app, waiting for my response.

I open his profile to gather parts of him I don't yet know—but there is very little Vatsal gives me to work with, a sum total of ten posts on his Instagram, all of them seemingly from his travels, with a few picturesque sights thrown in for good measure.

I'm three scrolls deep into a carousel post of him somewhere in Europe when: *catastrophe*. My fingers slip and I accidentally push like on a comment on his photo; him saying thank you to someone for their comment from three years ago.

I don't waste a second and instantly tap to unlike it—but it's already too late. The damage is irreversible. A message pops up.

Vatsal: caught you

My face flushes at his text like he's here; like he's physically glaring at me. His text feels like a poke in the stomach, a child being lovingly chided for being naughty.

Naina: idk what you're talking about
Vatsal: right . . .
Vatsal: you totally did not stalk me and accidentally like and then unlike a comment from three years ago
Vatsal: no, I must've just dreamt this up

I already hate how good-looking Vatsal is, but his cockiness, his upfrontness is even more infuriating, somehow. And so, I don't spare him either, rushing straight for the jugular.

Naina: just like I dreamed up you sending and then unsending and then resending me a follow request?

The typing sign stays buzzing for a full minute—I bet he had no idea I knew. Finally, Vatsal relents.

Vatsal: okay, we can call it even
Vatsal: two equally embarrassing faux pas
Vatsal: cancelled each other out basically

Naina: no, mine was embarrassing, yours was just
desperate
Vatsal: what if I am?
Naina: you're what
Vatsal: you know, desperate

I put my phone down, finding it tough to keep up
pretences, like the fact that he's so obviously flirting with
me is not getting to me. Before I can bring myself to reply,
or say anything that doesn't make me sound stupid, Vatsal
texts again.

Vatsal: what are you doing right now? still at the
coffee shop?
Naina: no, no, I've been back home for a bit
Naina: what's up with you?
Vatsal: wanna grab lunch together, maybe?

I don't know if Vatsal and I are 'grab lunch' friends yet,
or if we're friends at all. At best, we're two strangers
tied together by an extremely awkward encounter and,
unfortunately, a lot of strings.

Vatsal: listen I just figured that . . . we've gotten ahead
of ourselves
Vatsal: and I'd just like to make it not awkward,
preferably over a meal
Vatsal: also because I'm starving

I run the prospect of hanging out with Vatsal over in my
head, playing catch and release with yes or no. It's not an

entirely horrible idea—I *am* slightly sick of applying for jobs all day, every single day. Plus, Nipun did mention me running into him over the next few months, and so maybe it makes sense to make things a little more . . . friendly?

But then there are technical difficulties.

Naina: I'd love to but I have lunch at home :((((

I don't add: I'm afraid Rani didi will bash me to death with a *belan* if I don't eat it—especially when I requested her to make pav bhaaji ten minutes before she was about to leave.

'*Mai kaam chorr dungi* [I will quit],' she yelled from the kitchen. '*Tumhaari wajah se baakiyon ka kaam late hota hai* [I get late for my other jobs because of you].'

Before leaving, she'd pulled my cheek. '*Pav kamm hai. Mangwa lena* [There aren't enough buns, order more].'

Vatsal: :(
Naina: but
Naina: you could come over?
Naina: only if you also bring one extra packet of pavs
Vatsal: NO WAY
Vatsal: THERE'S PAV BHAAJI???
Vatsal: be there in 15

~

Vatsal shows up at my door in record timing—with three pav packets.

'I said *one* extra packet,' I say, opening the door to him.

'This one's for you, this one's for me,' he says, lifting his hand holding two packets. 'And this one,' he says, pointing to the third packet tucked in tight between his arm and his waist, 'is for emergencies. Now where's lunch?'

I let Vatsal in, and he finds the kitchen without any instructions, like he's been here a thousand times before. As he watches, I empty out the bhaaji from the *kadhai*, shift it to a bowl and hand it to him to heat up as I toast the buns.

'Enough?' I say, one and a half packets later, all sweaty from standing at the stove.

'A few more.'

'You can't possibly have that many.'

'Don't challenge me, Naina.'

I'm close to finishing toasting the second packet when I've completely lost my appetite—or the will to live.

'*Please* tell me these are enough for you,' I say, wiping the sweat from the steaming kitchen off my forehead.

'They'll do. For *now*,' he winks as he takes the bowl of bhaaji out of the microwave and lands it with too loud of a thud on the dining table. I follow with a tray in hand, decked with a massive pile of pavs that Vatsal playfully arranged into a pyramid shape. When one of them falls flat on the ground as I trip over seemingly nothing, I shriek.

'I told you not to play games with the pavs.'

'Horrible gross motor functions,' he chides as he picks it up off the floor and puts it on his plate.

Vatsal and I take seats across from each other on the dining table and he pushes the bowl of bhaaji towards me. 'Here, take.' When I don't move swiftly enough, he holds the ladle and pours me a hefty portion.

'I'm not going to eat this much!'

'Whatever you leave, I'll finish,' he says simply. Like we do this every day. Like he serves me food and clears off my leftovers after he pours me too much.

Over the next hour, Vatsal ladles a concerning amount of bhaaji onto his plate and the pile of pavs starts losing structural integrity until most of them disappear. He's not wrong. He *can* eat that much.

As for the conversation . . . initially, it feels like wearing training wheels, the overwhelming awkwardness of being in such proximity again washing over the both of us, presumably. But here's the thing: with every bite, I fall more and more into ease with him, his being here. All throughout, Vatsal speaks with food in his mouth—which on anyone else would be off-putting, but somehow, on him, is endearing—and with every pav, I see his exterior melting, giving way into the narrow softness of who he *really* is. Like how Vatsal is 'cool' only until you get to know him—inside, he's mushy. A little bruised, even, like a ripe apple hanging on a tree, glistening under warm sunlight.

Halfway through the meal, he licks his fingers as he says, 'You know, I hadn't had pav bhaaji until I was, like, fifteen.'

'What? That's not possible.'

'It is.'

'That has to be child abuse. Are your parents in jail?'

'It would be really awkward now if one of them *were* in jail, no?'

'*Please* say they're not.'

'No, they're just divorced,' he says, chowing down a huge bite. 'Which, if you live in India, is somehow worse?'

Suddenly conscious, I ask, 'How come?'

'How come they're *divorced*?'

'Yes?'

'I mean, they didn't really like each other all that much towards the end, Naina, isn't that why people get divorced?' he laughs.

'But what happened, exactly?' I ask. 'I mean, only if you want to share, obviously.'

'No, no, I don't mind,' he says, grabbing another pav. 'I don't know *yaar*, it was a love marriage that eventually became long-distance and then it ended pretty randomly, from what I remember,' he says, before suddenly hesitating. 'Just woke up one day and my parents sat me down for the talk, how they were no longer together but that we'd always be a family, how I was going to move to London with mom and then come back and stay with dad next year, etcetera, etcetera.' My face sinks into my neck as I sit there, taking it in. 'Oh my god, Naina, please don't feel bad about it. It was ages ago.'

'Still, it couldn't have been easy.'

He licks the plate clean of the last remnants of bhaaji. 'Yeah, but I'm over it now.'

Are you though? I want to ask, but I refrain. We're not there yet.

'Okay, but what does that have to do with you not having pav bhaaji until fifteen?'

'I moved to London with my mum, no, when they divorced, like I mentioned. And I don't know, I mean, London is not particularly famous for its pav bhaaji, you know? It just never happened.'

'Really? I could have sworn it shows up as the top ten things to do in London on TripAdvisor.'

Vatsal cackles slightly, his gaze still on his plate—like he'd rather not see that I make him smile.

'Nice try.'

Sitting across from him, I feel this sudden itch to scratch, an indescribable urge to really get to know him—beyond the pleasantries, beyond the physical intimacy we've already shared.

'How was it? Growing up with divorced parents?' I ask, careful not to prod, but curious still.

Vatsal pauses for a moment before he answers. 'It was . . . okay. Different. I'd go around asking my friends why their parents lived together because it wasn't normal in my life—two parents who share a house.'

'I'm sure that made for some weird sit-downs with your parents.'

'Yeah, they had to give me a talk,' he says, scoffing. 'Like anything in life, though, you get used to it. It was also pretty uncommon for that time.'

'I mean, it's India, so there's that.'

'Yeah, like, to this day, I'm the only person I know with divorced parents, so, I guess, it's, I don't know, isolating?'

'No, I get it,' I say. 'I mean, I don't understand, but I *get* it. Having a childhood different from everyone else's.'

'Your parents hated each other too?'

'No, they're actually quite lovey-dovey and all,' I say, fiddling with the spoon on my plate, knowing that I'm avoiding looking Vatsal in the eye, just like he did while telling his story. 'Just that I grew up without them, most of the time.'

'Oh,' he says. He waits for me to add the rest.

I point to ask if he's done and he raises his arms in response. I collect both of our plates and stack them together.

'Both are really high-profile neurosurgeons. Best in the country types, you know? So, naturally, incredibly busy.' Vatsal looks at me patiently as I walk him through the rest. 'I was raised by my nani, pretty much, because there was no way my parents could be home before 10 p.m. Like, it's weird, but I don't think my mom picked me up from school, like, ever.'

I don't normally talk about this—not when I'm drunk, not ever. This has always been the no man's land of my friendships, relationships; I never know how to tell this story, inconsequential as it is, and no one ever knows how to respond, either. And so, I don't tell it. Sarina has always known, yes, but even with her, there has never really been a need to put it into words. Like: *oh no, you grew up privileged and your parents worked their asses off to provide for you? Do you want a silver spoon with that cake of yours?*

'Hmm,' Vatsal hums, quietly.

There's this thing I do—that most people do—when someone opens up in a moment of vulnerability, which is to scramble to say something, anything, to make them feel like they're understood. We try to fill the gaps and spaces between these conversations because it feels heavy, scary even, to let things rest suspended in the air—for just a moment.

But Vatsal doesn't do that. He just looks at me and takes it all in.

'That must've been tough,' he says, finally, as I empty out the last bits of my leftover bhaaji back into the kadhai.

'Like you said, I got used to it.'

We're quietly clearing the table of the remnants of the lunch—*achaar*, a *katori* of onion, some green chilli on a plate—when Vatsal suddenly speaks again.

'You know, in between all that divorce stuff, my parents never taught me how to ride a cycle. Like, on my tenth birthday, when we were already in London, mom gifted me a cycle and I was all like, thanks, wow, I love it.'

'But obviously I didn't know how to ride it, so I just . . . didn't use it? So, when she asked me if I didn't like the gift because I wasn't using it, I had to tell her that I didn't actually know how to ride a bike.'

The story tugs at my heart— aches for this little boy who didn't want to break his mother's heart but had no other option—I want to pat tiny Vatsal's head. I want to ask if he wants to be my friend.

'What did she say?'

'My god, she sobbed uncontrollably. And then immediately made my birthday all about teaching me how to ride one.'

'One time, my mom found out that I'd been getting my nani's signatures on important forms under her name, so she shut herself in her bedroom and cried the entire night. I don't think I've ever felt worse than how I felt that day, making her cry.'

'But that wasn't your fault.'

'I know, but every time something like this used to happen, where she would feel like she's a bad mother, she would have a complete meltdown and go into this "I'm quitting, I'm giving up, I need to be a better mother, I don't care about being a doctor" spiral. Which was, honestly, a lot.'

'Would she? Quit?'

It's funny now that it's been so many years, but once upon a time, I remember how badly I'd prayed before going to sleep that I would wake up in the morning to find her home, sitting aimlessly on the couch.

'No, even then I knew it wasn't even an option. She loved her job. She spent too much time struggling to become a surgeon to give it up. Which I respect now, as an adult.'

'But as a child?'

'As a child . . . ' I say, practising the words over in my head, hoping they don't sound as brutal as they feel in my mind. 'As a child I think you just wonder why your mother doesn't have time for you. You don't really have any ability to thread together these two pieces of information into logic. You just think . . . my mother is too busy for me. And that's it. That's your worldview.'

We take the empty bowls and dishes back to the kitchen in silence; Vatsal and I lose track of the conversation amid the chores. Suddenly, he adds: 'It's funny how we've only talked about our mothers.'

Running the kadhai under the sink, I say, 'I've thought about this a lot. Fathers get away with it because we just *expect* them to be busy, you know? As a kid, that's what you're told, *na*? That mothers give the love; dads earn the money. So, when you're fed these ideas as a kid, it's tough to fully abandon them even in adulthood.'

'Hmm.'

'Even when you know they're wrong. I mean, my father was just as absent as my mother.'

As he wipes the kitchen countertop, our backs to each other while I put the leftovers back in the fridge, I hear his voice over the sound of the running tap in the sink. 'I don't usually talk about this stuff with people.'

He can't see me, but I'm nodding my head as I realize: same. I want to say: *You are the first person I've ever talked about this with, ever.* 'Yeah, me neither. Don't really see the point, it's the most tired story in the world. Like okay, your parents fucked you up, what else is new?'

I can hear the chuckle in Vatsal's voice amid the clatter of the plates he's wiping; I smile in return. Something about making the guy laugh. 'Side note, but I was dating this girl once and I was breaking things off because it wasn't right . . .'

'And she says something like, "That's probably what your parents taught you, to leave when things get inconvenient", or something along those lines,' he says and I turn around, my gaping jaw stuck in an oval-shaped hold. 'And beyond how absolutely fucked up it is to even say that, I was like, bro, I've known you for *two* months, it's not that serious.'

'My god, what a *bitch*,' I exclaim. 'One time, my ex-boyfriend said I spent so much time resenting my mother for being a busy career woman growing up that I can't see that I have become her.'

'Wow, what the actual fuck.'

'This is after I showed up late to a date.'

'That's it?'

'By five minutes, on a *weekend*.'

'I don't even have to see his face to know he's a dick.'

'Yeah, but, imagine if he sees me now. Fired and all. How wrong he'd find himself to be, calling an unemployed loser a career-obsessed woman.'

'Wrong, yes, because he was an asshole to you. Not because you're an unemployed loser, Naina,' Vatsal says.

Looking at me, like really looking in a way that I haven't been looked at before, Vatsal adds: 'You're anything but a loser.'

In the evening, when Sarina returns to literal morsels of pav bhaaji left for her, her suspicion runs wild—especially when I tell her where her portion went. 'Hmm. Steamy washroom make-out sesh followed by an intimate lunch?' she says, shutting the empty Tupperware box with a sum total of two pavs left for her. 'What could that mean?'

'Are you my mom?'

'I'm just saying that it feels like you two have . . . a little crush.'

'Crush?'

'Yeah, like, on each other.'

'Very funny,' I say, shutting her down. 'Today was mostly so that we're not so awkward around each other all the time. And I think it helped.'

'What I walked in on at the restaurant was anything but awkward, Naina,' she says, laughing.

'That was the *one* time,' I shriek, protesting. 'You know I had a horrible day and it was just . . . casual.'

'Mmm-hmm.'

'Anyway, now we're friends.'

'Friends? *Accha*?'

'Stop it. I actually think he's pretty cool. We're going to work together out of this cafe he works from tomorrow.'

'So you're planning on spending *even* more time together.'

'As friends.'

'Of course, *friends*.'

'All those EDM beats have fried your brain.' When Sarina doesn't say anything in response, I add, 'Besides, he's leaving in, like, a month. So, it would be totally impractical.' I emphasize the last part: '*If* there was anything happening.'

'Right.'

'Which there isn't.'

Sarina looks at me, unimpressed. 'I believe you.'

'Then why does it feel like you don't?'

'Because even you can see through your bullshit, Naina.'

'You're making a big deal out of nothing,' I say, looking away. 'Can't I have a guy friend?'

'Prove it to me,' Sarina instructs, her hands on her hips.

'Prove what.'

'That you're not into him.'

Sucking my breath in, knowing I'm not just lying to my best friend but myself, I ask: 'And how am I supposed to do that?'

'I don't know . . . go on a date? You haven't been on one since he showed up.'

~

I don't schedule a date one week after my conversation with Sarina because I think she's right. I do it partly to get her off my back, to buy myself more time to figure my head out, and mostly to get Vatsal off it—a task which is proving to be tougher with every passing day. If we're not hanging out, we're texting each other about all our failed Tinder matches. And if we're not texting, I'm thinking of things I *could* be texting him about until I stumble upon something reasonable enough to warrant a double-text.

So, let's just say it helps that today, I have another guy's texts to wait on: my date, Rohit, who I meet outside Wenger's in Connaught Place. Not your typical date location, but what can I say? I woke up with an intense craving for chicken patty!

I'm about halfway into the flaky goodness of my childhood dreams, my mouth greasy while simultaneously salivating, when I spot him from across the parking lot. I wave at him. 'You must be Naina,' he says, smiling as he walks closer toward me. I was worried I wouldn't recognize him from just having seen a few hazy pictures, but he has a striking face—not traditionally handsome but easily distinguishable, with large brown eyes and a suntanned complexion. 'I see you started the date without me,' he jokes.

'I got some for you too; it's like, the best chicken patty in the world,' I say, lifting the paper bag in my hand. 'The weather's nice, right?'

'Yeah, it doesn't feel like Delhi at all,' Rohit says, looking at his shoes.

'I thought we could sit and eat in Central Park? A picnic?'

I'm recounting this story for Vatsal as he's seated across from me on the living room couch a few days later. We've just stuffed our stomachs with Rani didi's colony-famous shahi paneer, the one I know she puts ketchup in to make it taste that good, and this story is all that is keeping the two of us from yawning headfirst into an afternoon nap.

'Rohit. Nice. Sounds like a freak,' Vatsal says, excitedly. 'I already can't wait to see where this goes.'

'What's wrong with Rohit? It's such a normal name.'

'*Was* he a normal guy?'

'Fair. Okay, so we find a nice spot in Central Park and we're just chatting and it's a . . . good conversation, honestly, because he has a start-up and we start talking about how he's solving for marketing and all, and you know me, I obviously had a lot to say about that.'

'My god, Naina, please tell me you didn't end the date with a job offer in hand.'

Ignoring him, I continue: 'So then I ask what he's looking for out of this date and all after we've spoken enough and what his . . .'

'NO, NO, NO! No, you didn't Naina, oh my god,' Vatsal exclaims, rising up from the couch and almost knocking over our empty plates in the process. 'What is *wrong* with you?!'

'What?'

'Who asks that on the *first* date?! You don't ask that even a couple months in,' Vatsal yelps. 'My god. You could've just proposed to him right there while you were at it.'

'Can you calm down? You haven't even heard the full story.'

'It doesn't matter. I'm telling you how guys are. I can't blame him for anything he did after this because I *know* you freaked him out.'

'You're really siding with a man you've never met over me?'

'Fine,' he says, begrudgingly. 'Proceed.'

'So, when I asked him what he's looking for,' I see Vatsal's face cringe again, but I carry on, 'he interrupted me, because he just happened to be receiving a call at the same time. And I *could* give you the long version, but the short version is that it was his girlfriend calling him.'

'Wait, what?'

'Yep.'

'No, wait, I'm confused.'

'Exactly what I said, too. But don't worry, Rohit had an incredibly logical explanation for it. He told me how she's only his girlfriend for another week, you know, until her birthday is over, which is when he's going to break up with her. So, what he was doing right now was actually totally okay,' I say animatedly, mimicking his tone.

'Oh. Wow. Okay. That's not where I was expecting this to go.'

'Me neither.'

'See, on the one hand, I have to respect the hustle,' Vatsal chuckles. 'Dude was out here ensuring his future dating life while his poor girlfriend has no fucking clue she's getting broken up with right after her birthday of all days.'

'That's one way to look at it. But somehow, after all of this, while I'm trying very, very hard to find a moment to leave, he somehow thinks I'm waiting for a kiss?'

'You're joking.'

'I flinched when he started puckering his lips towards me, like, physically flinched.'

'And then?'

'Then he has the balls to say, "Isn't that what people come to Central Park for?"'

Vatsal's eyes are open as wide as his jaw. '*Please* tell me you're kidding.'

'I wish I was. Anyway, after that I literally bolted out of there, just straight up went like: 'Okay, you're extremely weird and I have to go.' And that's why I have decided I will now let my parents find me someone instead, because, clearly, I'm attracting these people.'

'Might you be overreacting?'

'*Am* I though? Every man I have met in the last six months is either a liar or absolutely insane *or* unhealthily obsessed with his mother.'

Vatsal doesn't say anything, until I see the equivalent of a light-bulb moment splash with a grin on his face. He says: 'I have an idea.'

'An idea?'

'Clearly you have a lot of time on your hands,' he says, pointing towards the zero tabs open on my laptop lying aimlessly on my centre table in front of us, 'as do I. And clearly, you're extremely single, as am I.'

I feel my heart pounding in my chest—where is this conversation going? But I don't let it show. Instead, I ask: 'What exactly are you proposing?'

'I'm proposing a . . . dating camp.'

'A dating camp?'

'Yes.'

I should've known then that this was going to be a bad idea—but Vatsal looked so cute suggesting it, I couldn't help but nod along. The 'dating camp' would entail both of us coaching the other on our respective dating lives; he walked me through it like it was something he'd given a lot of thought to. Our app bios, photos, how we dress for the date, what conversations we strike up, the whole lot—*everything* was under scrutiny.

'What makes you think I need your help?' I ask, offended.

'What have your last few dates been like, Naina?'

'None of them have been *my* fault.'

'Maybe, maybe not. Or, like you said, you're luring in weirdos for whatever reason, and I can help you fix that.'

'And how am I supposed to help you?'

Vatsal stifles a laugh—like simply the proposition is preposterous. 'I said that part to be nice. This is mostly for you, Naina. I don't need help.'

'Fuck you,' I say as I throw the cushion to my right straight towards his face, which he somehow catches before it lands. Still, desperate as I am, I relent.

Over the next ten minutes, Vatsal scrolls through every inch of my profile, eventually determining it to be at least one-fourth as hot as I am in real life.

Hot. He calls me *hot*.

'But I wanna be fully hot.'

Looking up from my phone, he says: 'There have to be *some* thirst-trap pics, at least. This is all too cutesy, please-marry-me vibes.'

'*Haan, toh,* I am looking for a serious thing. If I post thirst traps, I'll only get the horny dudes.'

'Naina, *all* dudes are horny dudes.'

Eventually, Vatsal and I arrive at a blend of some hot and some cute photos of me, none of which give the impression that I am just looking for a lay—but if that were to be the case, I wouldn't entirely be opposed to it.

'It is a calculated science,' Vatsal says. 'The hotness has to be heavily implied but not entirely on display. You have to leave something to the imagination.' Luckily, I have a few photos I'd taken that match that exact description—back when I was newly broken up with and took to revenge-posting on Instagram like it was my part-time job.

'I like what you've written,' he says, still looking at my phone. 'Although, if I'm honest, most men stop at the photos, right here. All this funny stuff will not matter if the pictures don't hit.'

'What a shocker! Men don't care about my personality! Why didn't I think of that before?'

'I'm not saying they don't care, Naina. We care. I'm just saying . . . we're simple creatures.' Then he looks at me, assessing me just as intently as he was assessing my profile, and adds, 'But you don't have to worry.'

'Why?'

'Your face is . . . okay.'

'*Okay?*'

'Don't fish.'

When we're done with me, Vatsal hands me his phone so I, too, can have a go at him. And my very instant diagnosis of Vatsal's profile, on the other hand, is that he does not need my help. I don't say this—I *have* to act cool about it after he has just pointed out a minimum of fourteen flaws in mine.

'Vatsal, oh my *god*,' I shriek, half-shutting my eyes, half-hoping he doesn't catch me looking, still, from between the cracks. 'You can't have naked photos on here.'

'I'm not naked, what drama,' he howls. 'It's just . . . shirtless. On a *beach*. It would be weirder if I *were* wearing a shirt.'

It flickers something in me—a desire to see more, this need to not have anyone else see it.

'What made you think this was a good idea?'

I'm *sure* it's a good idea. I'm sure he gets swiped on a lot. I'm sure, on paper, it works. And that makes me . . . mad? Unexplainably furious? Desperate enough to want to delete every digital trace of this photo from the internet?

'This is a very fuckboy move,' I say, calmly. 'Like, the second I see a shirtless picture on a guy's profile, I *know* what he's looking for and I'm not going to swipe right.'

That's a lie. I would totally swipe right. I would do it in a heartbeat.

I watch from the corner of my eye the look on Vatsal's face as I press delete on the photo, this quiet recognition between us underpinning why I don't want him available like this for anybody else's perusal.

'This one's gone,' I say, missing it the second I make it disappear. 'What else do you have?'

NOW

This is how it has always been: time ceases to pass normally when I'm around Vatsal. One second it's 12 a.m. and I've just gotten home, the next, the clock strikes 2.30; Vatsal and I have been talking for two hours straight as Sarina and Nipun fill the room with their ridiculously coordinated snores. The entire time, I've been on the edge of my armchair—waiting, any second, for Vatsal to say that this is it, he has to leave, he has to go home, that this moment we're having for the first time in three years has now come to an end. Yet, with every new detour the conversation takes, I realize that he, too, does not want to leave.

'I think I should head,' he says, anyway, standing up, looking at his watch at the first and only sign of a yawn on my face.

'There's literally chain snatchers circling the block at this hour,' I say.

'It's a good thing I'm not wearing any chains then, no?'

'Shut up, Vatsal,' I say. 'Stay. Leave in the morning.' My voice suddenly flutters with indecision as I point him to my bedroom, even though he absolutely does not need directions. 'I would give you the third room, but the bed is currently home to half of Sarina's and my winter closet, and I don't think you want to sleep next to her ten different fur coats.'

I *could* give him Sarina and Nipun's room too—they're sprawled on the couch—but I don't want to.

'I mean, that does sound extremely comfortable,' he says.

'Oh, well, then, you know where the room is,' I add, hiccuping through my words, suddenly conscious that Vatsal can read through every thought on my mind like I'm made of translucent film.

'Naina, please chill.'

Inside my bedroom, we busy our hands. Vatsal unfolds the extra blanket I pull out for him from under my bed while I clear days worth of messes off my table to make my room more palatable to him—until there's only one thing left to do. Vatsal takes the lead, falling gently onto the right side of my bed, effortlessly and without a second thought, like he does this every night. As he gets in, he pulls the blanket over up to his chest.

'You sleep on the left, no?' he asks as he tucks himself in and I nod in response.

I follow quickly after, trying hard not to fixate on the idea of *Vatsal in my bed*. I lie down next to him, caught at an overwhelm of seeing him up-close and piecing together parts of him I didn't realize I'd forgotten: the denseness of his eyebrows, the mole on his collarbone, how his upper lip is asymmetrically higher on the left-hand side of his face. How his hair, although slicked back, always has a few strands that fall loose on the forehead, which don't roll back no matter how many times he tries to position them. How his eyes have never learned to focus on what's in front of them, how easily they wander. How sometimes, in the middle of a conversation, they wander to my lips. I sit there and all at once remember every small thing that made up the person he is, the one I fell in love with.

And then there are bits I don't recognize. Like the two symmetrical stitches on the back of his palm. Or this scent that is enveloping but a tad too musky for his past taste. Or this new laugh, this inflection in it where it starts high-pitched and then disappears into his throat, all of a sudden. Did he always laugh like this before? Am I forgetting or am I remembering wrong? Am I forgetting or did I just never know?

I keep count of the rise and fall in our chests as we lie next to each other; I try to commit every bit of this moment to memory because some part of me already expects it to never happen again.

Suddenly, a tiny murmur; I hear Vatsal's voice tear through the silence. 'So,' Vatsal says, breaking my thoughts, 'what else is up?'

'It's a little late for small talk, no?'

'I mean, are you sleepy?'

I turn to face him and say, 'No, not really.'

'So then tell me.'

'Honestly? Not much.'

'Dating anyone?' he asks, looking up at the ceiling. Instantly, I mirror him—staring right back at the wall, averting his eyes.

That he can ask me this with calm casualness infuriates me. I could never ask Vatsal if he's dating someone; I would never want to know if he is.

I push the feeling down as I laugh and say, 'I have decided to . . . *not*.'

'What? Why?'

'The more first dates I go on, the more faith I lose in love. And men.'

'It can't be *that* bad.'

'The last guy brought me to a restaurant where his mum was simultaneously at her kitty party.'

Vatsal throws his head back and bangs it on the headboard, giggling like he always would at my failed first-date encounters. 'Fuck,' he says rubbing his temple. 'There *has* to be a good explanation for this.'

'His logic was that if the date went well, he could just kill two birds with one stone and introduce me to his mom right there.'

'Listen, the guy is resourceful. You have to give him that.'

'Resourceful or not, I fake emergency-ed my way out of that date like this,' I say, snapping my fingers. 'Said my best friend got hit by a car and ran.'

Vatsal shakes his head, turning on his side to look at me, 'Naina, Naina, Naina,' he sighs as he palms the side of his head, resting his weight on his elbow, 'don't tell me I'm going to have to coach you all over again?'

'No, thanks,' I scoff. 'Your coaching got me nowhere.'

For the next hour, sleep evades us as Vatsal and I try to make up for lost time. We cover all bases: from life and work to travel and television. As we speak, I keep oscillating between warm familiarity for this person and feeling motion-sick, like I ate too much before a boat ride. Like I stood up right as the plane took off the tarmac.

'It genuinely did feel like what Hrithik Roshan's character shows it to feel like,' he says, recalling his diving experience in Spain—a bachelor trip with his grad-school friends. He tells me how the friend never ended up getting married, but at least they got a good trip out of it. 'I swear to god, I *know* it sounds dramatic, but I came up for air and then had a good cry.'

I chuckle lightly, not trying to hide the disapproval I feel. 'Found the meaning of life?'

Vatsal, though, doesn't seem to pick up on the sudden shift in energy in the room, not the way I have. 'Something like that.'

'Everyone goes abroad and starts acting like these experiences make life what it is,' I say, my tone suddenly sharp, cutting through the previous ease of our conversation. 'Like, you can discover yourself in India also. You don't *need* to scuba dive, you know?' Vatsal looks at me with his eyebrows raised, his skin bunching up in the middle of his forehead. But now the floodgates are open. I couldn't reign it in if I tried. 'This leaving and escaping thing . . . finding yourself, all of that is only good when it's in a movie. Real life is about staying. Figuring your shit out where you are. Not diving into the ocean to forget about said shit.' Vatsal's eyes stay fixed on me. 'I mean, you're not Hrithik Roshan and this isn't *Zindagi Na Milegi Dobara*, right? This is real fucking life.'

What I don't say is: How can you sit here like it's not tearing you apart on the inside? How can you be around me and so easily pick up from where we left off, not fearing it breaking you again like it broke me? Why are you telling me about your life in nostalgic recollection after making me feel like we would be living it together?

Why does this not bother you as much as it bothers me?

'Anyway,' he says, ignoring my intrusion. 'It was a good time.'

'I'm sure it was.'

'Is there something you want to say, Naina?'

'Nothing.'

'No, say it.'

While my eyes are still glued to the ceiling, I can feel him looking at me, his stare like pinpricking lasers on my bare arms. I turn on my side to look at him and as our eyes meet, my body flinches at the sudden contact, the intensity of it. So quickly has the conversation veered from small talk territory into whatever this is, whatever reckoning with the past we're doing right now, that I can *feel* the physical whiplash.

This is a badly written scene. An unnecessary time jump, a hurried climax. Everyone in the writer's room is clutching their heads, shouting, 'No! This is not how it's supposed to go! Give the characters more time to explore this conflict!'

But not everything goes according to script. Real life doesn't play out like perfectly scripted TV shows. Things left hanging in the air for years don't just disappear; they stay suspended until it's the right time. Or wrong, who can ever tell? And then they hit you in the face, right when you think you forgot—like a piñata hanging pretty. It doesn't even know the bat is coming.

'Talk to me,' he says, after a moment of silence has stretched into long, long minutes.

'Let it go, Vatsal.'

'I wasn't the one who brought it up.'

'Not like that surprises me.'

'Naina,' he says, sitting up this time, his back against my bed frame. 'Can we please just . . . talk like adults?'

'I don't think you're in any position to talk about being an adult.'

'I don't think someone who blocks people on social media has a lot of ground to talk about being an adult either.'

'Right. And that affected you how, exactly?'

'I mean, beyond how childish it was?'

I sit right up, enraged. 'You want to talk *childish*? How about the way you left? What was that if not *childish*?' I intend for this to come out angry, but tears line my eyes, my voice cracks as the words bleed out. 'This was a bad idea,' I say, turning off my bedside lamp, washing the room a dull grey. 'We should just sleep.'

I shift and lie down on my side, my back towards him, when the palm of his hand wraps around my elbow in the dark.

'Please, Vatsal,' I protest, but he jerks me in towards him until my arms are no longer glued to my sides but flat across his chest, his eyes piercing wounds into me, my heart ready to jump out of this trampoline park situation I've placed it in.

'What? What do you want?' I plead against his chest, short of thumping my palms on it in protest, to force him to let me go, even when the last thing I want is to lose this proximity. I forgot what his nearness does to me, how the warm touch of his hand on my skin feels like a searing hot flame I can feel down to my bones.

It's shameful—three years and a single touch later, I'm still discombobulating.

'Naina,' he sighs, his palm now resting on the bare part of my waist, my T-shirt riding up in bed, in a soft clutch, like he's still rehearsing his movements inside his head. All at once, his lips call to me. I find it impossible not to look, to imagine. It's hardly anything: a slight dance of the eyeballs, but he catches this movement, my body's sudden betrayal of my demeanour. That I want him, right now, even after all these years. That this is the effect he has on me, like radioactivity. One he is entirely aware of. Maybe that's what makes it all so easy for him.

Vatsal grabs my face, his hand cupping my jaw, his grip on my waist suddenly tight and intentional—like he's worried I'll slip away. Like it wasn't him who let go the first time.

'Stop, Vatsal,' I exhale, feeling my anger dissolve under his touch, as much as I try to keep it tightly lid, preserved.

'If you actually want me to stop, I will,' he says, simply. I don't say anything—I can't. 'Should I stop?'

I manage just about shaking my head no. *Please don't stop holding me, please don't go away again.*

'Are you going to talk to me?'

'What's there to talk about?'

'Stop being like this, Naina,' he sighs, frustrated. 'For fuck's sake,' he says, letting go of me and clutching his forehead. My chest finally loses its tightness—my body instantly misses the heat of his hand, the warmth of his nearness, the prospect of kissing him again, after all these years. He looks back up at the ceiling as he says this, like he can't stand to say it looking into my eyes. 'I've missed you. I have missed you every single day, Naina, and now you're here and we've lost so much time and I just . . .'

'What?'

'I can't stand being next to you and not having you.'

I breathe out a laugh. 'You managed just fine for three years.'

It's brave, what he does next—maybe because he knows I won't believe anything he says. As his palm finds the bottom of my jaw, Vatsal kisses me like no time has passed, like this is the default. It takes a single touch of his lips on mine for every rational thought, every wandering fear to vanish; my chest deflates, my shoulders lose their perpetual tenseness. This . . . this is the feeling I've been searching for all this time; having found and lost it once. This is the feeling I would let consume me whole, if I weren't older and wiser. If I were still the twenty-five-year-old I was back then.

'Stop,' I say, pulling away, suddenly remembering what came after this moment three years ago.

'Actually stop? He asks, his left eyebrow raised. 'Or is that a challenge?'

'No, actually stop, Vatsal,' I say, because I know he doesn't get it. Some still-logical part of me pulls me back to reality, to the truth of what we were and are. 'Because

I'm not doing this again with you,' I say, turning around on my side, my back to his face, putting an end to this night. 'I'm going to sleep, goodnight.'

I fall asleep waiting for him to say it back.

THREE YEARS AGO

Like kindergartners, where falling into friendship is random, completely dictated by the whims and fancies of a four-year-old heart, Vatsal and I, too, fall into the rhythm of always wanting to be around each other within a matter of a week. Soon enough, it doesn't feel like we've just met—I might as well have known him my entire life.

Now, we spend most of our days together—whether it's working at a cafe or him coming over for lunch. He swears it's not about me—that he just loves Rani didi's cooking—but I know that's nonsense. Rani didi forgets to salt food on most occasions.

So, ordinarily, my phone lighting up with Vatsal's call, probably to ask me to join him for work at the cafe or meet me for lunch at home, is a good thing. Ordinarily, it makes my day—just the proposition of it. Today, though, I almost don't pick up—not until the call entered its final lap. Then, something stirs in me and I swipe right.

'When are you coming?'

'I don't feel like working,' I say over the phone. 'You go.'

'Don't you have like a bazillion apps to send out?'

My voice quivers and a broken, 'Yeah,' comes out. 'I'll do it tomorrow.'

'What's going on?'

'Nothing,' I say. 'Nothing important.'

'Naina, you'll say nothing, I'll say tell me and we'll do this dance a couple times before you finally spill, so just tell me?'

I still don't say anything. I don't know if I can. What's there to say?

'Tell me. I'm here.'

When I can't force the words out, Vatsal folds. 'Okay, don't tell me. Just get ready and wear something comfortable. I'm coming over.'

'I'm honestly not in the mood, Vatsal.'

'Too bad,' he says and then the line clicks off.

~

The smallest things can derail a simple day, especially when the days are hanging by a thread to begin with. You just don't imagine your mother being the reason why.

As I'm rummaging through the open tabs on my laptop, trying to suss out the applications I'm applying to out of sheer desperation from the ones I'd actually like to see all the way through, my laptop screen starts jingling with the sound of my phone going off in the living room—where I'd placed it for a few distraction-free hours of work.

Mom, it reads.

It hits me unexpectedly: the realization that I don't want to talk to her, not right now. Why? I'm not sure, but I *know* I don't. And yet, I pick up the call anyway; the guilt of that feeling pulls me to the other direction, wanting to give a normal conversation with my mother a try. The regret I'll one day feel at never having tried makes me pick the call. It always does.

It goes well for two minutes.

'How is the job search going?' she asks, for the fifteenth time this week after a grand total of one minute thirty seconds of small talk—my mother, a woman sworn to brevity, who has lived her entire life being short of time for everything, often gets straight to the point. Tact isn't her strongest suit. 'Any leads?'

Irritated, I answer, 'I was talking about something else, but sure, it's going great.'

Silence on the other end, until she says: 'I'm sorry, Naina, but I'm just concerned. Being fired, unemployed for so long . . . this is unlike you.'

She's not wrong. It *is* unlike me. I grew up smart and responsible. The A-grade student. The class monitor. The dependable, reliable one when teachers needed help, nodding to their lessons in the front seat while backbenchers made a fuss at the back. I did that all on my own. There was no sibling to teach me fractions; no one sat me down to help me with homework. When it came to picking streams in tenth grade or getting admission in college, Sarina was there by my side. Not my mother.

So yes, it's unlike me; but how does she know that? Does she know what's 'like me' at all?

'Since when do you care, Mom? Do you even know what my last job was?'

'Behave yourself, Naina.'

'I can't do this right now. Can we talk later?'

'What is this "I can't do this right now" thing you've started? What are you going to do without a job? How are you planning on paying rent? Have you even thought of these things?'

'I really don't understand why you're acting up. I *will* find a job. I was literally doing applications when you called. You think I'm planning on sitting at home all day?'

'It's not about that, Naina.'

'Then?'

'It's about your attitude! Am I not your mother? Can I not ask what you're planning on doing now that you're fired?'

'You know, you don't have to say "fired" every second sentence, Mom. I know that. I lived through that. Are you *trying* to make me feel bad about it? Because honestly, I already feel bad about it constantly.'

'*Tum hi baat karo isse* [You talk to her],' I hear my mother grunt as she hands the phone to my father.

Before he can even say hello, I cut the call. Two minutes and my whole day is ruined; I shut my laptop off with a slam, hard enough to have probably cracked the screen. Pulling the covers over my head, I turn the AC on full blast and spend the next hour crying under the covers—quietly, as usual.

Even though no one's ever listening anyway.

~

Vatsal arrives at my apartment with a rented car and a winning smile on his face—I see it all from my balcony as we're talking on the phone.

'Get in,' he commands, looking up at me, pointing to the car.

'Why? What's going on?'

'I'm taking you somewhere.'

I groan childishly, 'Where?'

'You'll know when we get there.'

Rummaging through my closet, I grab the newest chikankari kurta I bought from an Instagram store that's sitting right atop my unwashed pile of clothes and my favourite pair of ripped blue jeans. I finish it up with *jhumkas* and some *kaajal* when Vatsal calls for the tenth time. There's no time for blush.

'I'm coming, I'm coming, my god,' I say over the phone as I hurry down the stairs. When I finally get to him, I'm panting. '*Now* will you tell me where we're going?'

'You look pretty,' Vatsal says, instead.

I hide my smile away into another question, 'And why have you rented a whole ass car for this?'

'Just get in, woman.'

'This feels like kidnapping.'

'Except you're not a kid.'

'Adults can also get kidnapped,' I add. 'So much for being a lawyer. *Itna bhi nahi pata* [Don't even know this much].'

'It's only kidnapping if you get taken against your will. And from the looks of it,' Vatsal says, pointing to my face, 'the fact that you got all dressed up negates any force of will here.'

'Wow, way to make it unfunny.'

'Just get in the car, Naina,' Vatsal says, circling over to the right-hand side as he gets inside this mostly busted-up Swift Dzire.

For the next ten minutes, we drive in silence as the soundtrack of *Delhi-6* blasts through the car. This feels good, being here with him. With someone who wants to do something about the fact that I feel like crap. As Vatsal manoeuvres out of a tricky, narrow spot with thirty cars sounding their horns at him, I look over, impressed. I don't let that on.

'Indicator,' I guide him instead.

'How do you know we're going left?'

'If we're not, you're *so* in the wrong lane,' I add. Vatsal looks over at me, suspiciously, before looking back at the road.

'I didn't know you could drive.'

'I didn't know *you* could drive.'

'What guy can't drive?'

'Um, hello? Sexist?'

'Not every tiny suggestion of gender in an argument means sexism.'

'That's exactly what it means.'

We conveniently approach a red light, so Vatsal can really drive home his point. 'No, it's a fact that more men than women know how to drive in this country. And that's not me saying that's right or how it should be, I'm not talking about the sociological reasons behind it,' he says. 'I'm just saying, as a plain fact, there are more male drivers.'

'What's your point.'

'My point is it's statistically less likely for a guy to not know how to drive than a girl,' he says, pressing on the accelerator as the light turns green. 'Which means that my statement wasn't sexist. It was statistical.'

I know I have a counter to that logic, but my brain around Vatsal is always at half-mast. I simply say, 'Anyway, I can drive.'

'I'm glad you can,' he says, nodding. 'Okay, Naina, now I'm going to tell you where we're going, but only because the car can't go all the way in, so I'm going to park right here, alright?'

He doesn't have to tell me. It takes one look at the blue signboards not too far away from our line of sight for me to piece it together. Where we are. Where he's gotten me.

I can't believe he remembers.

~

It was the morning of excursion day at school—the selection for sixth graders being Chandni Chowk. (In fourth grade, we got sent to a local fire station, so this was an upgrade.) The lore had passed down from seniors who had been there before us—waking up at the crack of dawn, showing up to school before day break so that we could almost pretend we're out at night, choosing a seat on the bus next to that boy I could swear I was in love with . . . all of it was out of sixth-grade Naina's dreams.

It was going to be the best day of my life.

I dressed myself in my cutest outfit possible—a new pair of jeans Sarina's mom had bought for me from the US and a white fluffy sweater that was once my Nani's. Because this wasn't a typical school day, some *kajal* and a tinted lip balm was unlikely to get us in trouble with the teachers;

and so, I'd circled my eyes with a thick rim of black and gaped in the mirror at how good I thought I looked.

I hadn't known then that in a few hours, I'd be driving back home, the kajal running down my cheeks with my tears.

All my parents—my mother, in particular—had to do was sign the consent form my class teacher had mailed weeks prior. I'd reminded her ten times; she'd promised me she would do it a hundred. And yet, on the day of, she held her head in anguish—she'd forgotten. *Of course* she had. A critical patient, an emergency surgery, urgent paperwork. All good reasons, I'm sure, but eleven-year-old me didn't care. All I knew was she'd ruined what was going to be the best day of my life.

I'll give it to my mother, she tried. She fought with the teachers, even tried to ring up the vice principal at 6 a.m. in the morning, but it didn't matter. There were rules and I wasn't going to get to go, that was that. I watched from the corner of my eyes—careful not to make eye contact with any of my bumbling friends as they hopped on the bus—as everyone but me drove off into the dark sky. I hung my head low on the way back home as my mother apologized and apologized—I could tell she felt horrible. I told her it was okay, I even faked a smile, but in my head, I swore I'd never forget.

I'd told Vatsal the story in passing the day he came over for lunch for the first time—with not even half of the full context—when he'd asked me what I'd choose between aloo and gobhi paranthas. The conversation had somehow veered to Paranthe Vali Gali in Chandni Chowk. Reciting the story, the drama of it all, I realized how ridiculous it sounded—it was just a day trip! Get over it, Naina! And

I was; I was over it. But the recollection of what mini-me felt like in that moment was stirring; I was so sure I'd never experience sadness as potent as I had on the way back home that day. Vatsal's face as I told the story had been stoic, and I'd shrugged it off, moving the conversation to gol gappas and the superiority of Delhi street food.

Standing here, though, a couple metres short from the streets I never got to wander as a child, I now know that it hadn't been just a story for Vatsal.

'Should we head?' he asks simply, like he isn't fixing something he had no role in breaking.

I nod lightly, gawking at him like a kid. '*Yes*, please.'

Walking the streets of Chandni Chowk, Vatsal and I fall into a comfortable silence, as we often do—making way for kids excitedly riding bicycles and *chai-wallahs* moving their stations from one location to another. We make ourselves small, shifting sometimes leftward and other times right, letting people go on with their days without interruption—just two observers witnessing Old Delhi amble about the way it has for decades, if not centuries. Every once in a while, our hands brush against each other as we walk the narrow streets—until finally our palms meet as Vatsal helps me climb over puddles or piles of trash. I *try* not to count how it takes him five seconds after we're already in the clear to drop my hand. I *try* not to let it mean more than it does to him—even though he keeps finding an excuse for proximity, like finding the tiniest gallis to waltz through just so we walk almost tethered. Even though every faint touch feels more electric, somehow, than the first time Vatsal and I ever felt each other's skin.

'I like how slow this is,' he says, quietly, as he takes a sip of the chai he bought us after we spent half an hour chatting with the shop owner. One thing led to another and we were tracing the owner's family tree—he told us how the shop had been his grandfather's and probably went way back more generations, how there was no work more rewarding to him than carrying his family's legacy onward, even though his father insisted he study, make a bigger life of his own.

'*Bhaag daud ki zindagi nahi jeeni thi mujhe* [I didn't want to be a part of the rat race].' He expressed regret that his kids had chosen that life, that they'd left these streets for parts of the city with the 'better' things for a 'better' life that he didn't think was all that great. 'But I understand it also, the world is changing. You need more to survive. Making chai is no longer enough,' he says, laughing at himself. A form of self-diminishment to make the decisions of his children not seem wrong.

'I like it slow too,' I tell Vatsal as I dispose of my empty *kulhad* in the trash can. 'But it's not possible, no?'

'Why not? I mean, that man is still living his life exactly the way he wants to, in the district his entire family spent *their* lives in, and he has no regrets.'

'I don't know, maybe it's possible for some people? And sure, I want a simple life too, but what happens when I look around and everyone's done these crazy things, bought the fanciest cars, homes . . . I mean, it's tough to not feel like you're doing something wrong then, no?'

Vatsal looks around half-distractedly, attempting to find us a spot to sit down. He points me over to a step-way and cleans it with his handkerchief so it's less dusty than we found it.

'You'll never be happy like that,' he says as he takes the third step while I'm on the fourth, our knees clanking against each other. 'If you keep looking around, of course there's always going to be something you don't have, you know? There's no end to wants.'

'Yeah, you don't have to tell *me* about it.'

He looks at me, his eyes asking: *Say more?*

'I mean, it's a daily thing for me, seeing how Sarina and Nipun have, like, the best relationship in the world while I'm constantly being reminded that I'm so, so alone,' I say, as both of us look onward towards the street in front of us. 'You wake up and you've barely even opened your eyes and there it is, in front of you, a daily reminder that you'll never find that kind of love.'

'Sucks a little more when it's the love of your life who has found the love of *her* life,' I add. I can only see a fraction of Vatsal in my peripheral vision, but I know he's listening intently. 'I mean . . . it used to be just the two of us against the world, you know? We've been best friends since we were like, this big,' I say, mimicking my height as a kid. 'And now she has her own person and I'm so, *so* happy for her, don't get me wrong, but it's tough not to feel . . . left behind? And then I feel like shit for being envious of my best friend in the entire world and that makes me feel even worse. Like, god, I'm a horrible person.'

'If that makes you a horrible person, then we're all horrible, Naina,' he says, matter of factly. 'That's like the most normal experience. It's like saying you're on a diet and you're entirely unbothered when someone next to you is eating a McSpicy Chicken. Like, no, fuck the diet. *I* want that McSpicy Chicken.'

'I could really use a McSpicy Chicken right now.'

'We're in Chandni Chowk. Have *some* taste,' Vatsal says, lightly kicking my waist with his feet. I feign laughter, looking around us to take it all in, when suddenly Vatsal adds, now joining me on the same step, 'You know you won't always be alone, *na*, Naina?'

'You don't know that.'

His eyes catch mine and he holds them, stuck on his, for a beat too long; I try to look away but I can't. He doesn't say anything, like he's going over it in his head, the things he wants to say but shouldn't. The consequences of saying things he thinks he shouldn't say. I want to tell him that he doesn't need to say anything. Not at all.

He doesn't need to say it because I already know.

'No, I do,' he breathes out finally, like a confession, and then looks away.

We're sitting parallel on the steps, and his pinky finger dangles against mine—the hands flirting, setting their own rhythm to this story. We're still not talking, not out loud at least, but the fingers touch. The fingers know. I look here, there, left, right, up at the sky—everything I can do to pretend that I'm not noticing, that this physical touch, this golden, warm ray of sunshine piercing into me is an ordinary feat. That we're sitting this close because it's packed here. That it's just another day.

Minutes pass before he grabs my hand. Slowly, he wraps his fingers through mine until there's no way to deny it, until there's no way to take this to mean something it doesn't. Hand in hand, closer than ever before, we just sit there and let the sounds of Old Delhi do the talking for us.

~

'Nipun, some cheat-sheet, *please*,' I beg.

'I don't know what you want from me,' he replies, shrugging.

'Can't you just give me, like, some blackmail material on Sambhav that'll make him fold?'

From the corner of the living room, Sarina asks, 'Isn't it his partner you're trying to impress, though? Nancy?'

From not getting to go to Chandni Chowk being the worst day of my adolescent life, going there for the first time ever as an adult quickly replaced that sullen slot in my mind. But while Vatsal and I were still exploring, my phone lit up with a call. Sambhav, it read.

'Hey, hi Sambhav,' I said, trying to act cool and collected, like job offers were lining up at my door.

'Hey, Naina, good time?'

Already, it sounded like a rejection—Like: *Hey! We really liked your application but sorry, no-can-do. Try your luck somewhere else, loser! Honestly, what did you even expect?* At least that's how I imagine rejections go. I wouldn't know, I've never been rejected. But I'd also once never been fired so, clearly, there's still time.

'About the interview,' Sambhav said, cutting straight to the chase. 'Could we do it tomorrow, maybe? I know it's super short notice, but I was hoping you'd be available. Nancy really wants to see you in person and she's flying out to Singapore for three weeks after this.' Sambhav added that Nancy, too, was intrigued by my profile—she was the finance head and Sambhav more the creative force behind the firm. 'We honestly aren't hiring at all right now because we just closed a major round, but I was impressed and I made a case to Nancy. Now you have to make your own case to her.'

And that brought Vatsal and my time at Chandni Chowk to a close—almost like my mother had waved a cosmic invisible hand over the entire scenario and gotten me a job interview to douse her own anxiety. Just as fast as Sambhav dropped the call, I made Vatsal drive us home so I could use whatever was left of the day to be as interview-ready as possible.

'He's literally already impressed with you, Naina,' Nipun says. 'I don't know why you're freaked out about him. It's Nancy you have to win over.'

'Because, if I botch this, I know he will have no reason to talk me up once I leave that room. I just . . . I want to be perfect. I can't fuck this up.'

And I am likely to. I am very, very likely to.

Here's the thing about me: I make a stellar third impression. You know, when the initial layer of awkwardness has melted off, when the small talk is out of the way and enough context has been laid for you to know, for sure, how this person will receive your jokes and your stories? Yeah, that. I make a great third impression at the random run-in after I've been incredibly aloof around you at a party. By the fifth time around, I'm a hoot! A couple more meetings and I could even make you fall in love.

I'm just not great at the *first*.

Maybe that's why all my dates have gone so terribly—maybe it's my own doing, a fatal flaw that no hot, eligible bachelor can correct.

Thick beads of sweat roll down my back as I overthink my tendency to leave a sour taste in people's mouth on my walk towards Marked's office in Greater Kailash, the uncanny November heat wetting my underarms after the auto-wallah drops me off at the main gate. *Stop it, Naina. Worry about global warming some other day.*

'*Iska aage nahi jaayega madam* [I won't go further than this],' the autowallah says, a tad too unkindly, dropping me off at the gate outside GK-II.

'Bhaiya, location *andar ki hai* [Drop location is inside].'

'Sorry, madam,' he says, reversing mercilessly and jetting off.

I map the location to Marked's office and it is a stellar fifteen-minute walk, which means that the buffer I usually leave for important meetings is suddenly completely nullified. I'll make it to the office, to the interview, in fact, right at the very second it's supposed to begin—if I don't get enough blisters from walking in these heels and bleed to death.

By the time I arrive at the gate, greeted by the bottle green hoarding with the calligraphic 'Marked' written on it, my feet are so beat up, I can barely stand.

Still, I brave a smile when I see Sambhav.

'Naina, hey, you're here early,' he says, finding me at the door as he's on his way somewhere—because somehow, injured as I may be, I have a penchant for never being tardy. 'Grab a seat and we'll be with you soon, okay? Nancy is just wrapping a meeting,' Sambhav says, walking towards the door to my left, presumably into the same meeting room that Nancy is in. 'Can't wait to get this started!'

'Same,' I say, smiling. Hopeful, for the first time in a while.

~

Nancy is the most intimidating woman I have ever met in my life. You know that woman in the movies, the one who is so unironically girlboss that she corrects you for referring to her as 'girl' boss and asks you, instead, to just call her what she is, which is a boss? Yes. That. She is fascinating to a fault and she fully looks the part—with her dark brown hair and golden highlights streaming down to her waist and her linen pantsuit that I'm convinced she literally has *just* put on because it has no discernible wrinkles from the day's wear.

Funny, though: I've never *not* found a man intimidating. That's the default expectation with a man, an aberration for a woman.

'Naina, so nice of you to come all the way,' she says, extending her hand to meet mine. 'Sorry to have kept you waiting.' Our scheduled interview was at 6 p.m. Nancy was in the room at 5.59 p.m. sharp.

'It's my pleasure,' I say, my words slurring. This keeps happening: when I meet someone even slightly better spoken than me, my command over the language disappears and I start babbling through my words like a toddler. *Get it together, Naina*, I scold myself.

Nancy wastes no time to jump in. 'Okay, I'll make this as quick as I can because I know your time is precious,' she says. 'I'm just going to get right to it. Sambhav *really* wants to hire you,' she announces, looking over at him and he smiles shyly at the ground. 'Personally, I don't think we have the bandwidth for another person, but he insists.'

'I understand,' I say, nodding, as Nancy takes a pause. At this point, I'm ready to walk out the door.

'The thing is, Sambhav rarely ever fights for something unless he isn't a hundred percent sure about them,' she says, continuing. 'So Naina, tell me, why should I hire you? And don't give me anything on your CV, or anything Sambhav could've told me. The fact that you're here, in my office, obviously means you're capable.'

This doesn't even feel like an interview, but a psychological assessment where every single word I say weighs more than I can tell; where answers *are* right or wrong, even if the questions don't make them sound like it. Every single thing I can think of saying sounds so sickly clichéd that I can't stomach saying it out loud in this room. So, I decide to be honest instead.

'I don't know if Sambhav told you, but I did get fired from the last place I was at. I was great, I can say this much with confidence, but still, I was let go.'

What the fuck are you doing, I read Sambhav's face, his eyes narrowed at me. I ignore him. Nancy, on the other hand, suddenly looks intrigued.

'The day I got fired, I was supposed to run my entire team through the most important presentation of our quarter, due a day after. Literally nobody but me had worked on that presentation and my manager let me go without thinking, for a second, that she would need me to hand things over. And I really wanted that to be my last laugh. I loved the idea of them scrambling to put something together a day before the meeting.'

'But as much as I wanted to, I couldn't do that. I couldn't see it through. And so, a day before the meeting, I mailed the presentation off to my manager. She didn't reply, but I know they used it because I saw every recommendation I'd

suggested make its way to the creative campaigns on all of
the brand's socials.'

I see curiosity rise in Nancy's eyes and take that as my
cue to go on.

'You asked for something that's not on my CV, so I'm
being as real as I can be—am I the best employee you'll
ever find? Probably not. But here's one thing about me: I'm
committed to a fault. So, I might not be the best employee
in the world, or the smartest, or the most creative, but I can
promise you, you won't ever hire someone as committed
to the job as me.'

'And I'm desperate. I've just been laid off and not
having something to do is driving me insane. Ask anyone
the kind of things they'd do to avoid the hell-hole that is
unending free time, and you'll realize desperation is key.
So. Yeah, that's about what I have.'

The room falls eerily silent as I cross one leg over the
other and wait for someone to pop the haze. Sambhav
looks at me like I've gone insane; Nancy doesn't give me a
hint of a smile. The interview is over before I know it—I
don't even have to ask if I've bombed it.

NOW

'OH MY FUCKING GOD,' I hear Sarina's voice jerk me awake at what can only be described as dawn. The door thuds shut as fast as her voice jolts us up, and Vatsal and I lie there, grumpy and confused at this sudden intrusion. Of all the things to happen after last night, Sarina walking in on what she *thinks* she saw makes for an arguably uncomfortable point of discussion.

'This is like ... déjà vu,' Vatsal jokes and I giggle along to pretend I find any of this funny and not absolutely cosmically mind-blowing. 'We could just pretend it didn't happen?' he suggests as I lie there, in thought and motionless.

'Because it didn't.' The edge of last night hasn't dulled.

'I was kidding.'

'I didn't see anything,' Sarina calls out from outside the room. 'Nothing at all. Take your time, no rush.'

Finally awake, Vatsal wastes no time to escape—at least that's what it feels like with how fast he puts on his shoes, folds the blanket, and opens the bedroom door to Sarina still standing right outside. He doesn't look at me—or say a word—as he does this.

'Why are you awake? It's 6.00 a.m.,' he asks her.

'The *doodh-waale* bhaiya came,' she says, flapping her hand in the air. 'Thanks for letting me fall asleep on the couch by the way. This neck ache is exactly what I needed after the weekend I had.'

'You expected me to airlift you and Nipun out of the couch and into your beds?'

'I expected you to not take my best friend to bed, let's start there.'

'Right, I'll see myself out,' Vatsal sighs, ducking out from under Sarina's hand blocking the path for him. Sarina doesn't let Vatsal go easy. As he heads towards the main gate, she shouts: 'I told you to *wait* for her to get home, not tuck her into bed.'

I don't hear Vatsal's response, but the thud of the main door shutting tells me he's gone. Just like that.

'You,' Sarina says pointing her finger straight at my skull, 'have a lot of explaining to do.'

I sigh looking at Sarina, scratching the itch on my forehead. 'It's not what it looks like.'

'Of course, the two of you just slept in the same bed all night and nothing happened.'

'Exactly,' I say, rising up off the bed now that it's sunk in, now that Vatsal is, once again, gone. 'Nothing happened. Nothing is ever going to happen between Vatsal and me,' I add, getting up off my bed and pulling her hand off my door frame on my way to the kitchen. The words I just said echo in my mind. *Nothing is ever going to happen between Vatsal and me.*

It's too heavy a thought first thing in the morning.
I need coffee.

~

Vatsal leaving undid the part of me that leapt head-first into
trusting him; this was the childlike innocence he brought to
every moment we shared together. He was like the friend
you make on the very first day of school—he feels like all
you've ever needed—until you move a grade up, change
sections and he forgets all about you. The fall hurts so much
because it always felt like a forever kind of thing from the
start; he made sure to hammer that point into my skull.

Three years ago, a week into being friends, he called me
his best friend.

'We're not best friends, Vatsal.'

'But we *could* be.'

'But we're not yet,' I said. 'You're, like, number fifty-
five on my list.'

'On your list of best friends?'

'On the list of people whose existence I'm aware of.'

He tilted his head then like a puppy waiting on a treat.
'And what's it going to take to bump me up to top five?'

'I mean, at the very minimum, time?'

Two weeks later, Vatsal was already the best friend
I'd ever had.

~

When Nipun wakes up from his afternoon nap, Sarina
jumps at his throat. 'You have to tell your friend to clean

up his act or I'm going to pull back his wedding invite,' she says, crossing her arms in front of her chest as Nipun sits there confused.

'What did he do now?' Nipun asks.

'Nothing. He did nothing. That's the whole point,' I say, defeated, throwing my head back on the couch.

'I'm going to need more than that,' Nipun says as he joins me, a loud thump in our broken couch seat as he plops down. 'Ouch.'

'I don't know, Nipun,' I say as I realize: I really do not know how I feel about this. All of this. Vatsal being here, again. Edging myself into falling in love, again. Fearing that it will end, again. 'It's like he has come back into my life like a storm, and I don't know how I'll make it through this time when he leaves again.'

Nipun and Sarina stare at me, then each other, in silence. A million unspoken words pass around between the two of them, the exact nature of which I'll never know. The secret language of couples, the intimacy of the eye-contact—my heart aches for that familiarity, remembering the strokes of it that I felt with Vatsal. That I still feel with him.

'I don't think he's planning on leaving again, Naina,' Nipun finally exhales.

'You don't know that, Nipun,' I sigh, resigning to the realization that this is going to hurt. All over again. No matter how much I try to keep myself away from him, he's back and by being back he has given himself the power to leave.

Nipun interrupts my internal monologue. 'The night of the Diwali party, Vatsal asked me if you would date him even though he was going away to London. That's the last thing I remember him mentioning before . . . '

'Yeah,' I say, not wanting him to finish the sentence. *Before all of that.* 'That doesn't sound right.' That's not even close to how the night went down.

'I know that's not what happened. I'm just telling you . . . *that's* what he wanted.' Nipun pauses for a beat before he says the next bit: 'Naina, I don't know, but Vatsal isn't the kind to just walk out on people.' I look towards Nipun, and despite my cautious brain telling me to stop, I find myself yearning for more. 'He moved to London with his mom after his parents divorced, studied there for a couple of years, and it was a few years before he returned to the same school as mine.'

'This was the era of Facebook, you know, and this guy was posting photos, sending updates, trying to keep in touch with all of us, but we got so damn busy with girls and math and just . . . being teenagers, none of us bothered to reply to his messages. We did, a little, but we fell out of touch.' I nod. 'I mean, we were kids and he was gone. We never expected to see him again so what was the point of making that effort?'

'I remember, on my birthday he made this video slideshow of all our photos and posted it on my wall I replied to it three months later,' Nipun says, mildly embarrassed at this social-media faux pas. 'And so, when we learnt that he was going to come back to India, all of us were so damn awkward about it, because we thought he'd hold a grudge. Anybody would. But honestly? We went right back to being friends. He pretended nothing had happened at all.'

'Sounds like him,' Sarina scoffs from the side.

Nipun continues: 'But I know he remembered. I *know* it hurt him. And none of us ever apologized. We were all just . . . okay with going back to normal.'

'Why are you telling me all this, Nipun?'

'I don't know,' he says, looking away. 'I'm just saying, I don't think Vatsal is the kind of person who walks out on people, you know? At least I don't think so.'

Sarina jumps in, enraged. 'But he *did* leave. And he hurt her, Nipun. How can he just come back and pretend everything is okay without apologizing for it?'

I want to pause and tell Sarina he tried—I want to tell her that it was me that put the nail in the coffin. But I can't; I'm not ready for Vatsal to not be the villain in our story yet.

'And I'm agreeing,' Nipun says, looking at me tenderly. Having been together for so long, Nipun has assumed the role of an older brother I never had, equally for how awkward and yet endearingly loving he is with me. 'He messed up. But . . .'

'But?' I ask, the longing in my chest threatening to put all fears behind and give into whatever this time with Vatsal holds for me. Just for the chance that in the process, I'll get to hold him.

'I'm just saying,' Nipun continues, 'a man who can't stop mentioning your name every other sentence is not a man who doesn't give a shit, you know?'

And right there, despite the heaviness, the fear, the irrepressible anxiety of it all, I find the tension in my jaw breaking. I feel the cracks of my smile lines filling.

~

Three suitcases line the wall of our entryway—one outfit in each for every event scheduled for Sarina and Nipun's wedding extravaganza in Goa. T minus two weeks. From inside the storage compartment of my bed, I fetch the final suitcase to complete the lineup: the sturdiest one of all, earmarked to carry Sarina's wedding lehenga.

Amidst the chaos of packing a houseful of stuff inside a few suitcases, Sarina and I stay occupied for days—long enough for Vatsal's name to not come up and for our conversations to successfully pass the Bechdel test.

'Come here,' I motion Sarina towards me with her unhooked wedding blouse that she is struggling to clasp shut.

'This is too tight,' she says, fidgeting as I try to bring the hooks together at the back, careful not to rip anything. 'Shit *yaar*, Rachna aunty really messed this up.'

'I told you not to make biryani for seven nights in a row this close to your wedding, but no,' I say, squeezing Sarina into her blouse.

'Is this what I've taught you? Giving up carbs for an outfit?' she says turning back around at me, her impossible elder-sister glare forcing me to take my words back.

'Not any outfit,' I fight back. 'Your *wedding* outfit.'

It takes some arm-twisting and very slight bruising, but somehow, I manage to hook together Sarina's blouse. She turns around and suddenly, even though we're no longer teenagers, we somehow also are. Suddenly, she's the girl wearing a lehenga for our school annual day dance at five in the morning and I'm the girl applying *kajal* in her waterline before we both take the bus to school. Time has done its thing and turned us older; but not even time has the power to dull all those years I've collected loving Sarina.

'This means I have to go through with it,' Sarina says, collapsing down on the chair next to me. 'Fuck. I still can't believe it's happening, Naina.'

I look down at her, this girl who randomly entered my life when I was too young to know what living even entailed, and then promptly *became* my life.

'I could swear you just got engaged, like, yesterday.'

Between Vatsal being back from London, and being back in my life, and the enormity of work now that QuickCart is officially onboarded, I haven't had idle time to think of what life will be like now that my best friend will be married. And moved out. Even though the moment is almost here, every time the thought occurs, I swat it away like a fly.

'So . . . pre-wedding jitters? Runaway tendencies? Say the word and I've got you,' I say, chuckling.

'Shut the fuck up,' Sarina says, twisting my arm.

'No, but seriously, how are you feeling?'

'No jitters, obviously. Just want it all to go smoothly.'

'You know it's an Indian wedding, na? Something is *going* to go wrong.'

'Yeah, but like, there's degrees of wrong also,' she adds. 'I can only handle a Category 1 disaster.'

Speaking of disasters, because we avoid the topic for long enough, Sarina owes me no warning before she jumps right in. 'So, you and Vatsal. Are you going to be okay being around him for three days straight?'

'Oh, we're talking about *that* now,' I say, motioning Sarina to rise so I can examine her blouse in full measure. As she stands there, I take a step back to admire my best friend, who I have seen wearing neon capri pants to school picnics, now wearing her wedding blouse. 'I think it fits perfectly,' I say, pulling down the sleeves of her blouse, needing something, anything, to do with my hands.

'Don't avoid my question.'

'I'm not avoiding your question.' I am. 'I just . . .'

Sarina waits, still as a statue, in anticipation of my answer. Like if she even slightly moves, I will decide against confiding.

'I don't *know*. He's exactly the same as he was before, Sarina. He's talking to me in the same way, he's flirting in the same way, I'm feeling the same things, all over again. But . . .'

'But?'

'But there's no way to know that it's different this time. Maybe it was casual to him then and it's casual now.'

'You'll have to ask him this to find out na?'

'*Nahi.* I'm not going back three years in the past and undoing all that progress. At best, Vatsal and I will find some way to stay friends because the two people we love are getting married. But I'm not getting my heart broken over nothing again.'

'You clearly don't think of him as a friend, Naina. Neither does he, not with the way he looks at you. And talks about you.'

'Even then,' I say, and Sarina takes it as my final word. Until she sees that pleading look in my eyes, the irrepressible need to know what he said about me when I wasn't there. Sarina doesn't even need me to ask.

'Couldn't stop asking when you'd be back home that night he came for dinner. "Does Naina have the keys? You're sure she'll be back home safe so late? Should we go pick her up?"' Sarina imitates Vatsal to near perfection; it feels like he's in the room with us. 'I think that's what put Nipun and me to sleep, the guy wouldn't shut up about you.'

There's nothing quite like being fawned over behind your back, I realize, as I say, 'Still, nothing is happening between us.'

'At least *try* not to blush.'

'Aren't we talking a little too much about my life when *you're* the one getting married, like, this weekend? What is this called, projection, I think?'

'Don't try and play smart with me, Naina,' Sarina says, looking at me like she's peering into my soul. 'You forget that I know you *andar tak*,' she says, her finger poking my chest, straight in the heart.

'*Theek hai*, madam, but first come help me close this thing,' I point to the overwhelmingly stuffed suitcase now holding Sarina's entire wedding attire. Blouse, lehenga, dupatta and all. We spend the next ten minutes not talking at all—if you don't count the incessant grunting—taking turns to sit on the suitcase to zip it shut.

'If it explodes, it's a sign,' she says.

'A sign you overpacked.'

'A sign I shouldn't get married.'

'It's a sign we need better luggage, Sarina,' I say, stacking the four suitcases we just shut against the living room wall, ready for Thursday when Sarina flies out. Just four large sacks of polyester holding the next phase of my best friend's life in them—and, by extension, mine.

While Sarina cleans the living room, my eyes don't leave the suitcases. They're just suitcases, but they mean that my best friend is getting married and leaving our shared flat, forever. That, whether I like it or not, real, hard, inescapable adulthood is coming, barreling at me in full force like a boulder rolling off a mountain. Only time will tell if it'll pass me by or crush me on its way down. We'll see about all of that.

Right now, I have to pack.

~

After two hours of sitting on Delhi airport's tarmac and another two hours of cruising at whatever altitude the pilot announced right when I was in my nap's sweet spot, I land in Goa—worryingly delayed—to the smell of moist soil after rain and the glint of a passing monsoon. The skies gurgle as we step into our cabs outside the airport, and I stare at them with bated breath. *Don't you dare think about raining this weekend*, I launch threats at the heavens. The thunder subsides, right on cue, as I load our luggage in the car. At some point in the cab ride, the cool wind and the hot sun knock me out—only for me to wake as the car jerks to a stop.

I wake to Sarina's manager, having bumped into him at the airport, chiding the driver, '*Arre* boss, *bass yahin* [right here],' as I open my eyes to all of my handbag's contents on the car floor.

'We've still got time, no?' Sahil asks as the sweet guard holds open the lobby gates and lets us in.

'You? Yes. Me? Not so much,' I say, rushing towards the reception.

A long hour of unreal panic induced by the fear of being late to Sarina and Nipun's mehendi and potentially missing out on even a second of it fills me up with adrenaline—and somehow, I manage to tie my mother's heaviest saree just in time, without any help. I only pause right at the end to pin the pallu up and look at myself in the mirror—not too bad, I think, as I dab the excess blush on my cheek and rub it off on my elbow.

As my hotel room shuts behind me, I beeline straight to the elevator to take me to the lobby. The mehendi is in the hotel's courtyard—all events facing the sea but not quite on the private beach that the hotel owns. Which is just as well—these heels would not survive loose sand. As the elevator hums on its way down, I finally take a moment to catch my breath, until the elevator dings open and, from across the reception, a familiar silhouette flashes in front of my eyes. A willowy figure that snaps me out of all my thoughts, puts my brain at a static halt like a TV that just won't turn on. A profile I could recognize in any dimly lit room. Arms so built and strong, even under layers of clothing. A smile blinding enough to blur everything else in its periphery. All his beautiful parts—Vatsal—dressed so immaculately in his lilac kurta and white pajamas with a Nehru jacket on, that I'm suddenly hyper aware of every single hair on my body.

'What are you wearing for Sarina's wedding?' I asked in one of our phone calls for Marked's commercial plan for QuickCart that veered, as usual, into overly familiar territory.

'Whatever the tailor cooks up from the fifteen different fabrics my mother told me to give to him.'

'You haven't given him a *design*?'

'What do you think, Naina?'

'Oh my god, Vatsal.' I couldn't fathom Vatsal looking poorly at Nipun's wedding—and so I hunted Pinterest to find mock-ups for his outfits and, after sending a hundred across, Vatsal landed on the five that he thought went with his 'style.'

'Which is what, exactly?'

'Cool guy who doesn't try too hard. Effortless charm, you know?'

I wish I didn't know; I wish he were wrong.

It's a special sort of hell, how good he looks in literally anything he decides to wear. But it's worse that he actually listened. His outfit is an exact replica of what we decided would look good for *this* specific function, before I got scared of our growing, cosy familiarity and flipped the conversation back to work.

Vatsal spots me too—the scrunch in his eyebrows softening their curious search as soon as his eyes land on mine. Like it was me they were looking for. And before I can stand up straighter, I find him walking towards me. He leaves me no time to rehearse what to say to him.

'Hi, Vatsal,' I say, shyly, as the contents of our last meeting come barrelling at me, how I left it all hanging, how it ended unceremoniously.

'You look . . . nice,' Vatsal says softly, and I think of murmuring a thanks but saliva fills up my mouth to the brim. His casual closeness, his musky cologne—it's all unnerving. My sentences come out awry; words sound fuzzy on my tongue. All of the confidence I've acquired over almost three decades of being alive melts away as I stand there, still, consumed by his gaze. Predicting his perception of me.

Eventually, I swallow up my nervousness until a soft sound emerges. 'You, too.'

He looks at me, right on the edge of saying something, but I can't do this right now. 'I'll just go check on Sarina?' I ask, hurriedly.

Vatsal dramatically holds his arms out open in front of me. 'Of course, she needs you,' he says. 'I'll see you there.'

Holding the pleats of my saree up, I scramble leftwards and then turn right towards the courtyard, until I finally stumble upon the signboards pointing me to the mehendi. I stop and gawk at the signage—'Welcome to Sarina & Nipun's Mehendi Celebrations'—like an admiring aunty.

Inside the courtyard, I walk into a floral canopy, one I'd seen references of on Sarina's iPad, with bright purple tables laid out and tulip centrepieces on them, until I spot Sarina already getting her mehendi put. From afar, I can see her protesting with the women applying it on her hands. My bet? She thinks they've made it 'too traditional'. Smiling, I walk towards my best friend, the love of my life, a vision to behold—dressed in her hot pink lehenga, massive amounts of cleavage on display to put at bay anyone's perception of Sarina as a typical bride.

'Excuse me, no one told me Karan Johar is shooting his next movie here,' I say, hugging her carefully enough to not smudge her foundation on my shoulder or get any mehendi on me. The didis hiss at me for this interruption. 'Actress *lag rahi hai* [You look like an actress],' I say, avoiding them.

Right as I'm at eye level with her, though, I spot the crinkle in her eyebrow, her concealer creasing in place. 'What's wrong?'

'It's Nipun.'

The fight or flight overwhelms me, but I try not to let Sarina see it on my face. 'What's going on? Is he okay?'

Sarina looks around us, a scan of the area before she scoots in closer to me, as close as the didis allow, to say what she says next. 'Nothing's going on . . . he's just,' Sarina says, pausing before she continues. 'I don't know, we had a fight last night and he's just acting off and now he's not even here and it's our mehendi, Naina, and everything just . . . it just feels wrong.'

'He's not here?' I ask, confirming, even though I heard her just fine—anything to buy myself enough time to squash the panic I know I'm feeling from showing on my face.

'Look around, do you see him?' Sarina cries. 'Naina, I'm freaking out.'

'Okay, look at me,' I say, grabbing her shoulders, instantly. 'Listen to me now. This is just a fight. You guys have had a thousand of those before. It means nothing, you know that right?'

'If it means nothing, where is he then? Why isn't he here?'

'I'm sure he's just getting ready,' I say, feigning confidence. Internally, the emergency meter is going off; my brain is racking up contingencies and their outcomes, all while my heart is holding on to the best possible outcome. 'I'll go check on him.'

'But how am I supposed to sit here without him?' she asks softly, her eyes bundling up with tears. 'I can't even text him right now.'

'You listen to the amazing music you've curated because this is *your* mehendi, I'll get someone to get you a wine glass with a straw in it, and you just . . . trust me,' I say as I squeeze her shoulders tight. The confidence I'm asking her to place in me is really the confidence I have in the two of them. In Nipun. He better not let me down. 'Because I *promise*, this is not a Category 5 disaster.'

Three Years Ago

'HOW WAS IT?'

'Can you call me from a quiet place, like, ever?' I say to Sarina over the phone, who is shouting so loud I have to turn my volume down to the very lowest digit.

'CAN YOU TELL ME.'

'And now I'm officially deaf in one ear,' I say, sighing, as my left hand flies dangerously into open traffic to get any autowallah to give me a ride. 'It was okay. Honestly, it was either the best or the worst interview I've given in my life. There's literally no in between.'

Sarina grunts over the call, still yelling, 'WAIT, HOLD ON.' I hear scrambling in the background and I figure Sarina is going inside the green room, a tiny area behind her set where she can get a moment to breathe.

'Do you know when you're going to learn if you bombed it good or bombed it bad?'

'Let's hope there was no bombing at all, but I doubt it's going to be before Diwali.'

'Correct, the only bombs allowed on Diwali are patakha bombs,' Sarina exclaims from the other end.

'Those are literally illegal.'

'Don't be a buzzkill. Speaking of Diwali, have you ordered Madan Bhaiya's milk cake for our party yet?'

Our Diwali Party. *The* Diwali Party. The one Sarina and I have been known to throw for as long as we've been friends—sometimes at her place, sometimes at mine, sometimes in the garden, and now, eventually, in our own flat. The Diwali parties have always been a thing; no matter the chaos that is ensuing in our lives, no matter how little money we have to sponsor alcohol for everyone.

It all started that one Diwali when my parents were out of town for a medical conference and Sarina's were too tired to parent two kids—and so we rang up some of our colony friends to have more bodies on the dance floor, opened all the stashed snacks in my kitchen's highest cabinet, and threw our very own, very first Diwali party. (When my mother found out, there was a feeble attempt at grounding, until I said something along the lines of 'Who leaves their kid behind on Diwali?' and there'd been a prolonged, mildly uncomfortable silence.) And the party's roaring success cemented its position as a tradition—we haven't missed a single one yet.

I turn my phone towards my face to catch the date— and wow, have the last couple of days flown. Diwali is in a week, our party is four days out. And I've done a grand total of zero things to prepare for it. As a less-than-natural party planner, *that* should be my worry. And yet, all that knocks on my brain is that Vatsal is leaving soon after Diwali. That it's been almost two months of being around him so often that it now feels like things have always been this way—how that's going to change within a span of a few days.

'I will get you your milk cake.'

'And I know for a fact you haven't even gotten started with the guest list.'

'You know, I really liked it when this party was a cute little gathering and not a grand event that we literally lost sleep over.'

'Too late to complain now. What would people even do if we didn't throw our iconic Diwali parties?'

'I don't know, get drunk and pass out somewhere else?' I say, laughing. 'You know I can't do this all on my own, Sarina, I need your help.'

'I told you, this season is crazy packed for me. Jonas went on a vacation without informing anyone at Bruno's and now I am covering all gigs, plus my freelance work too. Which means . . .'

'Which means?'

'You're on your own, kid.' I dramatically scoff, but she continues: 'Although, I can *maybe* think of someone who could help you out with planning the party, you know? Someone you're already spending most of your days with?'

'I'm cutting the call now,' I say, almost clicking it off.

'Another reason to hang out with Vatsal,' she says, teasingly. 'Such a shame, no?'

'Are you done?'

'Don't forget my milk cake.'

'Be nice and I'll think about it.'

I get off the call and open Vatsal's chat. Smiling wide enough to bruise my jaw, I send him a text to ask if he's free. He texts back: 'Always.'

One word and my stupid heart leaps up and down in my chest. *Naina, Naina, Naina,* I hear Vatsal's voice calling out to me, *you're falling in love with me, aren't you?*

~

Vatsal's voice right next to me sounds a little less inviting.

'Are you being serious?' he asks, a cringe contorting his beautiful face into a look of pure disgust.

'Too many balloons?' I say, squeaking one eye in to hide the horror of his abject disappointment at my question. I'm positive he'll discombobulate into teeny-tiny particles because he's straight up *seething*, short of fumes coming out of his nose.

Vatsal, to my surprise, is a little bit of a control freak—it's disarming, this realization. His exterior is so easy-going, yet so calculatedly casual, that I should've seen this coming. No one is this effortless without hiding something.

'I think you're freaking out a little too much over this,' I say, arguing with him as I'm scrolling through the Notes-app list of to-dos on my phone, the same list that has guided all the parties Sarina and I have thrown over the years. We're in the market next to my colony, looking for decorative tit-bits that will make our home go from 'three people who don't have a single interior-design-adjacent bone live here' to 'this could be a Diwali party out of a movie.'

It's always worked out fine.

Fine isn't good enough for Vatsal, though. He glares at me and says, 'I'm really, really not,' before turning to the shopkeeper. '*Bhaiya, balloons rehne do* [We don't need the balloons].' The guy makes a face—which, fair—I'd asked him to fetch me some black-and-gold balloon combinations and he'd disappeared into a hole in his wall. It had taken some concerning grunting for fifteen whole minutes before he was back.

'I don't get it, what's the problem?'

He clutches his head dramatically, his entire skull in the palm of his hands as he makes an animalistic sound; from the back, the shopkeeper tries hard to hold in his laughter. 'I don't know what's worse. The fact that you *think* balloons are Diwali decor or that you think black and gold is a good colour combo.'

'Hello? An Oscar trophy is black and gold? And Gucci bags?'

'Of course. The Oscars and Gucci . . . the epitome of taste.'

'But we've had black-and-gold balloons at every Diwali party,' I mumble, recalling that the idea had always felt ingenious to me. Balloons instantly meant 'PARTY!' and black and gold was *so* on theme for Diwali. 'People always liked them.'

He looks like he's about to melt and concede that I'm right. Instead, he pats my head and says: 'No, Naina, they just didn't have the heart to tell you the truth.'

'Okay, fine, gosh, no balloons.'

'Good,' he says, finally content. 'Now, what are we doing about food?'

'I was thinking Domino's?'

Vatsal looks at me like he's contemplating murder; like if it were legal, he would already be burying the body.

'Naina.'

'What?'

'You suck at this.'

And because Vatsal is infuriatingly attractive when he's taking the lead, I let him take charge. I just stand by and watch. A little too much.

~

'Oh my god, please tell me you're alive,' he asks, nervously. 'Fuck.'

'You couldn't hold me?'

'I tried, Naina, you were just extremely committed to the bit,' he says as he hoists me up. 'How's your head? Tell me how many numbers you can see?' he asks, holding up three fingers close enough to my face to pop an eye out.

'Five.'

'This is not the time for jokes.'

'Can we please be done with the decorations now?'

He holds my hand and pulls me up to sit on the couch. '*You* most certainly are.'

Turns out, being perched atop a flimsy ladder with Vatsal's intense instructions on where to fix the massive genda-phool garland was not the best idea for someone who is as flat-footed as they come.

'A little more to your right,' he said, and something in me, the impatient nerve to get this thing right while Vatsal was watching, a direct view of my butt in his eyeline, made me take a literal step to the right on his instruction—into the air, off the ladder. In my head, I fell in slow motion and felt the arms of death embracing me.

Except it's not that dramatic.

I fall, flat onto the floor, luckily saving my head because Vatsal cushions the fall with his hands just in time. I open my eyes to him looking right at me, his brows furrowed. There on, Vatsal carries me—loosely, with both his palms on my waist, because he's worried I've got a concussion—from the living room to my bedroom, his hands steadying me up while I grab my head, which is suddenly pounding.

'Can you chill, please? I'm walking, I'm okay,' I tell him, attempting—so obviously half-heartedly I worry he can tell I don't want to, not really—to squiggle out of his touch. 'Besides, concussions are a Western construct.'

'Concussions are a *Western construct*?'

'Yeah, I mean, I fell all the time in school, so did every last one of my friends, and we got right back up and started playing again. No one ever worried about,' I say, exaggerating in double quotes, '*concussions*. Totally made up.'

'Wow, that's actually so smart, I wonder why your parents didn't push you to become a doctor.'

'Shut up,' I say as I lie down on the couch in my bedroom, my feet resting on my bed straight across from me, and ask, 'Who's going to do the decor now?'

'You weren't *doing* much decor anyway,' he says, pointing to the single string of fairy lights hanging limply on the living room wall.

Sarina and Nipun walk in right as Vatsal concludes his hour-long decor exercise, all while I do my make-up in my bedroom. 'Oh my god, guys, I can't believe you did this yourself,' Sarina says excitedly, looking around the living room in genuine admiration. I walk out of the bedroom to join everyone. 'Like, this is some serious business, what do you mean we have actual Diwali decor for our party?'

Vatsal leaves no room for confusion: 'I did all the work. Your friend here is useless.'

'Hello, I almost cracked my head open at your instruction, how was that me being useless?' I say interrupting, and Sarina looks at me doe-eyed, as though wanting to say *Oh my god, look at you two being all cute and couple-y.*

Instead, she says: 'You hit your head and couldn't do the decor, but you *could* do that eyeshadow look?'

I hear Vatsal sighing so dramatically, you'd think he was a parent watching over his kid playing video games instead of finishing homework. 'Priorities.'

While Sarina and I lay out the pillows and cushions on the ground for teen-patti and arrange the bar set-up next to our main door, the doorbell announces our first guests—an olive-skinned boy in a khaki brown kurta and a girl wearing an Anarkali dress.

'Sana! Pranav!' Sarina exclaims, hugging them at the door. 'I'm so glad you guys could make it!'

'Naina, these are Nipun's friends from college,' Sarina says pointing to the two, who look so obviously like a couple—his arm around her waist, the blush on her face.

'So nice to see you guys,' I say, side-hugging both of them, and eventually moving back to let Nipun take my space.

Vatsal pinches me at my waist, stealing my attention. 'Siblings or dating?'

'Stop it.'

'Oh, admit it, you hate them.'

'No, they're cute.'

'And?'

'And I hate them,' I say, letting out a sigh. 'I really do. They suck. Why are they so in love?'

'They're *probably* not,' he says, but that's a lie. They obviously are.

'You said we'd be able to help each other out. I've gotten a sum total of *zero* good matches since you updated my profile,' I tell Vatsal, turning around to face him. 'I want my money back.'

'Really? I've gotten tons,' he shrugs. 'You were right. Removing shirtless pictures really did something.'

My insides screech at the idea of girls messaging him, him flirting back, scheduling dates. I can't bring myself to think of him actually meeting any of them—it feels like I'll burst at the suggestion. My smile goes ice-cold, but I somehow brave a response.

'See, at least I did a good job.' I hesitate, then ask: 'So, any good leads?'

Please don't say yes, please don't say yes, please, oh god, please don't say yes.

He shrugs like he's barely even considered it. 'Not really.'

For the next two hours, security is a non-concern as our house door remains in a constant state of open–shut, no latch, where people come and go as they please—some at eight sharp, others still trickling in at ten, some leaving for a smoke, others to hook up with someone they swear they're in love with. It feels like the party is at full capacity when suddenly, I hear a familiar voice echoing through the hallway—a voice that sounds like hope and possibility. Like the delicious ding of a monthly paycheck hitting the bank.

'Hey man,' I hear Sambhav from all the way across the room. I see Nipun and Sambhav do the 'man' version of a hug—where you do a side-ways high-five and then pat each other's backs—when Sambhav spots me.

'Hey! Naina,' he calls out, after catching me gawking at him like a puppy waiting to be thrown a bone at.

'So good to see you again,' I say, walking towards him and finally meeting him in a hug. 'I almost thought you weren't going to make it.'

'I had to, for you guys.'

'Okay guys, gather around. Teen-patti time,' Vatsal yells, beckoning all the guests to collect in one spot in the living room. I nudge Sambhav towards the set up where, on the floor, the mattresses are laid out next to each other—extra ones we rented from a shop nearby (also Vatsal's idea). I hold Vatsal's hand as I sit down, cross-legged with millimetres of distance between us. I can't get myself to concentrate on the game when I can feel the outsides of our knees touching; knowing there's only two layers of fabric that separates his skin from mine.

'Do we have to do this,' Sarina asks grumpily as she crouches down next to Nipun.

'It's a Diwali party,' I signal her to shush as Vatsal shuffles the cards without so much as even looking at them: 'Okay, everyone knows the rules?' A few voices mumble no and Vatsal smiles like he'd expected it. 'Okay, no problem,' Vatsal says as he passes around laminated sheets of a teen patti guide he'd gotten printed for the party. Eventually, the entire room pairs up to make the game easier for rounds. And because Vatsal and I are seated together, we are the obvious choice for each other.

'Don't ruin my game,' he warns, whispering into my ear, without looking at me, his mouth curved into a smile that betrays his otherwise focussed demeanour. 'This is serious business.'

'How do I know *you're* not going to ruin *my* game?'

'Boot,' Vatsal calls out, looking at me but instructing the whole room, and everyone puts in their chip for the first mandatory bet. This is what makes Diwali what it is: the chime of the poker chips clashing against each other in a glass bowl, notes of ten and twenty rupees flying around the room, kaju katli being passed as cards get sticky, and a light, hazy sheen of intoxication.

For the next half an hour, we go around the room in clockwise turns—some of us betting, some of us folding, some bluffing and others underestimating their hand—until it's just Vatsal and I versus Nipun and Sambhav left in the match. Sarina had smartly opted out right at the start—choosing instead to spend her time at the bar.

'Get ready to lose, Vatsal,' Sambhav playfully mocks us as Vatsal assesses our cards. Vatsal doesn't respond; his focus is unshakeable.

Sambhav whispers something in Nipun's ears and then Nipun raises the bar to forty—and I can see Vatsal's confidence persist. He raises the bet to sixty, in response.

'Fuck,' Sambhav mutters, ever-so-slightly, and I feel my grip tighten on Vatsal's forearm. 'Show,' Sambhav mutters under his breath and the cards come clean. Nipun and Sambhav had a queen streak, but Vatsal is all aces.

Vatsal wraps his arm around my shoulder, hoarding the massive pile of hundred-rupee notes in his hand. 'Come. We're doing shots.'

~

Three tequila shots in, Vatsal and I strike up a round of live matchmaking for each other. Our tongues split words fast and loose between us and it feels like dangerous territory—

slipping into talking about all this while drunk, inhibitions out the window.

'This is very Seema aunty of us,' I say, slurring my words. 'Not her,' I scowl when Vatsal points to Nidhi, Sarina's DJ-friend who is talking to Nipun near the bar set-up.

'Why not? You don't think I can get her?'

'Veto,' I affirm, trying not to combust with jealousy. Nidhi is single-handedly Sarina's coolest friend; an advanced scuba diver whilst being a full-time DJ while *also* somehow having the time to be a content creator. Of course I don't tell Vatsal these details.

'That guy?' Vatsal says, pointing to Nipun's friend from college, the one standing next to Pranav and laughing. He is a decent-looking guy, but he spent the entire night eyeing Bittoo and shrieking whenever he got even within slight vicinity of him. And that's not a red flag; it's a roaring fire alarm.

'Hilarious,' I cackle. 'Her?' I ask, pointing to the plus-one one of my school friends brought. 'She seems...lonely.'

'An extremely attractive quality in a person.'

'You're horrible at this,' I admit to Vatsal, the wine in my glass bouncing dangerously close to the edges. 'Like, shockingly bad.'

Vatsal glares at me, as though cautioning me, and says, 'Oh, hello, you've not had any hat-tricks either.'

From the corner of my eye, I spot Sarina walking from across the room towards me. 'Naina, these guys want to play Twister,' Sarina says, pointing to a group of her school friends—none of whom like me, I'm pretty sure, because of how Sarina would always dump them in lunch breaks to hang out with her much younger (and hence, uncool) friend. 'You have it in your room *na*? Get, please?'

I turn to Vatsal and command him to follow. 'Come. I need your height.'

'I'm literally just as tall as you,' Vatsal says, as we walk into my room, *awkwardly*—a quiet bliss away from the loud, roaring laughter of the Diwali party—all while still laughing about our failed dating adventures to avoid the fact that we are alone. In my bedroom. While drunk and compromised.

'I still can't believe you fucked it up with the surfer guy,' Vatsal says. 'Bad call.'

'Vatsal, we've been over this. One of the *first* three things he said on our date was how he's looking for a nice, simple, traditional girl who would become best friends with his mom.'

'Yeah, I keep forgetting that part,' he replies. 'So inconsistent with everything else about his personality, no?'

As I flail around my cupboard, trying to locate the box of Twister, Vatsal busies himself, scrolling through my Tinder.

'This one's cute?' Vatsal calls out, showing my phone screen back to me. 'Left or right?'

I turn back around to face my almirah—because if I look at him, he'll see the stupid smile pasted on my face. 'Left, for sure.'

It's Vatsal's profile.

We'd joked about it all this while—how we'd respond if the two of us managed to get the other as a recommendation. I'd said something along the lines of how it would mean that we'd officially eaten all the fish in the sea, and it was time to call this thing off. He'd suggested being a little less morbid given we were both only in our twenties and if I could please come up with better metaphors.

From the corner of my eye, as I tumble through the ten different board games in my cupboard, I see him swipe right on his own profile. I try not to smile, biting the inside of my mouth in preparation. Eventually, I give up on trying to find the board game and join Vatsal on my bed, lying on my stomach next to him while he sits upright with his back against my bed frame.

'Give me your phone.' Instantly, he tosses it to me.

'Ha!' I finally scream, pointing it in his face. It takes me thirty swipes, but I finally show up on Vatsal's Tinder. Instantly, I swipe right. Our phones ding with *You Matched!* notifications and the room falls silent in its immediate aftermath.

'Well would you look at that,' I say, giving him his phone back.

'All the fish in the sea ran out,' Vatsal says, sighing.

'We ate too much.'

'What to do now?'

This is how it feels in the moment just before.

'You tell me.'

'How drunk are you?' he asks.

'We can't keep asking each other this question.'

But Vatsal looks back at me with something different in his eyes, something more than just the longing I saw weeks before. This feels real; this feels like the real thing. My heart thump-thump-thumps as I feel our bodies move closer. All logic determines: *don't*. I run the list over in my head. First, we're friends. And good ones, too. At least I think so. And second, but more important, he's moving.

To London of all places. A whole new continent, literal oceans apart. In two months. That's nothing. That's not enough time for anything meaningful. And third . . .

I lose count when Vatsal tugs at my waist and pulls me in. I give in, making my body light enough for his pull.

'This suit is cute on you,' he says, the inflection in his voice leaving friend-territory far behind, bringing us right back to how it felt the first time we felt each other. 'You should keep it.'

'Yeah? That's great, because I took the tag off. Stuck with it forever, now.'

'Forever?'

'Hmm.'

'Suits you,' Vatsal says, and now that my left knee is resting on his right, now that I'm close enough that I know he can hear my scared swallows exaggerate every few seconds, I give in.

'What,' I ask as though I don't know where we're going.

'What.'

'What are you doing?'

'Nothing,' he says, coyly, while tugging at my waist even tighter, clutching me in, and in, and in. Like every time he pulls me in closer, he discovers new distances between us. Like he can't stand being even millimetres apart. 'Absolutely nothing at all.'

'We're supposed to be giving each other dating lessons.'

'You're right, we should be,' he replies, and my body reacts with the worry that he might pull away. 'But maybe we're not made for fishing, you know?' Vatsal says, his face now close enough to mine that I can spot the freckles on his cheek, the scar left behind from the cut Bittoo gave him on his forehead days ago.

'But I like fishing,' I protest. Asking for more, more proof he wants, needs, this as much as I do. 'Don't you?'

He bends in and drops his face to my neck. Into my ear, he whispers: 'Time to shut up, Naina.'

NOW

'I need you, where are you?' I say the second he picks up after three whole, excruciatingly long rings. 'Weren't you just at the reception?'

'I came to my room to grab my wallet. What's up? All okay?'

'Stay in your room. I'll be there in a second.'

'501, fifth floor,' his voice cuts through the receiver.

Once I'm outside Vatsal's room, I start knocking up a fury.

'You know there's this thing called the doorbell, right?'

'No time,' I say, shouldering myself against him, barging my way inside his bedroom.

'Okay, who died?'

'Not funny, Vatsal,' I say, sharply. 'Like supremely not funny right now.'

'Will you just tell me what's going on?'

'I need you to find where Nipun is and make sure he's up and dressed *right now* to attend the mehendi.'

'*That's* your emergency?'

'Oh, sorry I couldn't bring you something worse, I thought this groom-not-attending-his-own-wedding-function thing was big enough.'

'Isn't Sarina the one getting mehendi put? Or did I miss something?'

'It's *their* wedding!' I yell. 'Just . . . please go fetch him from his room and get his ass downstairs.'

'I can't do that.'

'What? Why can't you?'

'Because,' Vatsal says decidedly, crossing his arms across his chest, 'Nipun is not in the hotel, currently.'

'So you know where he is.'

'Yes.'

'And that's . . . not at the wedding.'

'Correct,' he says, nodding like this is all casual talk.

Saliva builds up in my throat; goosebumps rise up on my skin.

'Are you telling me . . . he has taken off?'

Vatsal bursts into an annoying cackle at the suggestion. 'Naina, you know we're not in a Bollywood movie, *na?*'

'I don't know why I thought coming to *you* would be useful,' and that, somehow, makes Vatsal roar even louder. 'You're laughing? What could possibly be funny when our friends' wedding is hanging by a thread?'

Vatsal points to the bed, signalling me to sit down. 'Sit.'

'Listen, if you're not going to help me, I'm going to go find someone else who will.'

Vatsal grabs my arm, positioning me next to him. 'Oh my god, woman, you need to chill. Breathe.' His hold is stern but the glint in his eye is gentle, requesting I breathe for my own good. '*Hogaya* drama? *Ab mai bolu* [Done with the drama? Can I speak now]?'

Our shoulders brush against each other as I side-eye him.

'*Bolo*,' I mutter.

'So you know how lilies and carnations are Sarina's favourite flower combo?'

'Does this completely random fact about *my* best friend have a point?'

'Can I finish?'

For all intents and purposes, Sarina was your prototypical Cool Bride. The only thing, *literally* the only thing she had requested of Nipun's mother—who had taken charge of planning the whole wedding—was for the flower arrangement to be lilies and carnations. Everything else she had given up any reign over.

'As long as they don't tell me where to honeymoon, I'm good,' she said, smiling, when I asked her how she was relinquishing that much control to Nipun's family on her big day.

Turns out, though, that neither the soon-to-be mother-in-law nor the wedding planners had taken Sarina's one request seriously enough. The floral arrangement was all tulips—which, while pretty, wasn't what Sarina had envisioned when she reached the venue of her wedding, a day prior. The second she saw it, she burst into tears, arguing through fat sobs with Nipun how the only thing she wanted for her wedding day wasn't taken into account. And while Nipun tried to funnily coax her out of that feeling, it didn't work. His usual dry humour made things worse.

'And so?' I ask Vatsal.

'So now there is a shop in Panaji that has prepared, at the very last minute, a literal human-sized lilies and carnations arrangement at the small, small cost of fifty thousand rupees, which Nipun is on his way back with in a truck. The plan is to surprise Sarina with it in the middle of the mehendi.'

What will she do with a human-sized floral arrangement is the first thought that comes to my mind. But I also know now that Nipun understands the way to Sarina's heart; even if his routes look different from mine.

'So he's not bolting?' I ask, feeling my shoulders relax.

'Of course not, Naina, are you crazy?' Vatsal continues: 'Nipun was spiralling last night. After she slept, he came to my room, he was properly having an anxiety attack. He felt like he wasn't the right guy for Sarina because all she wanted was one thing and he couldn't get her that.'

'But it's not his fault.'

'I know, I know, and I told him this happens all the time, how crazy weddings get, but he was just . . . losing it, thinking it's for the best if he lets Sarina find someone who can give her what she wants.'

'Oh god, Nipun,' I say, wishing I could hug him immediately. 'What did you say to change his mind?'

Vatsal finally gets up off the bed to grab a bottle of water kept on the table in front of him. Only when he leaves my side do I realize how close we have been sitting. He takes a large swig before he turns to look at me and says: 'I told him that he's always going to regret letting go of love. So even if he thinks he might not deserve Sarina, he might as well rise to the challenge.'

'And that . . . worked?'

Vatsal, shrugging as he latches the cap of the bottle back on, says, 'Seems to be the case, yeah.'

I feel the question at the tip of my tongue. I tell myself not to ask it.

It's not entirely voluntary, then, when I do. 'What would you know about letting go? Or regret, for that matter.'

He looks back at me and then around the room, like assessing an invisible audience that will clap or heckle at his response, parsing through what he can say, should say, and will say. Like it's a play; like we're at the cusp of the climax. It's so thick, the tension I can *see* piling up between us—my hands sweaty and anxious, his chest rising and falling.

'I think I know plenty,' he exhales, simply. Just like that. Like he knew I would ask. Like he said it *so* I would ask.

And that's my cue to leave.

'Where have you been?' Sarina's yelling jerks me to reality as I make my way back to the mehendi, disoriented from spending time alone with Vatsal—however little. 'I've been calling you for hours!' Sarina squeals in my direction.

'It's been, like, twenty minutes. And calling how, exactly? With what hands?'

'I mean, I asked someone to call you for me, but still, I've been looking for you *tabse*,' she says, pointing me towards the exact flower arrangement Vatsal just told me about—her face glowing, her disposition opposite to the one I left her with.

'I'm hoping, looking at this . . . *thing* that Nipun came through,' I say, fixing her *maang-tika* that's sliding down towards her right temple.

Sarina's smile is jaw-wide as she fawns at Nipun's floral arrangement in puppyish admiration; hidden underneath it is a sense of relief. I have never seen her *this* happy before. Maybe the happiness that follows bone-crushing fear is the most potent happiness there really is.

'He did. I don't know why I was freaking out, Naina.'

'I know why, you were catastrophizing the best thing that's ever happened to you.'

She scrunches her nose and makes a face, delegating the mehendi didi to pinch me. 'Very funny,' she says.

The mehendi goes on beautifully—Sarina spends most of the rest of it sitting on the porch, the design on her palms so intricate, you'd think it was the ceiling of the Sistine Chapel. I spend the rest of the time gaping at her lovingly—half out of adoration, half to avoid locking eyes with Vatsal, who has decided to look nowhere but at me.

~

'HOW ARE WE STILL NOT GETTING THIS,' my voice blares over the speaker blasting the song sequence for our dance performance at Sarina and Nipun's cocktail. The mehendi passed in a buzz—literally, everyone had enough champagne to put a horse to sleep—and now, with an hour to spare for the cocktail, I'm feeling the intense pangs of performance pressure. The group collected in the hall is a blend of our Diwali party guest list over the years, with a few of Sarina and Nipun's cousins added in for crowd thickness—and I, for some reason, have been deemed choreographer for this very last-minute dance performance we're executing as a surprise for the happy couple.

The only surprise at this rate is going to be how horribly uncoordinated all of their friends are.

'Guys, can we please focus,' I say, chiding everyone, but especially Vatsal, in front of the entire room. 'We have, like, half an hour *tops* to crack this.' A sentence delivered to the room, with careful attempts to avert his gaze that's been permanently stuck on me since the moment I showed up at the hotel.

The dance performance is a Bollywood cliché if there ever was one. There is everything: from 90s' hits to the more generic pop music of today, the sequence tracking the length and breadth of Bollywood's eras whilst featuring some fun techno-mixes, orchestrated by Sarina's friends at work. It *sounds* cool, but considering how badly Vatsal is fumbling the choreography, how terrible Sana is at dancing, and how miserably flat-footed Nipun's cousins are, the only thing that's going to be cool about the performance *is* the music. I make a mental note to ask the light-and-sound guy to dim the spotlights on the stage the second we're on.

The practice breaks into the final sequence—where everyone partners up for the classic arm roll-in and, by no surprise, I'm left with Vatsal because almost everybody else in the room comes coupled. As the last thirty seconds of the set blast through the speakers, Vatsal finds his groove. Suddenly, he's moving like the beat is powering through his body, until he grabs my hand and swivels me into his arms, his palm resting tight on my waist. I thud against his chest, startled. His sudden grip over the choreography, over me, takes me by surprise—by the time I'm against him, close enough to smell his cologne, it feels like we're the only people in the room.

'I thought you didn't know how to dance?'

'What can I say, I'm full of surprises,' Vatsal says, winking in my face. The dance ends and everyone clears equally to the left and the right, practising how we will make space for Sarina and Nipun's entry once we pull them onto the stage—except Vatsal and I. We just stand there, wrapped in a limbo, stuck in this liminal space between everything we used to be and everything we could become; the chasm between the past and the future, the unbearable now.

'My room,' he whispers in my ear, with confidence so frustratingly attractive that it makes me almost want to say no. To play it off, play it safe.

But I can't. Not with him. Not anymore.

'No, mine,' I say instead.

THREE YEARS AGO

Once you've had a life-altering moment, you assume it shows through the now-transparent film of your body—this impossibly glimmering sheen—that this once-in-a-lifetime thing occurred, how you must be questioned on every minute detail about it.

That's *not* what happens, at least not exactly—I walk out of the room, Vatsal behind me, my hair tousled, the dupatta of my suit crumpled, Vatsal's Nehru jacket buttoned in the wrong way, yet completely incognito. Quickly, we realize that everyone was too busy having fun to notice we'd been gone.

All, except one.

'There you are,' Sarina says, pulling me towards her, 'didn't I ask you to get me something?' Sarina is just drunk enough to have forgotten that I never got her the box of Twister, but not quite drunk enough to overlook my messy hair, my smudged kajal and lipstick, my intoxicated eyes. She was the one I ran to after my first kiss—she knows the signs when she sees them. 'Okay, where *were* you?' she asks, eyeing me, suddenly all sober and suspicious. 'Oh my god. Shut up. Shut up, shut up, shut UP!'

'I literally haven't said a word.'

'You guys DID IT, didn't you?'

'*Haan*, tell the entire party,' I say, pulling her to the side.

'That's a yes, *please* say that's a yes.'

Hiding my geeky grin proves impossible—'It's not a *no*.'

Sarina yelps, unable to contain the glee in her body, as she literally jumps up and down with my hands in her hands. 'I can't believe this. I won, Nipun owes me SO much money. I knew that this "friends" stuff was bullshit.'

'You guys *bet* on it?'

'The entire party bet on it.'

From across the room, as Sarina and I are talking, Nipun and Sambhav catch hold of Vatsal; Vatsal tears his eyes off them for a moment, turns to his right, finds me and smiles—as though saying, *what are we going to do about this?*

'What does this mean?' Sarina asks, pulling me back to the conversation.

'You know, we haven't gotten around to talking about that just yet.'

'Because you were so busy putting your tongue in his mouth?'

'Okay, slightly less on the descriptive side, please.'

'He's moving in a few months,' Sarina says, her brows furrowing up, her concealer showing through the cracks on her forehead.

'I'm aware,' I say, nodding. That hadn't been the most top-of-mind thing while Vatsal was kissing me, I'll admit. 'I don't know, I guess we'll just see?'

'So . . . situationship.'

'Sarina, we've literally *just* kissed. Can you, like, give me half a day to think about it?'

'Think fast,' she says. 'Tick-tock,' pointing to the non-existent watch on her hand.

For the next hour, Vatsal dodges me just as much as I dodge him—I can't so much as stand to look into his eyes without blushing deep purple, especially not with so many people around. And so, I stay glued to Sarina's side, even as she sits chatting with her school friends, who give me pointed why-are-you-here glares throughout the conversation.

'Hey, stranger,' Sambhav says, interrupting me mid-sentence right as I'm about to make some headway with her school friends. 'Been meaning to catch hold of you all night.'

'I'm all yours,' I say, trying my best to be casual, trying too hard to not try hard.

'Balcony?'

Cool November wind breezes past us as we step into the balcony, even as the sky is dulled by endless Delhi smog. Sambhav and I stand leaning against the railing, admiring the lit-up buildings in front of us.

'So,' he says, finally, looking at me.

'So.'

'If it wasn't already obvious, I want to talk to you about the job,' and the thumping in my chest tells me: it's bad news. I see Vatsal through the window, staring me down with unbelievable intensity, and smile at him, despite the nerves.

'Mm-hmm?' I ask, turning my attention back to Sambhav.

'Nancy . . .'

I can see it coming already. Nancy didn't like my over-the-top candour, even if that's what she asked for. She thought Sambhav never should've vouched for me.

'Yeah?'

'She loved you.'

'You're joking, right?'

'I'm surprised too,' Sambhav laughs. 'I'm not going to lie, I thought you'd bombed it by being *that* honest.'

'She didn't give me any other option!'

'I know, I know,' he adds, 'and *clearly* you know something I don't because Nancy didn't waste a second to tell me that you were hired, like, the moment you walked out.'

I force out of him every last bit of his interaction with Nancy after I left; he tells me how she'd said—her words and not his—that she saw a younger version of herself in me, that she felt like she owed it to me, somehow, to make it work. To get me on.

'Does this mean . . . ?'

'Welcome to the team.'

I leap like a frog and wrap myself around Sambhav in a hug, buoying horribly off balance because four-inch stilettos weren't made for gymnastics. But I can't contain it, this happiness. I'd hidden it even from myself—how much I'd wanted this job ever since I met Sambhav, met Nancy, imagined what it would be like to work in that office. And although it's Sambhav I'm hugging, although he has, in every way made this possible, my eyes catch Vatsal's through the window.

Who do you want to share your happiest moments with, Naina?

It's you. It's Vatsal.

At once, the realization clears every hazy thought in my mind: I am in love. I'm afraid that the second I see him in front of me, it's going to burst out of me. I'm also afraid I want it to.

I finish thanking Sambhav for the fiftieth time and finally make my way back to the living room. First order of business? Find Vatsal.

'Where is he?' I ask Nipun, who is standing at the makeshift bar, pouring himself another drink.

'I thought he told you he had to leave?' Nipun asks, Sarina perched on his side, glaring at him. 'Did he not?'

'No, I was outside, talking to Sambhav.'

'Wait, did he offer you the job? Is that why you were hugging?' Sarina asks excitedly. I don't even have to say yes, my face does it for me. Suddenly, it's a group hug—Nipun and Sarina squishing me in their arms like the de facto parents they are.

'Wait, but, do you guys know why Vatsal left?'

Nipun shakes his head, before his friend from school drags him away and then suddenly, it's just Sarina and me.

'What's going on?' she asks, her eyes concerned.

'I don't know, you tell me. What were you guys talking about while I was with Sambhav?'

With the precision of a best friend who knows to make mental notes of every moment before it even announces itself to be pivotal, Sarina narrates it out to me. How she was chiding him; how much he was seeming to enjoy it.

'I sent you two in there to get me a board game, you know,' she said, twisting Vatsal's arms.

'Guilty,' he said, scratching the side of his head. 'You got your Twister, though.' All while he couldn't stop smiling.

'A little too late,' she said, shrugging her shoulders, mocking him effortlessly. 'So.'

'So?'

'What are your intentions with her?'

'My god, babe, take it down a notch?' Nipun interrupted, adding levity to the conversation. But Sarina didn't budge. 'Chill *kar*, she's just taking your case,' Nipun said, looking at Vatsal.

'I'm actually really not,' Sarina interjected, her tone teeming with business. 'If you're fucking around, Vatsal, which I know you're likely to, you can't do it with her.'

Vatsal acted offended at that suggestion. 'Excuse me, how am I likely to fuck around?'

'Nipun's told me all your college stories,' she said, staring him down like they're sitting across from each other at an interrogation table. 'Naina is not going to be another notch on your belt; I'm not going to let that happen.'

'I swear she's making this shit up, bro,' Nipun said, eyeing her. 'You need to stop drinking,' he said, grabbing her drink out of her hand.

'I'm not fucking around,' Vatsal declared, confidently. 'I really, really like her.'

'Are you sure?'

'Oh my god, you're crazy,' he sighed into his drink as Sarina stared at him in suspicion. 'I promise,' he affirmed.

'So, what *is* going on between you two?' Nipun butted in.

'My god, *yaar*, we literally just kissed, like, half an hour ago,' he said, nervously. 'You both need to get off my ass.'

'*Arre*, I'm just asking,' Nipun said. 'No pressure, obviously.'

'I also don't know,' Vatsal shrugged. 'We haven't talked about it.'

'But?'

'But I,' he said, hesitating, 'I think I really like her. And I might want to be with her, like *actually* be with her.' Instantly, Sarina's face lit up. '*And* I'm leaving, so that's . . . just great timing.'

'Do you think she's there with you? Like, are you getting the vibe that she's feeling the same?' Nipun asked.

'You tell me,' Vatsal deflected, looking at Sarina. 'She hasn't told you anything?'

Sarina took a big swig of her drink in defiance of that question.

'Nice try, man, but it's like Fight Club between those two,' Nipun said, laughing. 'But, I mean, I see you two around each other and none of it feels *just* friendly, you know?'

Sarina watched then as the two men now took on the rest of the conversation. 'I don't know, yeah, I guess, I don't think so,' he said, sighing. 'I mean, we just kissed, for god's sake.'

'Exactly, so,' Nipun said, slamming Vatsal's shoulder in jest, 'I don't know, maybe talk to her? I mean, how hard can long distance really be?'

That's the point Vatsal went quiet, Sarina said, finishing the story. 'That's also when he turned around to find you on the balcony, but your back was against him,' she added.

'So? What's it going to be?' Nipun asked, bringing him, his attention, back to the conversation.

Vatsal didn't answer.

Moments later, he left.

NOW

'Room service,' Vatsal says, announcing himself as his arm rests on the door panel, the centre of his body curved inward. I open my hotel room to find him in his mehendi outfit, still—the top button of his kurta open, his chest hair and the mole right under his left shoulder peeking through, the flicker of a mischievous smile on his face.

'I don't recall calling for anything.'

'It's complimentary,' he shrugs. I half want to shut the door on him for being so unbelievably gorgeous and half want to rip off his kurta—but instead, I grab him by his collar and pull him in.

Vatsal pierces his way into my room, and I realize, into my heart, all at once—his palm grazing my jaw so delicately, as though the second he pulls it away, I might collapse. I'm worried I actually might. Our lips meet in a brave defiance of logic, rhyme, reason.

We shouldn't, I know.

We shouldn't because I don't know what he wants and the lack of knowledge here is dangerous. Vatsal's head latches to my neck, leaving his mark down in a spiral right towards my collarbone. We shouldn't because I will always be afraid of waking up one day only to find he has walked out the door. Vatsal picks me up, all his strength combusting into this one electric moment, and then drops me on the bed; he falls in on top of me, the weight of his body spread all over mine. We shouldn't because the wreckage my system suffered the last time has left me weak for seepage. But our bodies might as well be one because where do I end? Where does he begin? Where is he going to go next? We shouldn't because if this thing could be good, it could be so, so good that losing it sometime, anytime, would be an insurmountable pain—almost not worth the pleasure in the first place. We shouldn't because—

'We shouldn't do this,' I say, my internal monologue bleeding out of me.

'I know,' he replies, sighing.

'I'm serious,' I say, holding him away from me. 'You should go.'

'Naina.'

'What?'

Vatsal looks at me, longing. Defeated. With nothing to say, but his eyes carry the conversation onward. *Don't ask me to go, please.*

'What's changed?' I ask.

Vatsal steps forward and puts both his hands on my waist. He pulls me in with an agenda; it's odd how my body doesn't protest.

'Let me show you,' he whispers into my ears and every hair on my body rises. 'Please,' he says, pleading this time, as his lips meet the soft skin of my neck.

My brain tells me to say no, to leave and take time to think about this. To prepare myself for the flight, just in case there's a fall. But the beat of my heart is already anticipating the feeling of Vatsal's body all over me. When I think about it, there is no real choice here.

'We'll have to be quick,' I say. 'The cocktail starts in an hour.'

In one swift motion, he takes apart my nightgown and pulls my waist into his arms, before slowly inching his way down until his head is between my legs.

'Naina, after all these years, there's no way I'm being quick with you.'

I throw my head back. I let him take us where he wants to go.

Might as well.

~

It's so good. It's so bad. Why are we doing this? I don't know. Your hands are in my hair; my hands are inside your pants. Layers, too many layers. Need there to be none. Want to take this off, do you want to take mine off? Yes. Want to take all of it off, but only if it's not too much. Like being propelled by magnetic force, your hands on my chest, it's what they have always reminded me of—feeling pulled to you, having no say in the matter. Stay away from things that feel like this because what can feel really good once can feel really bad twice.

I try.

I try so hard. I reason with myself. I tell my better senses: I tried. I tried to keep away; I tried to stay unglued.

I tried. I tried. I tried.

Then you take my jaw in your hands and I forget how to say my own name because of how hard I am sighing yours.

'This is a problem,' he says, pointing to my blouse under the nightgown, to its impossible-to-undo hooks. 'It's a very, very big problem.'

'Of *all* the things you're good at, why do you have to suck at this?'

So much about Vatsal and I has changed in the years since I last saw him—but this one thing remains. His hands, how they talk while his mouth stays busy. I feel my flesh melting into my bones, dripping liquid all over him. Like the only thing holding me solid is that he's holding me.

'So. Fucking. Tough,' he breathes into my mouth while still working my blouse as I grab hold of his neck in a bid to pull him in closer. 'Why wear such complicated things?'

'Why not?'

'I'm going to take them off anyway,' he says, pulling away and staring at me so intently, I feel like I'm coming undone—that the progress, the moving on, everything from the last few years is, at once, blowing apart into smithereens as his touch unlocks a part of me shelved so high up, no one can access it. Not even me.

I decide to make it easy for him—I push him back, shoving his chest away, and undo the last hook he's unable to unclasp. Once unhooked, I take it off and throw it on the floor as he sits there, motionless.

'Not fair,' he breathes out, before reaching over to stroke his hands across the site of his struggle, digging his fingers into my skin like I'm clay.

'What's not fair?'

'For you to look like that.'

'Like what?'

'My god, Naina, fuck off, you know what you look like,' he says, frustratedly. 'Come here,' he commands softly, and I coyly resist, until he's suddenly impatient, grabbing my shoulders and pulling me onto his lap. 'I've missed you,' he says, tucking the strands of my hair behind my ear, like he did that one time. I realize it's a cliché because it works; it's not the touch, it's the tug at the part of my heart that's felt barren, that's stayed up nights wondering, crying, breaking over how he didn't miss me. 'You won't say it back?' he asks.

I would say it back, but I'm afraid if I start thinking, or talking, about how much I've missed you, we'll no longer be able to do what we're doing here. I'm afraid that the words that come out will end this thing for a second time, that you'll leave here having not had me, and that I'll regret all of this forever—for the second time in a row.

'I think . . .'

'Mm-hmm?'

'I think you should be talking less,' I say, gunning straight for his lips.

The thing about kissing someone as gorgeous as Vatsal is that the eyes struggle to stay shut—I keep wanting to look up, look over my head to see him, to let it sink in, that I'm *kissing* him. That this is happening. After all this time.

'Can you shut your eyes, you loser?' he says, laughing into my mouth. 'You're freaking me out.'

'How do you know they're open?'

'Because.'

'Because?'

'Because I can't stop looking either,' he says, sighing, and then pulling into me, this time taking the lead, his hand trailing south of my collarbone and journeying down my torso. Like I'm made of air, Vatsal flips me over and lands my back on the bed as he rests right on top of me. He's not much taller than I am, but when I feel the spread of his weight all over me, I feel miniscule in comparison. Unannounced, a rush of jealousy gnaws at my core, a fear thumping through my chest from the inside of my heart.

How many women have you done this to?

His lips find my neck and my head gives way to his intrusion, opening up, making space for him to nestle in, making himself at home. As he kisses the outside of my jaw, I say, 'I have something to ask you.'

'Can you multitask?' he replies moving down to my shoulder as I hold in my whimpering breath, an indication of how desperately I want more of him while I'm already getting all of him.

'How many . . .' I'm struggling to make up words as his face moves down to my chest.

'Mm-hmm?'

'How many girls have there been?'

Vatsal stops momentarily, until his lips return to my jaw and his hand moves to the warm space between my legs.

'Before you, after you?'

'Tell me before first.'

Unlatching from me, he counts them out, holding out one hand and eventually running out of fingers.

'Seven,' he says, finally. He then takes the same fingers and puts them to work, while his lips move down until he rests his chin on my stomach, his head locked between my legs.

'*Seven* before me?'

'Yes.'

'Of course,' I snicker, to which he twists the loose skin at my waist in revenge. 'And after me?'

What I will do with this information, I don't know; probably drive myself crazy about the fact that he's currently trailing the space between my legs, his tongue teasing the soft flesh between my thighs, all while putting to use tricks other women have lost themselves over, too.

He breaks for a moment, his mouth glistening, and asks, 'You really want to know?'

'Yes.'

I am heaving at this point. It's embarrassing. I want to scold myself; look in the mirror and ask myself to behave.

'Sure?' he asks, his fingers finding their way into me, his eyes hooked onto mine. I can't quite recall how quick or slow we've gone from him kissing my neck to this; time has ceased to exist—collapsing into everything and nothing all at once, seeming like a blip and forever at the same moment as our bodies coordinate their inhales, exhales, impatient sighs.

'How many women have there been for you to give me these many warnings, Vatsal?'

His hands, still busy, carry the job on, as he stares at me—a maddening look in his eye before the delivery of the grand punchline.

'What if I told you, not one?'

'Bullshit.'

Vatsal shakes his head, affirming his point. 'Not one that mattered, Naina.'

Maybe this is bullshit too—but I can't tell at the moment. Because even if it is a lie, it's one I need to hear. And so, I throw my head back against the headboard and let him take me—hoping I'm the one that finally means something.

~

'Get off, you've already gotten me so late,' I say, pushing Vatsal away to the other side of the bed as soon as my breathing returns to normal. His chest glimmers with sweat and I look at him, suddenly wanting him again. But we can't—Sarina will kill me.

By the time I make it to the venue of the cocktail, I'm solidly late. It's a full house already. The hall is glitzed up with fairy lights on the ceiling and a luminous bar counter on the right-hand side, with a glittering floor-stage in the centre. My first thought? Sarina will *love* this.

Right on cue, my eyes find her holding a glass of something cold, already having found me, too, looking furious. 'There you are,' I grab her arms, pulling her into a hug—and feel resistance.

'You're late,' she scolds.

'By like, fifteen minutes, can you chill?'

Sarina rips her arm away from mine. 'No, don't ask me to chill, Naina. Sorry for being that girl, but this is *my* wedding, you're *my* best friend, and you keep showing up late like it doesn't mean a thing.'

'Sarina, I'm fifteen minutes late. Because of something you'll find out very soon. Can we please not fight at your wedding?'

'Oh my god, I don't *care* if you and Vatsal are back together or if it's over again,' she snarls. 'This is *my* time. Be here. Be present.'

I meant the choreography, not Vatsal—but the details don't matter. Not right now, not at *her* wedding.

I grab Sarina by the shoulders, attempting to fire through my sincere apology via osmosis; find some way that she would understand this and not let it sour the night. 'Please, please, please forgive me. I'm so sorry, but I'm here,' I say, grabbing her face. 'And I promise to never be even a second late again.'

Here's the thing most people don't realize about anger: it only needs acknowledgement that it's allowed to exist. Like ice melting under the July sun, Sarina comes apart with my apology.

'I'm sorry,' she says, sighing. 'Shit, I don't know what's gotten into me, Naina. I'm just . . . I *thought* I was chill, I was cool, but this wedding has, like, turned around my idea of who I am. I feel like a bridezilla.'

'Sarina,' I say, holding her, 'you're marrying the love of your life, which is the best thing in the world, but you're also losing what used to be a life led independently for . . . I don't know, thirty whole years? *Plus* you're getting an entire new set of family members to be accountable to. This is *supposed* to feel like a lot. A lot of good *and* bad.'

Suddenly, with the look in Sarina's eyes, we're back in time to when she was fifteen and I was twelve—when she lost a game of football to the boys in class after teasing them endlessly that she'd win or when she didn't make the cut for the school choir because she wasn't 'musical enough'. I see the girl who has held me through my pain like I've held her through hers. I see a lifetime's worth of fumbling and falling to get to where we are today.

'What if this is the wrong decision? What if there's someone out there who can make him happier? With a much more normal job than mine?' she asks, laughing lightly.

What is love if not Nipun and Sarina both being afraid they're not good enough because they only want the best for the other?

'My god, Sarina, do you realize who we're talking about here? It's you and Nipun.' I point her to him standing and talking to her parents as her mother is on her third body-laugh of the minute. 'Look at him. *That's* who you're marrying.'

'The guy who doesn't give a shit about the open bar or his friends from college he's seeing after five years but has, instead, been warming up your parents every chance he gets because he knows *his* parents can be a lot,' I add, turning her shoulders to face him. 'And look, now, any second, he's going to find you,' I say, predicting Nipun's movements to a tee, 'and then tap your father on his shoulder, shake hands with your mom while cupping her hand with his left, and say something cheesy like, "I'm just going to go check in on your daughter."' Like clockwork, Nipun follows my command. 'And now he's going to walk over to you and say he's been looking for you all over the place.'

'Where have you been?' Nipun says, pulling Sarina into a hug, kissing her cheek to spare her lipstick. 'You know, for a wedding that's supposed to be about us, we're barely getting to spend any time together.'

What takes me five minutes takes Nipun five seconds. Sarina smiles and folds under his arms. I take that as my cue to leave.

~

I might as well have saved my time and not bothered teaching the choreography to anyone, because the end result is so all over the place that I feel borderline homicidal through it all. I am the only one dancing to the steps, Vatsal bumping along, trying his best to follow me, while the rest of the group moves about the stage like they're in a club. My plan to dim the lights on the stage comes in clutch; this is the worst possible dance 'surprise' I could give to Sarina and Nipun. But it doesn't matter. They look so in love, they barely even notice.

'SHOTS,' Sarina yells as soon as we leave the stage. 'We *have* to, that was like, the best dance performance ever.' Right off the stage, the entire group of Sarina and Nipun's friends and cousins circle around the bar as the bartender pours everyone a shot of some neat alcohol, then another, and then another. Five shots in, the horribly mismanaged dance is no longer spinning in my mind, especially as Sarina drags me to the dance floor while the DJ plays music from the predetermined playlist I'd handed him hours ago.

'Not a single song that's not on this playlist,' I'd warned him. Sarina was cool, but music, to her, was sacrosanct.

On the dance floor, hours away from her send off to the land of the married and committed, Sarina and I dance until our feet just about bleed from the stiletto straps digging into them. This goes on for hours—and by the time the party dies down, it's 3 a.m., my saree's *pallu* is all jagged, and sweat is coating crevices of my body I can't wipe with a napkin in public.

As the crowd thins, half retreating to their hotel rooms, half asleep on the hotel's reception couches, Vatsal beckons me away from the venue—right as Sarina and Nipun make their exit, right as I'm about to call it a night.

'Beach?' he asks softly under his breath—like he's afraid of really asking, in case I say no.

I *should* head to my room; I *should* get some sleep, considering Sarina's haldi is tomorrow at eight in the morning and showing up late is not even remotely an option. But a quiet beach under the night sky with Vatsal by my side is an offer too tempting to refuse—and so I nod, letting him lead the way.

'I love how quiet this is,' I say, walking next to him, my heels dangling in his hands as the crevices between my toes squish against the wet sand. My bare soles register a blistering ache, but the cushiony ground I'm walking on softens the pain. 'So, the dance was a total disaster.'

Vatsal turns to gape at me, offended. '*Hey*, I tried,' he says, open-mouthed. 'You spent so much time worrying about me, you didn't notice that not a single person in that group was a good dancer.'

'Of course, *meri hi galti hai* [It is my fault].'

'Of course,' he repeats, mimicking my intonation, slapping a sweet smile on his face as he looks at his feet. Neither of us seem to be able to keep a stare.

As we walk, our vision extends only a couple metres ahead of us—the horizon rapt in black-nothingness, interrupted occasionally with a glimmer of the stars in the sky revealed by the passing clouds, the moon reflecting silver on the water, the sight of a ship very, very far from where we are. At this moment, for a brief while, we are the only two people in this vast, unbelievably unknowable universe. Hands brushing against each other, we walk to the sound of the waves crashing with the sand—no need for conversation.

'I like this,' I say, suddenly anxious about the time spent with words unsaid, breaking the spell of quietude. 'I love how the ocean looks at night.'

Vatsal turns to look at me.

'I just feel small here, you know? Like . . . look at how much water there is, how far and wide it's spreading even beyond our vision. It's, I don't know, endless.'

'Hmm?'

'Did you know there's this part of the ocean, it's called the midnight zone, that's, like, completely dark, at all times? Light literally can't pass through it, so it's in a total state of, like, opacity, you know? That's how big the ocean is. It's absurd.'

'It just makes me feel like, I don't know, no problem of mine is big enough in this world, if you look at it that way. Everything is figure-out-able here, because there's such a constant sense of perspective,' I say, looking at Vatsal. I can barely see him—just the contours of his face illuminated by the moon. I try not to focus on how this is the best I've ever seen him look. Instead, I say, 'Anyway, I can't believe it's tomorrow. She's getting married. *They're* getting married.'

'I know, it's tough for me to reconcile that the guy who wore neon *chaddis* to school under his white uniform is going to be a husband.'

We giggle at the incredulity of it all—the fact that time passes without announcement, without warning, seemingly all at once, too—as Vatsal pushes two hefty rocks out of my way with his shoes.

'It's weird that we're at the age when people are starting to settle down, you know?'

'Are you?' he asks, softly, a quizzical look on his face.

'Am I what?'

'Starting to settle down?' he completes. Our hands brush past each other long enough for his pinky finger to find mine. Neither of us mention it, but now we're walking with our fingers intertwined, our hands half-clutched— just enough to pretend we're not doing what we're doing.

'I haven't thought about it,' I say shrugging, feigning ease that I'm not even close to feeling. 'I mean, the first step is finding someone.'

Vatsal laughs lightly under his breath, before he says, 'I mean, I hope you're not still looking,' as he flings away the sand under his feet.

And because I don't know what to say, I let myself stay silent, until suddenly, he drops my finger. I try to not let it show, the nervousness of being held and then let go, how daunting it feels, analysing every tiny part of him to find signs of certainty, confidence.

'Why would you hope that?' I say in this game of tug-of-war we're both playing. Who's going to give in?

'Naina, my god,' Vatsal says, ruffling his hands through his hair, 'I mean, I've just spent the last couple of hours inside you, you know. I *really* hope that wasn't casual sex for you because it wasn't casual sex for me.'

'*Obviously* it wasn't casual sex for me either, Vatsal.'

And then finally, in this version of the world where no one exists but us, Vatsal exhales: 'Then I'd really appreciate it if you stop . . . *looking* now.'

'Okay, let's consider this,' I say, halting our stroll and finally forcing us to stand eye to eye. 'I stop looking. Like, *really* stop looking. What if you leave again?'

'Naina, I never wanted to leave in the first place. You know that,' he says, sighing. 'Don't you?'

'But you did.'

'And I came back.'

'And then you left again.'

He pauses this time. 'Because you made me, Naina.'

'What if I make you leave again?'

'I'm not going to let you,' he says, so firmly that I fear I have no option but to believe it. Still, I stand there wordlessly gaping at his face. 'Naina, since the day I left, there hasn't been a single moment that has passed where I have not wondered what life would be like if I'd stayed, if I hadn't gotten so up in my head about it all,' he says, grabbing hold of my waist. 'And ever since I've been back, ever since I saw you after all those years . . . I just . . . '

'You what?'

'I just knew I couldn't stand it if we didn't make it work this time.'

I look away to escape his glare that's so decidedly fixed on me.

'You know I'm here, you see it, I'm crazy about you, tell me, am I going to leave?' I don't answer. 'Tell me,' he commands, clutching my jaw in his hand, forcing me to look into his eyes to find that speck of sincerity I so desperately need—to hold on tight to this. To us.

I think I'll spend my entire life searching.

'Don't leave,' I say, grabbing his face right back, as I cross my fingers behind my back. 'Please.'

'I'm never going to.'

The rest is lost between our lips—and under the stars on the beach.

THREE YEARS AGO

'Isn't that weird?' I look at Sarina in desperation. 'I mean, it's been three days.' Sarina, in turn, stares at Nipun for an answer.

When neither says anything, I repeat myself. 'I want you to tell me if it is weird that he hasn't texted me in three days.'

Nothing about Sarina's description of the events sparked concern; it also didn't make any sense why he'd left after a seemingly well-spirited conversation. Unable to contain the curiosity, I texted him an hour after he'd left—finding everything so mindlessly boring without his looming shadow trailing around me.

Naina: Home yet?

I fell asleep with the phone in my hand, waiting to hear back. He replied the next morning; ten minutes short of noon.

Vatsal: yes, sorry forgot to text. crashed

This shorthand was entirely unfamiliar to me; this wasn't the way he texted. But I was hungover and disoriented, wasn't I?—so I shrugged it off. We'd *kissed*, after all. We'd crossed that line, knowingly, together. There was nothing to be anxious about. And so, I closed my eyes for a nap after chugging half a litre of water, promising myself that these hungover feelings will wash themselves dry the moment I wake up. That when I wake up, he would have texted a bazillion times already, asking if he could come over, hounding me for another round of pav bhaaji, concerned about why I'm still not awake and replying to him.

Two hours past noon, I woke up to five notifications. Four from my network provider—my bill is overdue and I'm being charged a couple hundred bucks in late fees—and one from my mother, reminding me to wish a relative happy birthday—someone I last saw ten years ago.

None from Vatsal.

I gulped saliva down as I refreshed Instagram, scoured through WhatsApp; so sure that he'd texted and my phone simply forgot to report it. But nothing.

Naina: work together tomorrow?

Vatsal was online when I sent that message—and instantly, his chat box showed me the 'typing' sign. Phew. See? Everything was okay. He was probably just as hungover as I was.

I waited right there, anxiously, on his chat window until suddenly . . . gone. The 'typing' prompt disappeared; Vatsal was no longer online.

The rest of the day after the Diwali party passed in a feverish locking and unlocking of my phone—a Pavlovian stir caused in me by every notification that buzzed through my bedroom. I stayed glued to my bed, phone on my chest, so worried he'd text and I would miss it by being in the kitchen or playing with Bittoo that I refused to spend my time doing anything but waiting. The waiting made it feel like what I was yearning for would eventually arrive, that the fruit at the end of all this patience was the ding of his message. I hadn't known then that I had already begun my descent into insanity.

That night, I went to bed with an unshakeable heaviness in my chest, this irrefutable feeling that something had gone horribly wrong, so terribly sour I could taste it in the back of my throat. In the morning, I woke up to ten useless notifications. I only cared enough to open one.

Vatsal: hey, have to go to office today, some big presentation

The text timestamp read that it was sent ten minutes ago, and so before my eyes were fully open, I fired off a response, hoping, praying, he was close enough to his phone to warrant a reply instantly.

Naina: meet for dinner then?

Something inside me knew, sending that message, that the answer I was waiting for wouldn't come. Like the calm before the storm, the rustling of the fallen leaves before the hurricane, I knew it in my bones—disaster was upon my head. Vatsal's screeching silence wrote passages inside my mind, all of which concluded the story of us with The End. Overnight, Vatsal went from replying to my texts with the urgency of a toddler with a sweet treat dangled in front of them to the busiest intern in this goddamn universe. Meetings. Presentation. Chat with my boss, Naina. Dinner with my team, Naina. Too tired to come over, Naina. The frequency of his responses dwindled, the enthusiasm waned to a degree of disinterest I didn't know he was capable of exhibiting.

Had I hallucinated the whole thing? What other explanation could there be?

Shameless as I was, though, on the third day—I tried again.

Naina: so busy, hmm?

I stared at the screen and cringed at the person I was becoming, had already become. This wasn't Cool Girl of me at all. Quickly, I unsent the text in favour of something slightly less damning.

Naina: come over tonight? sarina nipun and I are doing a movie marathon

I thought it was smart of me—throwing in the bait of other people's company—just in case mine alone was no longer exciting enough, as much as it pained me to digest that prospect. Still, I so desperately craved his proximity that I was willing to compromise the concentration of it; I was willing to dilute it by bringing others into the mix, just so I could have a part of him. Silly me, though, for thinking that this would be a tempting enough proposition.

Pushing my phone in Sarina's direction, I whine: 'Tell me.'

Again, Sarina glares at Nipun and he looks at me and says, 'Maybe he's busy? He hasn't really been answering my texts either.'

'He hasn't been busy for a day in the last month but he's busy now?'

The room quietens like static, some movie plays in the background.

'Should I call him? I feel like something is wrong.'

'I mean, yeah, you guys definitely have that equation where you can do that,' Nipun says half-heartedly.

'But,' Sarina interrupts.

'But?'

'It sounds like he's giving you an answer without you asking for it, Naina,' Sarina says.

It hurts almost as much as it makes me angry that she would assume that that's the case. Because that can't be it—no, obviously not. Sarina wasn't *there* in the bedroom. She wasn't the one on his chest, wrapped up in his arms, breathing into his neck. She wasn't there; I was. And what I saw, felt, knew . . . that wasn't quantifiable by a simple lack of response to three texts.

No, we had to mean more than this.

I unlock my phone and search to open his chat. Instantly, I know what I have to do.

Naina: hey, hi. listen, you're being a little weird and you can try and tell me there's nothing going on, but you know that that would be a lie, so can we just talk about it when you get a sec? Because this is just feeling extremely . . . strange

Against my expectations, Vatsal responds instantly.

Vatsal: nothing is wrong, Naina . . . I'm just busy
Naina: vatsal, there is clearly something wrong
Naina: this is not how you talk
Naina: this is not how you are
Vatsal: I'm telling you there's nothing wrong
Vatsal: work has just suddenly gotten crazy
Vatsal: i promise

I'm laser-focused on our chat window as Vatsal takes his sweet time between every text—first a minute, then ten. At least the replies come, though, I tell myself. My responses, on the other hand, are seconds apart. All this while I can feel Sarina's concerned eyes on me, her mind whirring with thoughts I won't let her verbalize.

Naina: you're sure that's it?
Vatsal: 100%
Vatsal: please chill

My insides fume up at the suggestion. How can I 'chill' when he kissed me the way he did that night? How can I 'chill' when he held me in his arms and whispered commands to take off my clothes all while he watched? How am I supposed to 'chill' in the aftermath of feeling the heat of his skin against mine, knowing that *this* was how it was supposed to feel, falling in love?

Naina: ok if you say so
Naina: let me know when you want to hang?
Naina: i'll be working out of the cafe tomorrow
Naina: if you wanna join me!!

My phone dings as closing credits come around for the movie I have spent the last two hours avoiding, only looking at my phone.

Vatsal: can't, busy tomorrow

There's no full stop at the end of his text, but there might as well be. I consider and then trash the idea of asking him when he's free, then, or if he's ever going to be free at all anymore. I fear my heart, at this particular moment, can't tolerate another rejection.

The entire stretch of the weekend before I join Marked, I have the hours and the days laid out in front of me to wonder what—and where we, or I—went wrong. Like a dog with a bone, I hyper-fixate on his WhatsApp chat box, his Instagram stories—like an addict waiting for a single hit. At nine p.m. on Saturday night, the seventh day after the party, he reposts the story of a girl—it's a photo of him, his back against the camera, as he looks at the Qutub Minar from the roofs of one of those fancy restaurants in Mehrauli—the one *I* told him about after I went on a date there. Posted ten minutes ago. I take a screenshot so I can zoom into every part of the story. The way his hair falls. How his hand hangs inside his pocket. The way I can see the hint of a smile from the side of his face. Back on the app, I tap on the girl's profile; her name is Zoya, her bio says she's twenty-five and a lawyer. Zoya has an open profile, a dog called Whiskey, and hair that flows down to her waist. Her entire Instagram feed is an aesthetic curation—every post speaks to the one before, the colours littered across are a sensory jubilation, and I fucking hate Zoya but I also know, pretty much instantly, that I'm also obsessed with her.

On Sunday morning, I scroll all the way into Zoya's profile, deep enough to find the dog she had that died, the grandparent she's the closest with, that one friend she thinks of like a sister. I move through her feed like a cat across the floor—stealthily, careful not to hit like, diligent enough to spot where Vatsal's likes on her pictures begin and end.

Monday morning, I start work.

And because at this point my expectations have dwindled to a zero, I feel an actual rhythmic irregularity in my chest when his text finally pops up on my screen.

Vatsal: have a great first day!

I tell myself I won't reply for at least a day and a half. I reply five seconds later.

Naina: thank you! I'm so nervous :(

9.45 p.m. I'm left on read.

NOW

The morning of the haldi, Vatsal and I descended the steps into the courtyard together, my arm entangled with his. We were no longer kids; I didn't ask if he wanted to be my boyfriend, he didn't ask me to be his girlfriend. Yet somehow, all those years apart became an interlude in the story of us. Overnight, the pieces just fit—the beginning, the middle, the everlasting after. Vatsal also stood by my side and squeezed my hand tight as Sarina and Nipun finally walked off (to their hotel room) as a married couple—fading into the distance like the childhood I'd once clutched so tight in the palm of my hand.

'Still feels surreal,' I whispered in Vatsal's ear as Nipun tried to pop open the champagne for the crowd. 'Like, pinch-myself unbelievable.'

Vatsal was only looking at me, though; we could be absolutely anywhere else. 'I know,' he said, wistful, somewhere else entirely. 'Unbelievable.'

Once all the guests had been entertained and the party had thinned, I finally found a moment to pull Sarina aside.

'So, newly married woman, how does it feel?'

'Exactly how I expected it to feel,' she said.

'Which is?'

'Which is the same as before, except I really want to get out of this lehenga now.'

I pinched her cheek, unafraid of ruining her make-up.

'So,' she said, leadingly.

'Hmm?'

'You and Vatsal seem very . . . couple-y and all.'

'You just got married five seconds ago,' I replied, unable to contain my stupid smile. 'Yeah, I guess we are a couple.'

At first, Sarina smiled, but then her face hardened— the look of weary concern I had known all my life, her elder-sibling shining through. 'Have you guys talked about it? What are you two? Where is it going?'

'I mean, not exactly, but we're together, I think?'

'You *think*?'

'I'm pretty sure?'

'This is exactly what happened last time, Naina,' she said, her brow furrowing, her tone betraying the lightness of the atmosphere around us. 'You need to have a proper chat about your life, your future, so nothing goes wrong this time. You're not twenty-five anymore.'

Classic Sarina. No one could tell me I didn't know what it was like to have an elder sister.

'I feel like we both know we want each other,' I told her. 'And I think that's enough, no? For now?'

'So, what? Situationship? Friends who sleep together?'

'Don't make it sound so cheap, Sarina,' I added, tempering my irritation. This wasn't the time. 'You know how I feel about him. Of course this isn't a situationship.'

'Which is exactly why I'm saying talk to him,' she reasoned, grabbing hold of my hand. I didn't know what I spotted in her eyes—concern? Worry? Why, I didn't understand. 'Just . . . tell him what you want with your life, with your future going forward and make sure he wants that too.'

I didn't get what she was so worried about. Things were good.

'I will, of course, I will,' I said, squeezing her hand right back. 'You need to stop worrying about me.'

'Soon,' she added.

'Yes, ma'am.'

'And don't make me ask again.'

'Oh my god, can we at least let your wedding day be about you, please,' I yelled in her ear, brushing it off. With the sound of the thumping bass as a mash-up of Punjabi party songs played in the background, I clamped down on Sarina's concern as just something she does. She worries because she loves me.

Everything was good, everything was just fine, fine, fine.

~

Monday morning, you and I, my living room—a few weeks after the wedding, yet still in the fever of it all. The sun shines through the room and into a streak on my face, my eyes, through the crack of the open curtain. You get up and pull it shut. Minutes later, I hear the coffee machine gurgling, my ears perk up at the sound of the ceramic mugs clinking. The coffee arrives for me in bed and yet the first thing that meets my mouth is your lips—Sarina never did *that*, thank god. The room smells like last night's fried rice and chilli chicken and ground coffee—I drink it all up like it's the best combination in the world.

You stay over more days than not; we don't say we're moved in just yet, but your *chappals* are under my bed and your toothbrush is touching bristles with mine—there is no label but there is a bottle of shower gel we share and a perfume that suits both of us on my nightstand.

We develop a list of things we can prefix 'our' to—*our* morning routine, *our* load of laundry, *our* bag of groceries, *our* favourite brand of coffee that costs an arm and a leg to buy. It feels like falling, but falling into place; I'm falling, but the landing is smooth, the ground prepped with a cushion.

Friday morning, you cook an elaborate breakfast before work, and the photos pour in. A Google Drive link, ten thousand photos, *our* slow Wi-Fi takes an hour for all of them to load. Mehendi, cocktail, haldi, the gorgeous wedding. Your iPad tethered to the nearest socket, we swipe right on them as the coffee in your hand loses steam, flattens to a cold mess. *Our* mess.

'They look so fucking cute,' you exhale in a whisper and I nod in agreement, nestling my head into the crook between your neck and shoulder, retreating into you like a tortoise does into its shell. I turn back to the bright yellow photo on the screen, the morning of the haldi. Sarina and Nipun look the happiest I have ever seen them—they look like they're in love. Then you look at me and smile, because we're in love too, aren't we? Even though we haven't said it yet. This is what love feels like, right?

I scooch in closer and find that the nearer I get, the further I feel—like no proximity in the world can ever dull the fear of losing you again.

'We look so cute,' I say, sighing into your ear, as we finally approach the end of the scroll, the collection of photos fading into Sarina's *vidai*—to her hotel room—and then some portraits the photographer was kind enough to take of Vatsal and I at sunset. And then, the end. I scroll all the way back to the start because I'm not ready for it to be over. Not yet.

'I can't believe it's done, you know?'

'I bet Sarina can, look at her face in this photo,' Vatsal says pointing to Sarina cringing at the smell of mehendi, like she did the entire time when she was getting it put.

'Still, I mean,' I say, nudging him at his waist, 'Sarina and I grew up talking about it and now . . . she's married. She's *actually* married. She did the thing.'

'You grew up talking about it? Getting married?' you ask, poking me right back in my stomach—is it strange that the touch of your hand always gives me butterflies, even when your hand has explored all of me?

'Yeah, we were those typical kids, playing pretend-wedding in the living room when no one was watching. We would alternate between being the bride and groom,' I reply, my mind dialling back to how Sarina looked in my red bedsheet tied around her waist like a lehenga. 'It was adorable but also a little desperate now that I look back on it, how much both of us dreamed about getting married so early on. But, I mean, that's what you're taught to dream about when you're a girl.'

Vatsal doesn't say anything; he just listens.

'Did you grow up thinking about it?' I ask, curious. There are so many pieces of you I don't yet know, so many pieces left to fit into the spaces between the ones I already have accumulated over the years.

'About weddings?'

'About marriage.'

You ponder over it, reflectively looking around the room as you reach for my hand and then mutter, 'Not really. I don't think I've ever thought about it.'

'You haven't ever thought about marriage?'

'No, I guess I haven't.'

How does one not think about it, ever, I want to ask. But I don't.

Instead, I say, 'But, I mean, you would want that someday, wouldn't you?'

I can see it in the way you sit still, the way your body stiffens next to mine. Your fingers taut, your arms glued to your waist on either side. This conversation . . . like a pin to this sweet bubble we've been in until—pop.

'I don't think so,' is all you say, now that it's been too long to keep the question hanging. Now that the silence has already made your answer clear.

'You don't think so?' I repeat—the cadence of an innocent prisoner reading back their life sentence.

'No, I don't think I would want that,' you say. 'I just . . . I've seen the worst of it, Naina.' And I know now that we're not just talking about the philosophical idea of a marriage. We're talking about us. Our future. The one Sarina asked me to talk about—before it was too late. 'I just know that it's the one thing that ruins a good thing and I don't . . .'

'You don't *what*?' I ask, breathless.

'I don't want to ruin this,' he says.

And just like that, it's like no time has passed.

~

You expect it to be different.

Against all logic, damning evidence, the beat of your heart telling you that it won't be, no, not really, you still *expect* it to be. You expect the hurricane to not strike again and take the awning with it. You pray the bear only sniffs. You wait for the best, knowing that the worst is statistically likelier—because if you start believing evidence that not everything works out in your favour, you won't make it past Monday.

But god, I really thought this time was different.

'Don't you think that with the right person it would be . . . different?' I ask and he grabs my hand—as though saying *You are the right person, silly*—and squeezes it.

'I don't know, Naina. I just don't think I can see another marriage fall apart. Especially not my own.'

'Right.'

'Naina, you know this doesn't mean I don't want you, right?' *Does it not?* I sit there motionless, wordless, until he says: 'Naina, talk to me?'

But what do I say to you? What do I say now that I know the ways I want you in, the fullness I want, no, need, of having you, will always remain unattainable? That no matter what I do in life, I will never have it all.

I will never be first.

'I don't know if that's what I want, Vatsal,' I say through my tears. I realize I'm crying only after the fact—like my body has begun responding to the end before my brain has even signed off on it.

'What are you saying?' you ask, startled. You mean: what are you saying Naina, when my shoes are in your rack and when my clothes are in your cupboard, what do you mean this will not work?

'We want different things,' is all I can mutter, the only way I can make a million springing thoughts align in one tight line. 'I can't . . .'

'You can't?'

'I can't imagine not being married to you,' I say. 'And you can't imagine being married to me.' I wait for you to take it back, call it a misunderstanding. I give you three whole seconds. But you don't. That's when I know.

I get up off our couch. I walk straight on.

'Naina,' you call out from the living room, but I shut my bedroom door on the way in.

You knock twice.

I don't open the door.

The next morning, your shoes are no longer in my rack.

~

'Didn't eat anything or what?' are my mother's first words as she opens the door to me; my sunken eyes gaping at her before they fall down to spot Bittoo.

A day after Vatsal left, I dropped Bittoo home with my parents—lying that I was too sick and needed their help taking care of him. A week in, though, the separation pangs started to hit.

'Bittoo,' I whisper, knowing how much he hates loud noises, until suddenly I hear the pat-pat-pat of his paws, him running towards me.

'How was the wedding?' she asks as I rub the soft part of his skull right as he lands into my arms. We haven't spoken a lot since.

'Nice, it's been a while, though,' I answer. 'You should've come.'

'I wanted to, but . . .'

'Surgeries, I know,' I say, scratching Bittoo's belly as he lies down to show me his stomach.

My mother stands there as I'm keeling over Bittoo, when she says, 'You've come to just see him only no?' shutting the door behind her. '*Maa-baap se bhi baat karliya karo* [Speak to your parents also].'

'Can we not do this today, please?'

'*Harr cheez se* problem *hai* [You have a problem with everything],' she says, tch-tching—like I'm fifteen, still. 'Look at Sarina, does she throw all these tantrums with Laila?'

'Okay, sorry.'

'Don't say it if you don't mean it.'

'Okay.'

'Why are you in a mood?'

'I'm not in a mood.'

'You know, you can sometimes confide in your parents too. Sarina isn't all that you have,' she scoffs. 'Especially now that she's married.'

I say it, I almost do. But then I don't.

Not until she says: '*Theek hai, mat batao* [Fine, don't tell me]. But when you have a daughter, then you'll realize how tough it is . . .'

I feel the earth shift. I hear the words forming. I see the explosion.

'Oh my god, mom, for the last time, I DON'T WANT A DAUGHTER.'

This is a decibel unexplored in our house, where the loudest sound on most days was the running refrigerator or the bell ringing at 11 p.m.—my parents' usual time of getting home.

'Will you calm down? What has happened to you?'

'I'm just sick of this,' I yell. Bittoo gets up and scrambles away from me. 'If you don't want to talk nicely, just don't talk. But don't give me unnecessary taunts, because I can also do the same.'

'What does that mean? *Itni kyu naffrat hai tumhe mujhse* [Why do you hate me so much], Naina? All I've done is give you this life, this fancy job you have, this . . . this cat, what makes you so angry at me all the time?'

'There's more to life than giving me *things*. Did you ever think that maybe I just needed a hug?' I ask, fuming, my eyes stinging. In seconds, the anger has melted into quiet hurt; the fate of a child who never thought she *could* be angry. 'That instead of being patted on the back when I gave my math exam in a fever, that you should've said, "No, Naina, you need rest, stay home", and then just stayed home to take care of *me* for once?'

She gapes at me like I'm describing a stranger—like I'm not reading out the script of my childhood from painful recollection that just never fades.

'How many parent–teacher meetings did you attend in the fourteen years I was in school?' I ask, but in vain. Zero isn't a number. 'None. That's how many. You just sent Nani,' I say, scoffing. 'Nani was more of a mother to me. Laila aunty was more of a mother. She came to pick me up from school when my period made me feel like I was dying, and you were too goddamn busy to answer your phone.'

'Every one of my friends went to Chandi Chowk,' I say, wiping my tears off the back of my sweatshirt. 'They took so many photos, they talked about that day for weeks. It was the only thing I'd looked forward to and you *knew* it. But you couldn't do a simple thing, you couldn't remember to do one thing for me which was to sign a stupid form.'

My voice croaks as I say, 'You left me all alone. You didn't even give me a sibling to lean on. *I* found Sarina. *I* found support. Where were you?'

Finally, my mother yells back: 'You think it was *easy* for me? Working all day? Providing for this family when your father wasn't getting promoted for years? Where is all this anger for him? Why am I the villain?'

'I'm not saying anything, Mom, I'm not even saying you did something wrong, all I'm saying is please don't ask me why we can't have a normal conversation or why I can't confide in you,' I say, the anger finally losing steam. Now, I just feel empty. 'It's because we have never *had* conversations. It's because you have never been in my life, you have no idea what goes on in my life, you don't know what a normal conversation looks like between us. Other than Sarina, you can't name a single friend I've ever had and it's not like you've bothered asking.'

Standing face to face, we pull the curtains off the pretence I've lived under my entire life. She looks at me, perplexed. Hurt. It hits me, finally, what I've done. But I can't get myself to regret it.

'*Tum aise* behave *kar rahi h*o [You are behaving] like I tortured you, Naina.'

'*Nahi*, I'm just saying you didn't love me enough to put me first.'

THREE YEARS AGO

'Any plans tonight?' Sambhav asks as I shut my laptop and shove it into my bag.

'It's 10 p.m. My only plans are to sleep.'

It's been a month since I joined Marked—and while that should be the only thing that really counts, my mind can't help but throw up the fact that it's also been a month and seven days since Vatsal and I stopped being what we once used to be.

On the Uber ride back home, I play my favourite game of retracing evidence. 'Pyar Diwana Hota Hai' blasts from my earphones as I shut my eyes, my head against the headrest. I start at the very beginning: the first time we locked eyes in Django, right outside the washroom. I keep digging and digging and digging until I'm certain I wasn't dreaming through it all.

When I get home, it feels like I've dug myself back into the past.

I unlock my home to find Nipun and Vatsal sprawled out on the couch, watching football.

'Oh, hey Naina,' Vatsal says, noticing the jingling of my keys, the creaking open of the door, Bittoo's little paws on the marble floor responding to the sound of my entry.

Hey?

'Hi,' I mutter at my shoes, looking anywhere but at him. I consider running away to my bedroom with Bittoo under my arm—but it's like the second I consider that possibility, he jumps and finds his way next to Vatsal, drawing my eyes to him no matter how much I want to keep them off.

'We're just watching the Premier League, want to join us?' Nipun asks.

'Thanks, but that sounds awful,' I say, hanging up my keys on the hook Sarina just set up next to our main door in one of her home-improvement sprees. 'I'm actually just going to crash, super long day,' I say. 'Bittoo, dinner,' I call out, pouring his meal into his bowl before disappearing inside my bedroom. Only when I shut my bedroom door and hear the sound of the TV turn back on do I let myself take the thirty inhales I've pushed down the last few minutes.

He's here.

Ten steps away.

He's here and it's nothing like what it was before but there's no one to talk to; no one who can understand how insane it really is *but* him and yet, he's the one I can't talk to. I'm spiralling when suddenly, Vatsal pushes open my bedroom door. The fact that he barges in without knocking, without requesting entry doesn't surprise me.

'I'm sorry, but the door seemed open,' he says, coming in. It wasn't open at all, I'd made sure of it.

'Yeah, no, no problem,' I say, collecting myself. 'Need something?'

'I was actually wondering if you're free,' he says, finally. 'To talk, I mean.'

'Oh?' I say, when I actually should be saying: *You want to talk? Now?*

'Okay if I shut this?' he says pointing to my bedroom door. I only nod—pretending, I hope *well*, that his proximity after all this while is not a doorway into absolute insanity for me.

'What's up?' I throw to his 'Hey!'—my first line of revenge. In my mind, I keep reciting: be cool.

'Nothing, I just . . . I got done with the internship today, so I came to see Nipun.'

'Oh, that's nice,' I say, holding back any reaction that shows I care. He's done. He's going to leave. This is his goodbye—and it wasn't even meant for me. This is just . . . by the way. 'Back to Bangalore now?'

'Yeah, day after, then London soon,' he says, sighing, as he rests his weight against my study table. My perfume bottle from the morning rumbles under his weight, falling over on its side. He picks it up as he asks, without looking at me, 'How's the job?'

'It's fantastic,' I say, beaming. 'Honestly couldn't have asked for a better place to be at.' None of this is a lie. But I don't say all of this *because* I mean it.

'That's good to hear,' he murmurs. 'I'm really happy for you.'

I give him a stiff smile, unsure what to say back.

'I actually wanted to talk about . . .'

I interrupt, because I know where it's going.

'We don't need to talk about it,' I say, cutting in. I don't realize how much I mean it until the sentence actually makes its way out. *Really.*

'Naina.'

'I'm being serious, Vatsal,' I say, standing up to face him. I don't want to be on the receiving end of his explanations, his logical reasoning. I don't want to claim the victim tag in our story, even though it's been thrust upon me.

'Can you just hear me out, please?' he asks, his eyes begging, his eyebrows furrowed. He looks at me in quiet desperation, showing me a part of him I don't recognize or understand.

'What do you want to say?'

'I'm sorry,' he exhales, finally, after a moment passes.

His admission makes it worse. It attributes intentionality to what I thought was something I'd made up in my mind.

It also, somehow, makes me laugh.

'Are you seriously saying *sorry* after all of that?' I ask, snickering.

He shakes his head. 'I'm not being . . . this is not me . . . I don't know Naina, I don't know what to say. I'm just, I'm sorry.'

'For what?! What are you sorry for? We're cool,' I say, casually. 'Totally cool.'

He grabs the outer corner of my wrist and pulls me in. 'Naina,' he insists, holding onto me. 'I fucked up. I was overthinking it all and I fucked up and I get that you're mad at me but please, just, please talk to me.'

I swing my wrist away from him. The sudden action
jolts him.

'I really don't understand why you're doing this now.
You had a whole month to tell me what you were thinking,
and you chose to ghost me, instead.'

'I didn't ghost you, Naina. I just needed time to think.'

'Oh? Right, then you should've acted like an adult and
said that.'

'I didn't know what to say,' he screams, frustrated.
'I didn't want to do anything but be with you, Naina, but
I didn't know what to say to you to make you understand
what it's like inside my head when I think about doing this.
Like, *really* doing this.'

'You had plenty of time to chill with Zoya though.'

'Zoya? What?' He says, like he doesn't understand,
because he hasn't lived inside *my* head the last month.
The obsessive thoughts, the maddening tendency to stalk
anyone remotely in his periphery, the overbearing need
to keep tabs on him, one way or another. 'Naina, what's
wrong with you? I'm trying to *talk* to you.'

'And I don't understand why. Your message was heard
loud and clear, you really don't need to repeat it to me.'

'Listen, I know I fucked up with how I handled
everything, but whatever you're assuming out of it was not
what was going on,' he says. 'I wasn't . . . ghosting you, I
wasn't—'

'I don't care what you were or weren't doing,' I say,
a decibel too high, a touch too frustrated. 'All I know is
you were a dick to me a day after taking me to bed and
that's just gross. I thought you were better than that,' I add,
scoffing. 'I thought I wasn't one of your casual lays.'

'Stop it, Naina,' Vatsal adds, angrily. 'That wasn't what it was, and you know it. Stop making me sound like someone I'm not.'

'Oh, do I? Do I know what it was? Well, I must have forgotten because it's been a whole month since it happened and you haven't said one word to me that means shit. So, *I* must be getting it wrong, obviously.'

'Naina, have you maybe considered that it isn't easy for me to fall for you one month before I'm packing up my life and moving continents? Have you *possibly* considered that maybe I freaked out about that?'

'Wow, you can save me the clichés.'

'How the fuck is this a cliché?'

'How is it not? Oh my god, the fuckboy got scared one day after hooking up with the girl and ghosts her for a month? You're the template.'

'Wow,' he says, sighing, looking down at the floor.

'What?'

'I didn't know you thought so low of me.'

'Yeah, I didn't either.' It feels like this is it, but I don't want this fight to end. 'You know, you could've just said that it was casual for you,' I laugh mockingly. 'I didn't need you to take me to fucking Chandni Chowk and make me fall in love and then pull your bullshit.'

'For fuck's sake, Naina, it wasn't casual. I *told* you I freaked out. I *know* I fucked up. But stop calling it casual and making it sound like I don't care, because that's not true.'

'Do you, Vatsal? Because you know what adults do when they get scared?' He stands there, quietly gazing at me. 'They *talk* about things.' When he doesn't respond, I say, 'You wouldn't know, though.'

'What's that supposed to mean?'

'Nothing, just that your ex was right,' I spit out—the worst part of me coming to the fore while he just stands there in disbelief.

He mutters, 'What?'

'All you know is how to leave,' I say, finishing with a soft whisper to our mighty fall.

Moments later, it's a self-fulfilling prophecy.

~

That same night, I do whatever I can to not look at my phone, to not think of anything that has to do with Vatsal at all. It's almost 3 in the morning when I finally finish rearranging my entire closet, digitally cleansing my laptop of all old, irrelevant Zupiter files, and clearing out every last promotional email from my inbox.

I pad towards my nightstand to turn off my desk lamp, when I find a piece of paper with my name scrawled atop it. Instantly, I know what it is—I feel the urge to toss it in the trash.

I don't. Instead, I tuck it under a folder inside my drawer.

I decide that the end of this story isn't one I want to read.

Naina,

In some ways, I feel like I've known you my entire life. In that respect, I don't feel like I need to fill you in on every part of me. Somehow, I assume you will just get it. And you do. You almost always do.

And in some other ways, you don't know the deepest bits of my heart, simply because I have kept them hidden. Here is one piece, before I offer an explanation for everything I've done wrong because of it.

I was seven years old when I first realized my parents were in love. I'd heard the word around; I'd even said it to mummy, occasionally to papa. But there was no real way of knowing what it meant—love.

Every single day, without fail, papa would come home with a bouquet in one hand and a bar of Cadbury in another. He would ring the bell twice and then the third time after a pause so mummy knew it was him—so I knew not to open the door. Not like I was allowed.

Mummy would greet him with the fattest smile on her face as I watched from the sidelines; she was the one who taught me what it meant to smile with all of your teeth on display. On the other side of the jaali would be my father, beaming right back at her. At once, he would walk in, handing her flowers, as usual, and they would wrap their arms around each other. Every day, one of them would initiate a kiss on the cheek, the other would happily accept. Sometimes, when they thought I wasn't looking, they'd kiss like real people do.

Papa loved mummy in the loud ways; the ways that papa's friends, if they ever witnessed even a flicker of it, would hundred per cent bully him for. He went nowhere without her—parties or hangouts with his friends—and on the rare occasion that he did, he would come back home before mummy would even have a chance to notice he was gone. Mummy loved papa too, at least I thought she did.

So when mummy left for London, an opportunity of her dreams to curate a new art gallery that had received some big money, there were tears, yes, but there wasn't ever fear—mummy loved papa, papa loved mummy, and distance was a shabby hurdle for a love so strong. I don't remember knowing a lot, but I knew that much.

'How hard can long distance be?' Papa had said kissing mummy on the forehead, and she'd smiled coyly, like she always did. He'd pushed her to accept the offer. 'Imagine, we'll get to tour London with Vatsal when I visit you.'

This next part, I'm not supposed to know.

The phone rang in the living room at ten in the night—it was mummy's thing, picking up the phone, but she was no longer around, so papa and I split it amongst ourselves, the responsibility.

When I picked up the landline and set it against my ear, I heard gasps over the phone. Breathy, loud wailing. The sound of my mother crying. I don't know how I knew it was my mother—I'd never heard or seen her cry before—but who else could it be?

'Calm down, Meera,' I heard my father's voice whisper over the phone. Cupping the receiver, I sat down on the couch—my ears perked up with curiosity more than concern. Why was mummy crying? 'What has happened, talk to me?'

'Please forgive me, Rakesh,' she squirmed into the phone. 'Mujhe please maaf kardo,' she repeated over and over and over. My ears hurt from her screeching; I itched to ask her to stop it.

'Meera, come back to India and we'll talk about it,' is all my father said. He was calm; he sounded the way he always did. 'We can't do this over a phone call.'

'I don't know if I want to come back, Rakesh,' my mother breathed out finally—once enough time had passed that I'd wondered if she'd dropped off.

My father asked, 'What?'

'Rakesh, I want to stay here. With him,' she exhaled loudly into the receiver. She wasn't crying anymore.

'You're . . . you're crazy, have you lost your mind? You want to destroy everything for some man you just met?'

I didn't understand what it meant that my mother did not want to come back; I didn't know who this 'man' was. All I knew then was that my mother might never come back.

'You don't understand,' my mother pleaded from the other end. 'Please, Rakesh, mujhe jaane do.'

'Aur kitna jaane du? You've left the bloody country!'

'Rakesh, please,' she said crying, again.

At this point, I could hear my father both, through the phone and from across the house. 'And what about your child? What about our family?' His agitation, still unclear to me in its exact source, shone through his tenor. 'Paagal hogayi ho kya?'

'Vatsal can come here, he can study in a really good school,' she speedily said. My heartbeat started rising the second I heard my name in the exchange. 'Life is so much better for him here, also. You know that.'

'Aur mera kya? I'm just supposed to not see my son again?'

That was when I put the receiver down. I turned the light off in the living room, walked straight to my bedroom, pulled out the remote-controlled helicopter I'd gotten for my ninth birthday and decided, this time, to fly it straight into the ceiling. It crashed into the wall and the little pieces of plastic came raining down all over the bed.

A week later, for the intra-school speech competition, one I'd been asked to represent my section for, the chalkboard read 'What does love mean to you?'. I rescinded participation and hid behind the football goal post the entire time. A few weeks later, I moved to London.

Ever since that day and for as long as I can remember, I have run away from love, very intentionally so, because the prospect of ever ending up where they ended up was terrifying enough to make a solitary life seem like a pretty good deal. Two people falling in love and then falling out of it caused my life to fall apart in cataclysmic ways—so much so that I couldn't afford to risk it all, on the off chance that it doesn't work.

That is what I was thinking when I left that night—abruptly, stupidly, realizing that the thing I'd run away from my entire life was finally happening to me, and how little say I had in the matter. And that fearful thought is the one that has kept me from reaching out, that has kept me cold and distant and honestly, cowardly, all this while. It's that thought that's kept me from asking you how your first day went at your new job, how all of your days are going, or just saying good morning to you, no matter how much I want to.

Until I woke up to find that my master's scholarship had come through and I realised that the only person I wanted to share this with was you, Naina. I hadn't learned, until that very moment, that staving off love also meant depriving myself of the best thing that has ever happened to me, will ever happen to me.

I couldn't possibly say these words to you now, having treated you the way I have. I can't stand to look at your face, knowing the hurt I've caused due to something that isn't even close to being your fault, and then ask for forgiveness. So, I'm being a coward again and asking you in the only way I know how. Here it goes: Naina, I'm so in love with you. This is the first time I'm saying it to you, but I swear I've meant it for as long as I've known you. And I'm so incredibly sorry. Is there a chance you'd forgive me and be mine, even though I'm leaving?

If the answer isn't one that will break my heart, you know where to find me.

Even if it is, though, find me anyway.

Just have one last conversation with me. Please.

Vatsal

NOW

'Who's going to make me coffee in the morning?' I yelp like a kid being sent off to boarding school as Sarina packs up the last bits of what remains in her bedroom. Things she could've easily left behind. But we need this moment, just her and I, for the last time, in our home together.

The wedding was a month ago—the chasm between the before of my life and now, the after—and this part of my life, this 'now' is taking getting used to.

It's been three weeks since Vatsal and I have spoken.

'I'll come over every morning just to wake you up and give you coffee,' she says, smiling, as she shuts the drawers on her nightstand. 'Wow, my employment contract was just randomly in here,' she says, trashing it in the dustbin now that her stint at Bruno's is finally over.

The room is now, officially, empty. It has all its original structure—every piece of furniture intact—but it could be anyone's room. It's empty of what really matters—it's no longer Sarina's.

'I can't believe this is the last time I'll be in this room,' she says.

'Okay, can you not be dramatic? I literally still live here.'

'Yeah, but you're going to get a flatmate and then I can't just walk in here like it's mine.'

'You can just stay here, you know? Lots of people do that.'

'Do what?'

'Like, when the elder sister gets married, the younger sister sometimes goes to live with her and her husband.'

'So, I'm the elder sister now?' Sarina asks, poking me in my stomach.

I want to say: yes. You are my entire family. But I don't, because she won't be. No, not forever. She'll be someone else's entire family now and I'll have to find something of my own.

'You're definitely more than a best friend.'

'Oh my god, Naina, you can't hit on me, I'm married.' She looks around her empty room—and I know this is tough for her, too. Bidding goodbye to the last bits of who she used to be, so she can become who she wants to be. 'Do you want to talk about it?' she asks, nudging my hand gently.

'There isn't anything to talk about.'

'Naina . . .'

'I swear, Sarina, I'm fine, I'm doing okay,' I say, grabbing her hand right back and patting it with mine. 'I already have people lining up to take the two rooms.'

'You know that's not what I'm talking about.'

I look away from her and rest my eyes on the mirror, at myself in it—overdrawn bags under my eyes, the crack of a tired smile, the slumped shoulders. This girl in the mirror, the one staring back at me, who is she? What happened to her?

'There's even less to talk about when it comes to that,' I say. 'You were right, I should've talked about it before I got my hopes up.'

'Naina . . .'

'I'm serious. He's gone and I'm okay and this is the end of the story and I just . . . I just want to find a way to be okay on my own, Sarina.'

Sarina clutches my hand tight. She drops her head on my shoulder.

'It feels like I've been waiting all my life for someone to make *me* their entire world. And I'm only now realizing that no one's going to do that, no one but me, for sure,' I say—talking more to myself than to her. 'Even you. For so long, I know I've been everything to you, but that wasn't going to be the case forever. Nipun came around and soon there's going to be kids . . .'

'I've gotten married, like, a month ago and you're already talking about kids? You're worse than Nipun's mom.'

'You know what I mean. It's just . . . I keep expecting someone, anyone, to decide that I am all they need, ever, for the rest of their lives, and I keep getting hurt when I realise that's never going to happen.'

'Naina, you *are* all I need. Ever. Nipun is the love of my life, he completes me in ways that I didn't even know possible, but there's no great dependency there. He knows that. I love him and he loves me just because.'

'But you . . . I *need* you. I cannot do without you. You know this. You've always known this,' she says, looking at me as I try hard not to let the tears in my eyes trickle down to my cheeks. 'You are my home.'

There are so many lies we tell each other to keep life going, to keep the going sweet. I'm grateful that this is one Sarina tells me, even if she doesn't know it's a lie yet. Even if I know everything will change one day.

'I'm going to be okay,' I tell her. 'I promise.'

'I know you are. Because I've got you.'

Sarina and I sit there on the same bed we've eaten bucketfuls of popcorn on, where we've spent every night pretending it's a sleepover that'll end when day breaks, but it never does—where I've then sat between Sarina and Nipun as we did all of the same things together, but somehow different.

Good different, but different, nonetheless.

Maybe this different will be good too. Maybe I'll just have to wait until I find out.

'I'm going to miss you,' I say, finally breaking down.

'I won't give you a single second to.'

~

The house is unbearably quiet the moment Sarina leaves. I perch myself up on the couch, unmoving, and stare at the ceiling, when moments later, the buzz of my phone ringing cuts through the quiet. I let it ring into a fade; I let myself be, for the moment at least, unreachable. Only when the phone goes off again do I pick it up.

It's my mom.

'Why weren't you picking up?'

'I was sleeping.'

'It could've been an emergency.'

'How? I'm not one of your patients.' I regret it the moment I say it. 'Sorry.'

'Is Sarina done moving out?'

'Just, she took the last of her stuff a while back.'

'Do you have anyone coming to check out the rooms?'

'*Haan*, I have a few leads, but it'll take about a month until something is finalized.'

'*Accha*,' she says. 'Papa and I were thinking we'll help you with rent until you have new roommates.'

'Thanks, Mom, that really helps.'

She's quiet for a moment, then.

'I actually wanted to talk about what you said the last time.'

'Please forget it, I wasn't feeling good, and it came out on you—'

'However you were feeling, there was some degree of truth to what you said,' she says, interrupting. 'I just wanted to say . . .'

'Hmm?'

'I can't . . . I can't change how things were when you were growing up. In my head, I was doing the best I could . . .' And then she says the words that don't suit any parent. 'I'm sorry, Naina.'

The words undo something in my brain, a rewiring of sorts. Years of anger I've kept clipped tight under my feet, like a wild dog disciplined with a leash, finally feels like it's disappearing.

'Mom, you don't have to say sorry,' my voice breaks. 'I know you were trying your best. I had a great childhood. I don't want you to feel like I didn't. *I'm* sorry for the things I said.'

'No, I'm glad you said them,' she says. 'Nani died before I could ever have a face-to-face conversation with her, like what you had with me. I thought one day I'll sit her down, tell her how I feel, say, "The person you birthed and the person I am today are two different people, we need to find a way to accept these new versions of each other", but that day never came.'

'I don't want that with you, Naina,' she says, gently. I can tell she's breaking down too from the other end of the line; how hard she's trying not to let it show. My mother, the *strong* woman, the uncaring antihero.

'I don't either.'

'So how about . . .'

'Hmm?'

'How about I treat you like the twenty-eight-year-old woman you are and you . . .you love me as your mother but try and see me as a woman, too?'

I giggle through my tears at the silliness of it all, but I say, 'That sounds good,' anyway.

'So, tell me.'

'Tell you what?'

'Anything,' she says. She means: fill me in. Give me parts of you that you've kept hidden for so long. Treat me as a friend, Naina, please. Let's try, before it's too late.

And so I do. I give her a piece of me. It's a small one. Maybe one day I can give her the largest.

~

We do this thing now that we've never done together as a family, except on those lone weekends when my parents did not have shifts slotted—every Sunday, at 2 p.m., we have lunch together.

I knock on my parent's door, knowing that the doorbell doesn't work. I know these things now; these silly little details that my mother shares over texts she sends like 'Ate chicken for lunch. Too overcooked' or 'Papa is not fixing the doorbell because he's fighting with our electrician. Can you please speak to him?'

My mother opens the door instantly—like she's been standing against it, waiting. The wafting aroma of kaali mirch meeting garlic and onion greets me along with her smiling face.

This will never not feel like an unfamiliar sight.

'*Arre wah*, right on time,' she says. 'Come, I was just setting the table.'

I pad indoors as I drop Bittoo to the floor so he can do his exploring; it's taken four visits, but he's learning to fall in love, again, with the contours of the home he was brought up in.

We're both learning.

'I've bought some kibble for him,' my mother says from the kitchen, as I spot a bright blue cat bowl adhered to the wall right outside the kitchen. I don't even need to tell Bittoo; I look down and see that he's already found it.

'Thanks, Mom,' I say, as she puts the bhindi down on the table—bright green, barely cooked. Just the way I like it. 'You bought him a bowl also?'

'It was coming for free if I added an extra pack of the food,' she says, shrugging.

'*Accha*,' I say, nodding. 'Papa *kahan hain* [Where is Papa]?'

'*Arre*, I forgot to tell you. He's gone to buy a new bell for the house,' she says, scoffing. 'Finally *ladhai solve kar li unhone* [the fight is solved] with the electrician.'

I giggle as I sit down at the same seat I've sat in for all my lunches after school—except this time it's not Nani sitting across from me.

'So, tell me, what's going on,' my mother says as she fills my plate with a scoop full of bhindi. It's the same question every time.

I fetch a warm *roti* from the casserole and break it into a morsel.

'Nothing,' I say, shrugging. 'Same old.'

'*Kuch toh hoga naya* [Something must be new].'

With my mother, I have now covered it all—the ex, the firing, Marked, Sarina's wedding, the before, the after, everything I can recall being of any relevance to my life. Bit by bit, I have divulged parts of me that have never been hers, and she has done it too. How it felt having me at twenty-three, why she could never give me a sibling, why her and Papa slept in different beds for a few years. Brick by brick, conversation by conversation, we're building, together, a new relationship.

But I haven't yet told her about Vatsal.

'Okay then, tell me how's your dating life?'

'Mom,' I say, rolling my eyes. 'Please, no.'

'*Arre*? You're, what, almost twenty-nine now, I think we can talk about this like two mature women, Naina.'

I play with the bhindi on my plate, averting her gaze. 'What's there to talk about?'

'*Iska kya matlab* [What does that mean]? You're a young, desirable woman in her twenties, of course there's so much to talk about.'

'I don't think so,' I say, staring at my plate, feeling the numbness take over. This happens every time I think about him now—it happens, sometimes, even when I'm not thinking about him.

'What's wrong?' she asks. 'Naina?'

'Nothing, nothing's wrong,' I say, sniffling at the involuntary announcement of a lone tear whenever the thought of Vatsal arises. Which doesn't take much effort—his memory is always looming around me. Suddenly, my nose is watering, my eyes are betraying my demands. 'I swear.'

'Tell me, *na*?' My mother's tone isn't demanding. It's not intrusive. 'Naina?' she says, grabbing my hand. '*Kya hua* [What happened]?'

'There is someone,' I say, wiping my nose. 'I mean, was.'

'Was?'

'Yeah, it didn't work out.'

My mother's clutch on my hand tightens. 'What happened?'

'I don't know,' I say, sobbing. I thought I knew, really, but I don't, not anymore.

'Something must have happened no?'

'*Pata nahi*, I think we wanted different things.'

'Different things *matlab*?'

That's a good question. What does that mean, that we wanted different things? We wanted each other, in the end, didn't we?

'He didn't see himself ever getting married to me,' I say, finally, when the silence has worn off.

'To you or to anyone in general?'

'To anyone in general,' I say. 'His parents divorced when he was very young, so he just . . . doesn't like the idea of marriage.'

'And then?'

'And then what,' I say, looking at my mother, perplexed that she doesn't get it as intuitively as I need her to. 'How can I date someone who doesn't want a future with me, Mom?'

'Is that what he said?' she asks, letting go of my hand.

'What?'

'Did he *say* he doesn't want a future with you?'

'No,' I say, looking away. 'He wanted a future, he just didn't want to get married.'

'How long did you date him, this guy?'

'We were friends once, three years ago,' I say, drawing back the timeline. 'And then, I don't know, we dated, you could say, for a few weeks after Sarina's wedding.'

'And you broke up with him because he doesn't want to get married?'

I feel my mother and I on the precipice of a fight—but I don't want to push the boulder off.

'Shouldn't you be encouraging me to be with someone who *wants* to get married?'

I watch my mother practise the words in her mind before they make their way out, what she says next. 'I'm just saying . . . I don't know, I feel like your entire life, Naina, you've clung on to things that felt safe, that felt . . . risk-free, certain, even if you didn't particularly enjoy yourself. Isn't that why you stayed at your last job all this while?' She tucks a loose strand of my hair—one that's been irritating my eyelash—behind my ear as she continues. 'Didn't you stay with that stupid boyfriend of yours even though he was horrible to you, just because you felt like that stability was better than actually finding someone who understood you?'

'It's not that simple, Mom,' I say, fidgeting out of her touch, worried about being seen.

Except it *was* that simple, wasn't it? It was simple every time I looked at him and found that his entire face softened the moment his eyes registered mine. And it was simple, how it felt, right? How my shoulders relaxed when he was around, even if not exactly nearby, how I'd realize, only once I'd unclenched it, that my jaw was clenched tight the entire day until I finally saw his face? How did something so simple get so complicated, then? And how do I make everything simple again, now that the knots, instead of being untangled gently, have been ripped out, the connection severed?

'Isn't it? That simple?' she asks, locking eyes with me. 'Does he make you happy?'

I sigh, not wanting to answer this question.

'It doesn't *matter* if he makes me happy, it's too late now.'

'You can still answer the question.'

I don't have to think about it, not really. 'He does. Did.'

'Do you wish he were here right now?'

I fight back my tears. This one question I *can't* answer.

'Then it is that simple, Naina. No one knows what they really want in the future. He probably doesn't either. So shouldn't you just do what makes you happy right now?'

'I don't know,' I exhale. I don't think I know anything anymore.

'This life that I have today, Naina, it's not everything I wanted,' she says. 'But it's the best life I could've had, despite it all. And when I look back at all of the things I wanted in this life . . . things that I thought I absolutely could not live without . . . well, I have lived without all of them, haven't I?'

The doorbell rings again. Thrice, this time—and a new sound.

'That's your father, make sure you tell him you like the new bell, okay?' she says, getting up to open the door.

SOMETIME LATER

'Are you at least going to tell me his name?' I ask Sarina, pushing open the door to Django.

I can feel her shaking her head from the other end. 'No, let him find you.'

In the last few months, Sarina has taken it upon herself to be the Cupid of my love life. Sitting all the way in Bali, the place she currently calls home, she swipes right on some dating app on my behalf, conducts small talk, arranges dates and blocks the slot on my calendar. All I am instructed to do is show up. Safe to say, not a single one of these dates has gone even remotely well.

We're on thin ice and potentially the last leg of this tradition as I ask, 'And how will he do that?' like I always do.

'Duh, I sent him a picture of you,' like she always does, as well.

'How will I know once *I've* spotted him?' I ask Sarina as I elbow myself through the long line of people waiting for a table at the entrance, making my way for the bar. 'That's also kind of an essential part, you know?'

'He's going to be wearing black.'

'That's extremely helpful, Sarina, thanks, so is every other guy in this restaurant,' I say, scoffing.

'Can you be game for this thing for once?'

'I am being *so* game, especially since this is the last time I'm letting you do this to me.'

'I won't need more attempts, I promise,' she says.

'That's what you said the last time also,' I say, shifting my phone to the other ear. 'Really, now, how do I find him?'

'Naina,' Sarina says, softly.

'Yes?'

'You just need to look.'

And then the line goes off—I stare at my phone, slightly confused. On Sarina's instructions, I look around the room, hoping that when my eyes land on who it's supposed to be, that I'll just magically know somehow.

My phone rings in my hand, once again.

'What did you finally wear?' my mother's voice trickles in from the other end.

Twenty-nine years into our relationship, my mother has been testing every last clichéd question on me lately. With every one she now asks, I realize how she's never asked it before. She was just never that kind of mother. Laila aunty took me shopping; Sarina took over when we were old enough. My mother would just stand there, puzzled, when I wore a new top and ask, 'Where did you get that from?'

It feels different now, the question. Not an inquisition, but curiosity. A genuine want to know. Maybe some part of her is realizing the kind of mother I needed her to be. And so, she is trying. I, too, am realizing now that it was her first time being a mother. And so, I am trying too.

'That pink dress you bought me last month,' I tell her. She does that too, now.

'Excited?'

'Nervous, slightly. I don't even know what the guy looks like.'

'Sarina *bhi na, paagal hai* [Sarina is crazy].'

'Anyway, let me call you back once I'm done. Most likely won't be a long time,' I say and shut my phone off as my mother laughs, shoving it in my pocket as I place myself atop a high chair at the bar. The bartender places a tequila soda in front of me on my request and I take a few, light sips to line up some courage.

'Waiting for someone?' he asks, shaking a cocktail in a mixer, the ice sounding up a storm inside the steel container.

'Something like that,' I say, a touch too loud, so I'm audible over the commotion at the bar.

He stops and asks: 'Should I pour him a drink?'

'I don't know what he takes,' I say, when suddenly, the empty space gets taken up, right as I feel the tenor of a sound all too familiar fill my ears.

'I'll have what she's having,' the voice beckons the bartender, who nods on command, as I turn to face rightward.

A sight all too well-known. Hair buzzed down to the sides. The top two buttons of a black shirt running loose. A sly smile. The same narrow eyes, the same puppy-like mischief in them.

'How many times?' he asks, my phone in his hand.

'How did you even,' I say, grabbing it back, shocked, as usual, at his ability to be so overbearing and somehow so discreet, all at once. I don't let myself digest that it's *him*.

'I keep telling you,' he says, jumping right up on the bar stool next to me, his left thigh brushing against my right. 'It's not safe in your pocket.'

'And yet you're the only one who has ever stolen it.'

'It only takes one thief, Naina,' Vatsal says, his glittering smile reflecting off the black marble slab of the bar counter.

'So,' he mutters, lightly, once the shock has subsided, replaced by everything, all at once: joy, sorrow, fear, calm, anger, forgiveness. A blend of every mutually oppositional feeling in my chest. 'Here on a date?' he jumps straight to it, defying the awkwardness of the idea. His speed makes it easy to answer yes.

'First date?'

'Mm-hmm.'

'Do you think there's going to be a story after?'

'I mean, going by my record?'

Vatsal laughs the same way he always did. He shakes his head and lets out a breathy exhale.

'What about you?' I ask, softly. Hoping he doesn't hear, hoping he doesn't answer. It's a 'yes' I can't stand to learn. 'Also on a date?'

Please say no, please say no, please say no.

'Something like that,' he says, grinning.

My heart thuds to a fall. But I manage to say, 'Right.'

'So, where's this date of yours?'

I tell him that's a good question. 'I actually have no idea. Sarina has this thing where she sends me on stupid blind dates now, so I have no real clue who he is. The guy is just supposed to find me, I guess.'

'So he could be here and know it's you he's supposed to meet, but you'd have no idea if *he* were here?'

'When you put it like that, it feels like the plot of a pretty gruesome serial-killer documentary.'

'I'm sure it's not going to be that bad, Naina,' he says.

An awkward silence lingers as both of us stare at our individual drinks, then around the room. We don't know how to be around each other anymore—not quite strangers, not quite friends, definitely not lovers.

'So, when's *your* date showing up?' I ask, wanting to pop the haze, this dull ache between us.

Vatsal looks up from his drink and then twists his neck to gaze right at me. Without looking at his phone, without moving his attention even a little away from my eyes, he says, 'Oh, I think she's cancelled.'

'And you're still here?'

'Apparently so.'

'What do you plan on doing for the rest of the night, then?'

'I guess I'll spend it hoping your date doesn't show up?'

'And if he does?'

'Then,' Vatsal says, finally looking away.

'Then?'

'Then he's just going to have to wait, Naina,' he exhales. 'Because I've been first in line for a long, long time.'

I don't let the flush on my face show. Instead, I ask: 'So what do you suggest we do until he shows up?'

'I don't know, maybe we start from the beginning?'

'The beginning.'

'Yeah, you know, the part that comes before the rest of the other parts and the end, usually.'

'They teach all this smart-talk at law school?'

'No, this is all self-taught,' he chuckles, remembering. 'Can we?' he asks. 'Start at the beginning?' His eyes are so fixed on mine, I have to stop myself from feeling crushed under the weight of their hold.

'We tried, though,' I say, interjecting. 'I don't know what's changed now.' I despise myself for not continuing this game of push and pull, laying all the cards out at once. Give or take. Win or lose. Now or never.

'You're right, nothing's changed,' he sighs. And maybe once again, maybe for the millionth time around him, my heart breaks. 'Nothing about the fact that I'm so, so in love with you, always have been, always will be, has changed, Naina.'

This is the first time one of us has ever said it.

'Vatsal,' I begin interrupting him, but he grabs my hand before I can.

'No, let me finish. I love you. I always have. I want to say I've loved you since the moment I saw you outside that washroom,' he says, pointing straight ahead, 'at this very restaurant, but back then I was mostly petrified that a gorgeous woman is going to think I'm a disgusting pig.' I giggle as he pulls my bar stool closer to his. 'But I have loved you since that day and I know this because I have not crossed paths with anyone else since and thought they'd ever hold a candle up to you, Naina. I love you. I have gone three years without saying this but I have felt it every single day.'

I don't say anything. Not as tears brim my eyes. Not as my throat tightens.

'I will give you literally anything you want if that means you'll be mine. I swear, Naina, I'll ask you to marry me right now if you'd let me.'

'I don't want that,' I say, mascara tears flowing down my face. 'It's not *about* that, Vatsal.'

'Then tell me, what is it about?' he asks, wiping my cheeks dry.

'I just need to know you're here, that you're not going to leave,' I say. 'I need to know that I won't have to spend another day waking up in the morning and not having you by my side.' I don't let him interrupt. 'I thought all this time that I needed to be married to you to have that certainty, like it would physically chain you from ever leaving me.'

'Naina, I don't want to ever leave you.'

'But I'm always going to be afraid that you will,' I say, terrified for my life.

'How long?'

'How long, what?'

'How long are you going to be afraid for? Is forever enough time?'

I slap his chest away. 'Don't try your lines with me.'

He pulls my stool in closer. 'Naina, remember you asked me how many women there were before you and I told you, what, seven,' he adds.

'Still so fucking furious about that number,' I say, laughing through my tears.

'And then you asked me how many women after you.'

'Yes.'

'Do you remember what I said?' I nod. 'What was it?'

'None,' I say, faint as a whisper.

'Good, you remember. Now ask me how many there will be after you.'

'Why?' I say, pulling one hand away, already knowing the answer, not needing to hear, knowing now that no matter how far away either of us try to run from the other, we'll find our way back here.

'Just ask me, Naina.'

'How many women after me?' I say, half crying, half laughing.

He doesn't answer. He kisses me unprompted, right there in front of the bartender, in the middle of the same restaurant from three years ago, inches away from the exact spot where my life changed, all at once, forever.

No blind date comes looking for me that night. Only Vatsal, in the same black shirt I first saw him in—outside the washroom, that one night, years ago.

That night, for the first time in the entire while we've known each other, Vatsal and I have our first, proper date. Later, I take him home, only for him to never leave again.

Five years later, he still calls it a coincidence.

EPILOGUE

You wake me up in the morning with a cup of coffee and ask if I slept well. 'Of course,' I say, 'I was sleeping next to you,' and you smile, because you know to expect the same answer no matter how many times you ask. We get up off the bed and you lead us into the living room where you have already laid out your newspaper, my magazine subscriptions that have just come in the day before and Bittoo's breakfast. You spoil him dirty, I often tell you this.

'How come he eats at the table like us?'

Sitting down, you pat the empty space next to you, saying, 'Come?'

Although it made me nervous to live alone in a house filled with so many memories, I'm glad I kept the apartment after Sarina and Nipun moved out and left Delhi entirely—Nipun now works freelance with SaaS startups, whatever *that* means, Sarina takes on a gig wherever they're travelling, and I'm . . . well, I'm still here. Before that day at the restaurant, I was so sure I'd fill the gap they left with flatmates I'd never learn the birthdays of. I believed I was fated to live and die in this apartment, alone, one day—surrounded by however many kids Bittoo leaves behind.

But it was a dry renting season. My broker had some unresolved issues with the landlord. Sarina and Nipun's room had too much seepage damage. There was every reason to fill those rooms—yet they stayed empty.

Until you.

Until us.

And then, everything else.

So this house remains: with all its memories intact, newer ones forming daily in the shape of upholstered couches and sage-green walls that we painted together. I no longer worry they'll have to scrape my dead body off the ground, except on those fearful nights where I dream of a world where you somehow get taken away before me.

This morning, like every other morning, I pad towards you, pausing to browse through a stack of magazines you've collected in a neat pile on the table for me, before taking my spot next to you. Sometimes I'm in a *Vogue* mood, other times it's *The Economist*. You say it depends on what I dreamed of the night before. It doesn't make sense to me, but it makes sense to you.

You sit cross-legged on the couch and Bittoo hops and nestles into your lap in the gap between your legs, so his body rests on the cool leather couch. He sits there, aimlessly, his chin placed on the edge of your knee, like he understands the ten different headlines you read out to him. When you've scanned the first page, your free hand scratches his head and he purrs; since you've been around, he never purrs for me anymore.

Having decided that today is a *Vogue* kind of day, I finally scoot in next to you two—impatient for your eventual dream analysis. I place my coffee, the one you get for me in bed, every day, right next to your mug—two of a set of four we bought from the same shop we got our Diwali party trinkets from, years ago.

Placed together, the mugs look like they're holding hands. Instantly, I take yours away from Bittoo's head and clutch it in mine. Looking at us, you wouldn't be able to tell that only yesterday, we had a fight—something about us having to go to your work friend's party, something about me saying that your friends don't give me great vibes and 'Urgh, do we really have to go?' You got cross at the suggestion. You didn't say 'I don't ever say no to going to one of Sarina's gigs', but I heard it anyway. Sarina is different and you know that, but I get it—that's not the point. So we go to the party; you're mad and I'm bored, and we have an awful time and come back home and fight.

The fight veers into dangerous territory. Something kids, something future. How did we get here? Just like we always do.

'I don't know if I want any,' I admit, sitting on the edge of our bed, terrified.

'You don't want children?'

'I don't think so,' I reply. 'Do you?'

'Yeah,' you mutter. 'But does it matter?'

You're angry that I always want things my way; I'm mad that you think that, when everything I do is to make you happy. Neither of us is right, enough evidence abounds in our relationship to prove that, but it doesn't matter. We go to bed furious. We don't cuddle. I fall asleep, fearing this is the end. It feels like the same fight, every time.

On nights like these, I barely get any sleep; sometimes I wake up at 3 a.m. with a shortness in my chest, this inescapable worry that I would wake up to find that you are gone. But my eyes crack open and you're always there, right there, your hand on my stomach, under my T-shirt, clutching my skin tight. In the middle of the night, in our unconscious states, your body searches for mine, mine relents, unflinchingly. At daybreak, we wake up intertwined—just like we did this morning.

'What did you say we had to do today?' I ask you while you're hyperfocused on this one news clipping you keep going back to. You don't respond.

I have this joke I make around friends—you tend to leave me 'on read'. You laugh along, but deep inside it bothers you that I make this joke. I don't always understand why, but then I realize that you're always fixing old mistakes; you're never not worried about making them again. You think I'm wounded, sometimes, and I think you're wounded, too, and we try to dress these invisible wounds with words and touch to make them more bearable. But other times, I want to tell you: you don't have to worry so much about me. I'm good. Me and my heart, we're good now.

'Huh?' you ask, because you weren't listening. 'Sorry, what did you just say?'

'You were saying something right as I woke up? What did you want us to do today?'

'Oh, *haan*.' You fold your newspaper and put it away, fix Bittoo's position in your lap as you turn to look at me. 'I was wondering if you want to change the curtains.' They're old; a faded white bought off Amazon, back when Sarina and my budget was really tight. We thought we'd change them once we saved enough money—eventually, we just stopped noticing they were around.

'You really hate those, don't you?'

'They're just so . . . blah.'

'How dare you.'

'I mean, if dirty white is your choice of interior decor, I'm not judging you, but I *am* saying that we should then have a veto system and I would absolutely use my veto on that one.'

'Fine. What colour do you want to get?' I ask, when it hits me: I don't think I know your favourite colour.

That's how we get to know each other. Bit by bit. On accident. Because I knew the second that I saw you, I never needed to know more. That you existed was all I ever needed. Everything else, I could spend the rest of my life learning.

'Incorrect, you barely gave me a thought the first time you saw me,' you chide me in my head, and then I say, for argument's sake, 'Okay, fine, the *second* time I saw you, I knew you were all I needed.'

Sometimes I learn things about you that would have made me run if it were anyone else. Like how you don't like ketchup with anything but an aloo parantha. Or that you think pav bhaaji is superior to gol gappe. Or that you despise the look of white sneakers. And how you listen to music, yes, but only exclusively old Hindi songs.

'Even love songs?' I ask, and you nod. '*Especially* love songs.'

'That's slightly cringe, no?'

'Get out of your colonial hangover high horse, Naina. *Hindi mai pyaar karne ka mazza hi kuch aur hai* [There's a different sort of fun in falling in love in Hindi].'

'Pyar Diwana Hota hai' plays in the background on a set of speakers we bought together as our first big collective purchase once I retired Sarina's hand-me-downs. A parrot we named Hari chirps at our windowsill. The bell rings once, twice, and we take turns to answer the door. In the gaps in the middle, we sip our coffees silently. I forget some days how long it's been, but I could swear I've known you my entire life.

Sometimes this is how love happens; unbeknownst to you, a shooting star traces the night sky just as you're making a wish. And then it appears—everything you never even knew you needed, bundled up alongside all that you've ever wanted. Love, by chance, by fate, by accident.

A coincidence.

God, it was humming in the background the very first night, wasn't it?

Aa hi jaata hai jispe dil aana hota hai,
Harr khushi se harr gham se begaana hota hai.

ACKNOWLEDGEMENTS

Writing my second book was nothing like the first one.

The first one popped out of me easily. This one, on the other hand, was an all-nighter; kicking, screaming, crying in labour, begging for it to be over. Basically, in my mother's words, the second one came into existence exactly how I came into the word. In writing this, I celebrate its birth the way my mother did mine—with a huge sigh of relief.

And so, first and foremost, thank you to my parents for the simplest joy of giving me life. And then for scolding this novel's submission out of me. If it weren't for your relentless follow ups and occasional chiding, this book would probably not hit the stores on time. Thank you to my sister for taking your metaphorical red pen to all my words and striking off anything you thought was beneath the quality you expect from me. Thank you to my grandfather for letting me live his literary dreams—and guiding me so passionately along the way. And to Saharsh, my brother-in-law, for adding humour and banter to my life—some of which has hopefully bled into this book. My grandparents who have passed and my dog I so desperately miss everyday, thank you for teaching me love after life, how it lingers, how it stays buried deep in the cracks of your heart long after every physical trace of it is gone.

To all my friends—the old, the new, but mostly, the ones who have stuck around—the friendships in this novel are a patchwork quilt of all of the love you have shown me every single day. Lord knows what I've done to deserve it.

To Arjun: if I start thanking you for things, I'd run out of ink and paper. You know though, don't you?

Thank you to Gurveen for commissioning this book—the belief you showed in me has quietly changed my entire life. Thank you to Oorja for making sure it was error-free. Thank you to Shadab for an expectedly breathtaking cover design. Thank you, so much, to everyone at Penguin who has repped *Fool Me Twice* everywhere—Chaitanya, Saumya, Mishti, Naina, Khushi—free of charge and full of a lot of love. You have made my first year of being an author an experience I will never forget.

Thank you to the lovely folks at Omo Cafe for letting me linger around for a year, at the same table every weekend, to finish this book.

This book was written in a state of turmoil, heartbreak, exhaustion and shame. It packs—in nooks and crannies and jokes and text messages and oddly specific references— moments of my life and people that I wish I could forget, yet have chosen to immortalize. That's a writer's curse, unfortunately; you can't say no to good material, no matter the probable cost. Relatedly, if there's anyone reading this book wondering if I wrote it about them, the answer is in my words. If you have to ask, you weren't reading closely enough.

And finally, Dear Reader, thank you, again, for choosing to enter a new world with me—for letting me write, for being there to read the words that make it past the first draft, for being kind, generous, accepting. If the first one was youthful and naive, this one is older and wiser. If the first one was grief and rebirth, this one is heartbreak and healing.

I hope it fills your cup. God knows it took everything out of mine.

Scan QR code to access the
Penguin Random House India website